A Job You Mostly Won't Know How to Do

A Job You Mostly Won't Know How to Do

A Novel

PETE FROMM

COUNTERPOINT
Berkeley, California

A Job You Mostly Won't Know How to Do

Library of Congress Cataloging-in-Publication Data
Names: Fromm, Pete, 1958– author.
Title: A job you mostly won't know how to do : a novel / Pete Fromm.
Other titles: A job you mostly will not know how to do
Description: First hardcover edition. | Berkeley, California : Counterpoint,
  2019.
Identifiers: LCCN 2018050852 | ISBN 9781640091771
Subjects: LCSH: Domestic fiction.
Classification: LCC PS3556.R5942 J63 2019 | DDC 813/.54—dc23
LC record available at https://lccn.loc.gov/2018050852

Jacket design by Steven Attardo
Book design by Jordan Koluch

COUNTERPOINT
2560 Ninth Street, Suite 318
Berkeley, CA 94710
www.counterpointpress.com

Printed in the United States of America
Distributed by Publishers Group West

10 9 8 7 6 5 4 3 2 1

In memory of my father,
Daniel Fromm, 1926–2018

When the groom lifts the veil from her
delicate temples, I'm thinking someone
should warn them: a future of funerals, car
payments, taxes, kids throwing up in the night.
It's a job you mostly won't know how to do,
your naked arm deep in a jammed kitchen sink,
burnt rinds of eggplant, crazily adrift.

—JOSEPH MILLAR, "American Wedding"

A Job You Mostly Won't Know How to Do

PROLOGUE

Taz is on his knees when she tells him, his arms abuzz with the repeated hammer blows, tingling and tweaking. He looks up, ears buzzing too, the pry bar and his fingers wedged underneath another six inches of the damned kryptonite subfloor.

Thumbs hooked into her tool belt, like now she'll just get back after all that pesky lath, Marnie watches him, smile just waiting to bloom, and says it again.

He blinks, lifts an eyebrow, and wriggles his fingers free, rubs away some dust. "For real?" he says.

Fighting back the grin, she reaches into the pencil slot in her tool belt and eases up the pregnancy test, just a peek, pushes it back down. "The eaglet has landed."

Taz glances around the living room; the wall facing the kitchen just studs, plaster littering the floor, nail-hole freckles where the lath used to be, the whole room's old fir trim taken down, stacked beside the shop out back, waiting for him to catch enough time to strip the gazillion coats of paint. More plaster peels away from the gaps where the trim used to be. Ancient cloth-wrapped black wiring sags between the naked studs, ringed here and there by dingy white porcelain knobs and tubes. The floor looks exploded, broken shanks of the plywood splintering up in the air, the maple underneath glue-streaked, filthy, like some pharaoh's treasure finally touched again by light. Dust motes drift through it all, wherever the sun penetrates the gaps around the doors, the double-hung windows. He takes it all in, just a glance, but still, too long.

Marnie's face shifts, the bloom fading, and he says, "Oh my sweet baby Jesus," and struggles to stand, his knees older than they were a second ago, all his joints tightened. He wraps her up, dust puffing wherever he touches. "Oh my sweet baby Jesus," he whispers into her hair.

"So, you found religion?" Marnie says, pulling back to study him.

"Born again," he says.

"Not even born *yet*," she answers. "Just heading our way."

Over her shoulder, he keeps studying the room this baby will land in. The dust-coated tools scattered through the carnage; the dulled and nicked inch-and-a-half chisel, the battered Sawzall, its bent blade, the indestructible crowbar. Like trying to baby-proof Baghdad. He gives Marn a kiss, a long one, wondering, and they're in the middle of it when Rudy walks in through the kitchen, just showing up, wrecking bar in one hand, longneck bottle in the other. "Oh," he says. "That's nice."

They break apart, in no hurry, Taz still staggered.

"You could get a room, you know," Rudy says.

"We may have to," Taz answers, but Marnie pulls him back, whispers in his ear. "Clam up," she says. "Until it's safe."

Taz nods, but *safe?* Seriously? He wants to say, *Nothing is ever going to be safe again.* But he keeps nodding, turns toward Rudy, and says, "You brought beer?"

Rudy shoots him a *wtf?* Says, "From your fridge. Want one?"

Marnie shakes her head, and just catching it, Taz does, too.

Rudy raises an eyebrow, glances for a watch he doesn't own. "It is Saturday, isn't it?" he says. "I mean, I know I'm late, but not that late, right?"

"No, it's still Saturday," Taz says.

Rudy takes a swig, lifts his bar. "Well, okay then, suit yourselves. Just show me what you need wrecked."

"Demoed," Taz corrects.

"Whatever you want to call it." He stabs the end of the bar into the wall, breaking the plaster, pulling down the next few pieces of lath.

"One of these days," Taz says, "we're going to have to, you know, start building, not just tearing down."

"Beyond my skill set," Rudy answers.

"We're beyond just about everything," Taz starts, and Marnie gives him a poke in the side with her hammer handle.

She goes up beside Rudy, digs in the claw of her hammer. Taz comes up behind and starts to slip the flimsy dust mask over her head.

Marnie lifts her hand to ward him off. "Thing's a pain," she says, then stops, giving herself a tiny slap upside the head, and adjusts the elastic strap, takes a few deep-sea-diver breaths, in, out. They all three of them get back to tearing the place apart.

Hardly more than a month before, after another of Marnie's mother's visits, the demolition held off for it, her mother sent a note saying she'd bought a new bed for them. Mattresses, the works. All down at Wagner's, waiting to be picked up. "You should not have to sleep on the floor," she wrote to Marnie, but aiming straight at Taz. Out back, in the converted old garage he'd scabbed a shed-roof addition onto and declared his shop, even though the ruptured and rotted concrete floor made moving tools almost impossible, he was working the tung oil into the bedframe he'd been obsessing over for months. The best pieces of cherry he'd magpied off jobs for years, scoured the state for, every board gone over like Sherlock with his magnifier.

But they did pick up the mattresses. And, without a second of hesitation, Marnie pocketed the return money for the bedframe, said, "She'll never even think to miss it." A bounty undreamed of.

And, then, well, jesus, the new mattress and all, they had to give it a try, take it for a test drive or two. Three. More. And now, this.

T-MINUS TWO MONTHS,
AND COUNTING

Taz tried—Marnie standing sideways before the bedroom mirror, shirt pulled up to her neck. He oohed and aahed, pushed out his own stomach, said, "Oh my god, you're ginormous," but really it was just Marn, a silhouette he could trace blindfolded. He came up to run his hand down her stomach, and she shoved him away, said, "It's there, jackass. Any fool can see it."

A month later he told her she looked like a rope with a knot tied in the middle. He got the look.

But, by the time they blow out of Missoula, seven months down this new trajectory, there's no denying anything. Ditching the interstate, they follow the Blackfoot upriver, the narrow twists of the first canyon, then into the flats of Potomac, the mist still hanging low in the pasture, fingering into the spruce and lodgepole, the Angus standing like shadows. They climb the hill, swoop back down over the Clearwater, then back into the turns of the next canyon, the ponderosa crowding the road on one side, the river on the other, and Taz catches her leaning over, studying the river, looking for fishing holes, or figuring runs for the kayaks. She was nuts for all of it, from the very first day, the college kid from Ohio. All he had to do was show her this stuff he knew like breathing, from when he could take his first steps. It drove Rudy wild, the ease of the courtship. "It's so not fair. I could show her all that. I could take her fishing and we'd actually catch fish."

She turns, catching him smiling, says, "What?" and he says, "Nothing. Just the first time we came up here."

Back out on the higher flats toward Ovando, the Scapegoat peaks rear up to the north, gray and parched with the drought, their snowpack gone since April. Smoke palls the farthest peaks, the fire season taking hold in the wilderness. Taz takes the turn-off at the gravel piles, leaves the main fork of the river and the pavement behind, dust coiling up after them on the dirt, then into the trees, hammering over the last broken bits of anything that could be called road. A swimming lesson, Marn calls it, and Taz pulls the truck in tight to the chokecherries, the lone gigantic ponderosa that marks their secret spot, no one else, as far as they could ever tell, macheteing through the thick stuff to discover the drop and pool, never even a fisherman's tracks, though once they did find a grizzly's in the mud, water splashed across the rocks, still wet. They opted out that day. But now, grizzly-free, they snag their rods and fly boxes from the bed of the truck and snake through the willow and scrub, keeping to rock, never leaving a trail for others to follow. As soon as they see water, Marn drops her fly rod and sheds her clothes like a skin that no longer fits. It's what they've always done, from the very first time they stumbled into this place, back when Taz still couldn't get over it, how easily she stripped down, as if they'd known each other forever and, as usual, Taz gets caught gaping, has to rush to catch up.

The water, even in the scorching July heat, is at first breath-taking, and they gasp and giggle their way into it, then paddle deeper, pushing up to the drop and drifting back down, cir-cling through the eddy, their breaths steadying, his arms around her belly, and they watch the clouds stream over, harmless as brushstrokes, no water coming from them in months. There's no smoke to see here yet, just the tinge of it in the air, pleasant almost, like a campfire.

Her belly bulges—an elbow or knee sweeping beneath Taz's hand—and his eyes widen and Marnie laughs. "She's going to swim like an otter, this one," she says, her wet hair like a pelt itself, draped across his shoulder.

"Or he?"

"Don't be an idiot," she says. "Solid double X."

"Really?"

He feels her nod. "Sacagawea," she says. "Lewis can follow her along. Maybe even Clark. Hogging all the glory. Men, same old, same old. "

Back at first, wowed by the way they just knew all these places she could barely imagine, she'd called him and Rudy Lewis and Clark. They'd only been twenty. Seven years ago, but already it feels a lifetime.

———

They dry raisin-style in the sun, then dress and pick their way upstream, the water so low in the drought that they crunch over whitened cobble they'd never before seen dry. When they reach the wall of the last little canyon, Marn flashes Taz a look, a question, and he glances down at her belly, raises an eyebrow. "Sacagawea carried her baby all the way to the Pacific and back," Marnie says, and she goes first, stepping up onto the foot-wide ledge of cracked and crumbling stone. She clings to the stone, a root here and there, some wild bit of buffalo brush taking seed in the rock, cracking its way in. Below them, the river, channeled tight, races through the drop, split by boulders, and Taz follows inches behind, ready to grab, to dive in after her.

But they make it through, dropping from rock to bunchgrass, the little meadow the canyon keeps hidden, and they stroll through the brittle stems, scattering grasshoppers all the way up to the beaver ponds. Water trickles through the bulwark of sticks and mud, the first pond glassy beyond it. They catch their breath, set up their rods, and Marnie, looking around for any kind of a hatch, runs her finger across the flies in her box, pulls out a tiny one, a midge, and names it out loud.

Digging through his own fly box, Taz says, "Maybe, but I think a hopper can't miss."

"No," Marnie says. "Midge. That's what we'll call her. Her name."

"Midge?"

"Yeah, just this tiny thing, but what sort of holds the whole deal together."

"Really?"

She smiles. "It's perfect."

"The food chain? You want her at the *bottom* of the food chain?" He laughs. "That is so *not* perfect."

She looks at him.

"And you're going to explain that to her later? 'Yeah, jeez honey, we just wanted, you know, for you to be at the slaughter end, what the whole world preys on.'"

Her look narrows.

"Come on, Marn. If you want to go all native, how about, I don't know, Cutthroat? That'd be cool, make the other kids leave her alone. Or Otter maybe."

She squints down toward scary and Taz says, "Or, you know, Midge is good."

She rolls her eyes and he says, "Midge," like a punch line, and they cast out and he's thinking Maddy maybe, or Carly, or Sandy, or maybe Sarah, or Sybil, running with the *S*'s, but not Sybil, you'd never know which one she was, and if it's a boy, because, seriously, she can't really *know*, maybe Bruce, for Springsteen— that'd drive Marn wild—or Eminem if she wants a compromise, or if she wants to run with the animal thing, go totally native, maybe Tatanka, but that'd go to Tank, which would make him sound like the asshole jock of some shitty comic book, and then the first fish hits and, as always, they pull in a dinner's worth of the little brook trout.

They gather sticks, Marnie building up the start while Taz breaks bigger branches, swinging them against the edge of a rock, and they cook the trout over their twig fire as the sun lowers, dappling through the cottonwood leaves, the willows, the long needles of the ponderosas scattered up the slopes.

"She's going to love this place," Marnie says, pulling the last little slab of fish off the skeleton, her chin shiny with the oil.

Taz leans back on his elbows, says, "Why wouldn't she? It's like we live in a painting."

Marnie says, "If he could see us now, that Van Gogh guy would cut off his other ear. Or one single person from Ohio catching a glimpse of this? They'd die weeping, if Cleveland's air hadn't already finished them off."

"Can hardly believe you survived," Taz says.

She gives him a little swat. "Can't believe you never knew what you had till I showed you."

It's the usual, but then she adds, "Or that your parents ever left."

Taz squints against a drift of smoke and it's a bit before he comes up with, "I don't guess New Zealand's so hideous."

"Full of hobbits," Marnie answers, but it's a lot just mentioning his parents, these people she's never met, and she hands him the last trout and sits cross-legged beside him, cleaning the bones with her lips.

Taz feeds the last sticks into the fire and they go silent, watching the flames take hold, the blue leap and dance of them as mesmerizing as ever, and the sun drops behind the mountains, casting them into shade, and soon the first slightly cooler breezes start their evening fall down from the tops.

They both know it's time to go, but Marnie sighs, says, "This kind of night, you know. Sure isn't making going home any easier."

Taz thinks of bringing a baby up here, hauling her through that canyon, keeping her out of the pinecones, out of the creek, the ponds, listening to her crying right when everything goes so silent, wonders how many nights like this they have left. "I could hump it back to the truck," he says. "Get the sleeping bags."

"That's not what I mean," she says, voice changing as she stares into the fire. "And you know it."

Taz rubs her back, bites off his own sigh. "We'll get the house finished. I've got time right now."

"If another job doesn't come up, time's *all* we'll have."

Taz pulls his hand away, leans toward the fire, pokes at it with a branch no bigger around than his finger. "Work always shows up, Marn."

"Well, now'd be a good time." She pitches the trout skeleton onto the coals. "That's all I'm saying."

With the tip of his stick, Taz pushes the skeleton deeper into the fire, the tiny, fragile bones glowing more than burning, and then just gone.

———

They roast on the drive back, windows down, the rush of ninety-five-degree air less cooling than baking. "Jerky," Marn says, shifting herself, rolling her neck the way she does any time she's uncomfortable. She looks down at her belly, blows out a long sigh. "Buffalo jerky."

Taz steps harder on the gas.

They slog into the house, the sheetrock up, but not yet taped or mudded. Still, the living room, as soon as they push open the door, looks like an actual room, not just an open skeleton. The Visqueen covering the sanded maple crinkles underfoot, and Marnie slides onto the broken-down couch the college students had pitched, just some place to sit during construction, something they'd pile onto the dump load as soon as the main room was finished. They'd scabbed in the electrical, the tangle of knob and tube still in the truck, under the sheetrock scrap. He'd mud this week, tape the seams, cover the screw heads, then dust like a fiend, paint, peel up the plastic, dust some more, put the poly-urethane down until the maple gleamed like glass. Marn didn't know, but he'd made reservations, two nights, the C'mon Inn, where she could bob in the pools, teach Midge to swim, where neither one of them would be breathing in all those fumes. Or gilling it, whatever Midge did in there. He pictures her floating, the umbilical cord her deep-sea diver's air hose, a little brass helmet covering her head, the paned-off round window of the face mask. All twenty thousand leagues. He does not tell Marnie any of this.

He glances down to her slumped on the couch, eyes closed, pale, sweating, breathing like a diver herself. He's learned better than to ask if she's okay, but he does anyway.

She peeks open one eye, stares at him. "She's going to be a giant," she whispers. "A Titan. You try carrying her around."

"In a heartbeat," he says, actually kind of meaning it, think-ing, before he stops himself, that he could do better, that he'd just bear up, wouldn't make such a show of the *exhaustion*, the *misery*, make such a fricking burden of the whole thing. But she purses her lips, blows a tired raspberry, and he has to admit that he doesn't really have a clue.

He goes to the kitchen, as unfinished as the day they bought the place, worse. They weren't in the house a week before they tore into the bedroom, *The only room we'll need*, she'd said. Sure the kitchen would be next, they'd emptied their paint brushes against the wall above the sink, Marn painting in this gigantic green smiley face, adding white fangs with the ceiling paint. A joke then, but work had caught up with them, the bank account, and the face, three years on, had become her picture of the house itself, eating them alive. If there'd been a way to paint it over without her noticing, he'd have been on it yesterday.

He stares at it as he pulls open the freezer, twists an ice tray, breaks out the cubes, brings the water in a pint glass. She holds it against her cheek, her forehead, rolling it back and forth. "We never discussed heat waves when we planned all this," she says. "Drought."

Planned? Taz keeps himself from saying. "Two more months," he says.

Eyes closed, she says, "Yeah, the timing hasn't slipped my mind."

He sits on a sawhorse and watches her, leans a little closer, ready to snatch the glass if she nods off.

Minutes later she opens her eyes, sits up a bit more, holding the glass in both hands, resting it on her belly. "We have to get serious," she says.

Taz braces.

"I mean, look at the accounts, add and subtract. All that abacus shit." She waves a hand around. "And this place. We've got to get a real schedule going. We can't bring her into this mess."

Taz doesn't even have to glance around, though he's always liked these first days with the sheetrock up, the rooms echoey. And, really, it *is* a room. Shelter. They have plumbing. Power. Their bedroom's been finished for years, and now the other, the baby's room, is just waiting on paint, trim. The bathroom, stuck off the hall between them, has a door at least, hiding all that waits inside, the plumbing, the fixtures they can't yet afford, the tile. The kitchen, though, doesn't even have a door, just the opening he's turned the couch away from, so she doesn't have to see all that still waits in there, those appliances so far out of reach they haven't had the heart to even start tearing down the plaster. Still, it isn't like she's going to drop this baby in a cave. But he says, "I know, Marn."

She stares at him. "You always say that."

"I know," he starts, then closes his mouth, pushes up off the sawhorse, just as dog-tired as she is.

He walks out to the shop, keys the padlock, and pushes the door open, flips the lights, walks around the tool bench, one thing, along with the relic of a table saw, that his father couldn't ship overseas. He pulls back the tarp keeping the dust off all the non-woodworking tools, and digs through the buckets of plumbing stuff, electrical, until he finds the taping box, collects the mud tray, the eight-inch knife, a roll of drywall tape, mixes a batch of mud.

She stares at him when he comes in, his every move. "That's what you think I mean? When I say we have to get real, make a plan?"

He doesn't bother to answer. Just dips his knife into the mud. Turns to face the wall. Gets to work.

He's rolling the tape out along the belly band when, behind him, Marnie says, "You know, not talking about money doesn't mean we have any."

He pulls the tape back against the knife edge, tearing it off, then dips the knife into the tray, walking backward, spreading the mud out over the tape.

... AND COUNTING

Taz picks up a week of work, a week and a half, all more handy-man than carpenter or cabinetmaker. It helps, but not much for the way it stalls out the work at home. Only a month out, the living room and baby's room floor still plastic-covered, the walls' every screw and seam smooth with sanded mud, he presents Marnie with her packed bag, tells her about the week-end at the motel. She stares, shaking her head, asking where he thinks money really actually comes from, but eventually lets Taz usher her into the truck, saying that they've got arrivals to think about, that the money's something they can worry about later. He leaves her bobbing in the pool, like a manatee, she says, and he races home, grabbing Rudy on the way. Together they throw up the paint, living room first, Rudy rolling at light speed, Taz cutting in the corners. They barely speak, moving around each other like they're the married couple, knowing each other's movements, thoughts.

Until Rudy, eyes on his rolling, says, "How'd she take it?"

"Take what?"

"The whole banishment thing."

"Banishment?" Taz stops. "You think she should be breathing this shit in?"

"What, *I* don't have brain cells?"

Taz laughs, leans as far as he dares, slides his brush along the ceiling line. "Just a few terrified survivors."

Rudy takes a swig from his beer. "They can run, but they can't hide."

They work, falling back into silence until Taz climbs down, resets his ladder, climbs back up.

"You tell them yet?" Rudy asks.

Taz turns, finds Rudy loading the roller in the tray, not looking anywhere near him. "Tell who?" he says.

"About the grandbaby and all?"

Taz dips his brush into the paint. "Yeah, I told them."

"So, they're racing up here?"

Taz runs the brush along the ceiling line. "Not exactly," he says.

"Happy at least?"

"Mom's thrilled. My dad just wondered *How the hell you plan on supporting a family?*"

"Nice to see him mellowing."

Taz reloads his brush, reaches as far as he can.

Rudy says, "You told them you bought this place, right? They don't think you're still living at my place? Still finishing high school?"

"Even told them I got married."

Rudy eases the roller onto the wall, up first, then back. "Wow, full disclosure."

"Mom'd come," Taz starts, but leaves it at that.

"No doubt," Rudy says. "I just kind of wondered if a baby might be enough to make it happen."

"There's nothing bringing him back."

"The, um, current administration?"

"Could be Bozo the Clown. Wouldn't make any difference."

"Well, pretty much is. Bozo, I mean. But, still, a baby. Kind of a game changer, right?"

"They left me here with you, Rude."

"And my parents," Rudy says. "Not exactly raised by wolves."

Taz resets his ladder, climbs, dips his brush. "He got wiped out. Holds the global economy against the whole country. The whole globe. You know how he is."

"Dude does have some anger-management issues."

"How much difference you think a baby is going to make?"

"My folks left, too. The crash smacked us all."

"Arizona, Rudy. They hated winter, not themselves."

Rudy finishes his section, and they shift over to the front wall, the one they saved for last, the windows eating up that space. He waits for Taz to get the corner in, stands leaning against the roller pole like a wizard's staff. "What'd Marnie say?"

"She's never done more than seen them on Skype. I don't think she had any big ideas."

"Doesn't bum her out?"

"She lived here six months without heat, Rude. I don't think much else is going to phase her."

"It was summer," Rudy says. "Mostly."

Taz laughs. "She could handle him."

"And anyone else."

"I'm sort of just kind of glad she doesn't have to."

Taz gets the corner in and Rudy finishes with the roller. "Baby room next?"

Taz picks up his ladder, starting that way. "But it's not the baby's room anymore. She's calling it *the nursery* now. For real. Marn."

Rude kneels to change roller heads, switch paints. "Calls the baby room the nursery," he says. "Totally insane. I mean, like, where does she even come up with this shit?"

Taz opens the new paint, something called Gemstone, blue or green. Both maybe. Marn's going to stencil dragonflies in around the ceiling, mayflies and stoneflies, and, of course, midges—another bridge he's decided to cross when they come to it.

————

The next day, they start with the floor, predawn, pre-coffee. "What!" Rudy says, and Taz says, "We can get all three coats in if we fly."

"Three?"

"Place is going to last forever."

"Overkill," Rudy says, but takes a knee on the front porch, works the lid off the five-gallon bucket.

"Coffee's on me while the first coat dries." Taz says, "Promise."

Rudy gives him a look and stands back to let Taz stir, and without a word of planning, both of them knowing the drill, they open the door and start. Rudy pouring while Taz spreads, they finish the living room and move into the hallway between the bedrooms without so much as lifting their heads. They slick down the hall into the nursery, stepping around each other as they shimmy through the doorway, the maple popping out so golden they smile all the way into the back wall before they realize what they've done.

Rudy says, "No way."

Taz, "We didn't."

But they've painted themselves in, no way out but through the nursery window, Taz first, Rudy handing out the bucket, the roller pole, both of them laughing till they can hardly stand. Catching his breath, Taz gets out, "Marnie never hears a word," and Rude's eyes widen. "To our graves."

They get into the kitchen through the back door, the sun still not up yet, but the east lurid with the smoke from the wilderness. Taz builds coffee and has almost a whole cup before going out to the shop, getting a few more pieces marked out for the bed he's making for the nursery. A surprise. Rudy leans in the shop door, sips his coffee, watches a while before asking, "Do you even sleep anymore?"

"Time for that later."

Rudy walks in, pulls a chair out from the gigantic dining room table Marnie had found, some Civil War leftover, something peace treaties could be signed at, leaf after leaf after leaf, a dozen chairs, all of it shoved up against the jointer, the band saw, the shaping table, which are all shoved up against the back wall. "Later," he says. "Like after the baby comes? I hear that's a good time for sleeping."

They get the second coat down before noon, starting in the nursery this time, and a third before nightfall. Half dizzy from the fumes, Taz braces himself in the doorway of the still-1917 kitchen, Rudy cleaning brushes in the stained and rusted farm sink, the linoleum pattern beneath them long, long gone. Aching and exhausted, he admires their work, the reek of fresh paint wrestling with the drying poly. Behind him, Rudy shuts off the water, pops a beer, then a second. "And they said it couldn't be done," he says.

"Not by mortals," Taz says, and they click bottlenecks. "Not a chance."

He turns to the kitchen's rough old plaster wall and raises his bottle to Marn's fanged smiley face. "Here's to Marn, too," he says. He had, he has to admit, guessed they'd have the kitchen wrapped in a few months, the whole house in six. Been fool enough to tell her so. Out loud. Six months. Three years ago.

"When are you picking her up?"

"Tomorrow, I suppose. Maybe the next day."

"Coward," Rudy says.

Taz smiles, though to himself he admits it's been a relief, having her gone a few nights. "Just depends how long it takes to air out."

"We'll be able to open the windows soon. This heat? It'll be a few minutes. You hear about the fires?"

Taz nods. The wildfires breaking out of the wilderness, raging, zero percent containment. Seeley Lake already evacuated. Lincoln prepped for it. Holed up in here, he can't really remember what all. He could sleep standing up, if he had time. "Want to poly the baseboard tomorrow, the door trim?"

"You already got it?"

"They were tearing out the old bleachers at Loyola."

"All that clear fir? They didn't sell it?"

Taz glances his way, smiles. "Not all of it."

Rudy stares, says, "Dude," but can't come up with anything else. "That'd be a surprise for her. Coming back to find you in lockup."

"Just re-sourcing, Rude. If they sold it, it'd just wind up as crap somewhere."

"But you, you're serving a higher purpose?"

Taz taps the neck of his bottle to his forehead.

"And you've got it all milled already? Ready to go? When the hell did you do that?"

"Nights."

Rudy keeps shaking his head. "And you still got all your fingers? Wonders never cease. Marn know?"

"It'll be a surprise."

Rudy slaps his hand against the tabletop, fumed oak, nearly black. "You want to get this bad boy in too, get it all set, plates, salad forks, teacups, candles lit?"

"Got to let the poly harden up a little first."

"But, seriously. You're going to try to have this all finished before you bring her home from the motel?"

"No, even god couldn't do that."

"So, what's the rush?"

Taz blows a long, sorrowful foghorn across the neck of his bottle. "*What's the rush?* There's a baby coming, Rude. I told Marn the whole place would be done two years ago. Maybe three."

Rudy turns to look Taz in the eye. "Her mother," he says, and Taz turns away. "She's on her way. Am I right?"

"Not till the baby is born."

"Oh, jesus, and Marn's holding your toes to the fire, get this place all Martha Stewart before she gets here."

"The main rooms, anyway."

"Well, what time do we start tomorrow?"

"The crack."

Rudy groans.

"Whenever you want to show up, Rude. You know that."

"Yeah, but with Moms on her way, we better scorch."

Taz tosses his bottle toward the garbage can across the kitchen. "Might be time for you to take a break anyway, Rude. I got no idea when I can pay you next. Not a clue."

Rudy opens up the fridge, backs out empty-handed. "Pay? Man, that'd be a novelty," he says. "I'll see you in the morning. I'll bring some beer."

Taz follows him out, watches him walk down the drive, a wave over his shoulder, then turns to the shop, flips on the lights, starts brushing stain on all the trim he's made out of the stolen bleachers.

HOLDING

She comes to the nursery door, huge, hands on her back, and stands there watching him work at the foot of the twin bed he's just surprised her with, a matched pair, mostly, to the bed he'd made for them, something he'd got after at night, buried in the shop, slipping into bed late, smelling of wood, something she actually kind of loves. "It's gorgeous," she says. "Walnut?"

Taz can't not quite grin. "The wood of royalty. Most of it from that rolltop job."

"Way not to get ahead of yourself," she says, fighting back her own smile.

Taz leans back, looks at her.

"Like, two years or so."

"What?"

"Taz, that's a big-girl bed. Best big-girl bed in history, but ..." She sees his face, stops. "... but it's so perfect, I might sleep here myself."

"You will not."

She laughs. "We're going to need a crib for a while."

Taz looks around the room. "Well, we could use this one ourselves. Like if she's sick or something. Or can't sleep. If we have to be here with her."

"Do you have mattresses?"

He twists his mouth to the side.

"So we're going shopping," Marnie says, as if money were no issue at all.

In the final days, Marn helps with the trim, just the standing stuff, door casing mostly, though Taz comes in from the shop once and finds her putting the cove moulding down along the bottom of the baseboard, lying stretched out against the wall, huge, not even using the air gun, because she likes tapping in the little finish nails. He laughs, says, "Should I call the stranding team?"

"The what?" With the nails pinched between her lips, it's a little Elmer Fudd.

"You know, the people who roll the whales or dolphins or whatever back into the water."

"Come over here," she says, a nail held up, her hammer. "I want to see your toes for a second."

Taz crosses to the opposite side of the room. "You sure you should be doing that?"

"Lying down? It's what I do best."

He puts down the last pieces of the baseboard, giant ten-inch planks he couldn't have touched without the bleachers, checks the fit. "Think your mom is going to like it?"

Marnie chuckles or hums, or maybe just chokes on a nail.

Taz says, "You okay?"

She spits out her nails, still chuckling. "You know exactly

what she'll do," she says. "Walk in here, say, 'Oh, nice,' and go straight to the kitchen, her white-glove deal, say, 'Oh,' in that other way, then the bathroom, not even saying 'Oh' anymore, just that lip-purse thing she does." Marn does it herself, like she's just taken a big juicy bite out of a mostly rotten lemon.

"That," Taz says, "is so hot."

Marn rolls onto her back, flops her arms to the sides, her belly like a mountain, her boobs the jutting foothills. Her lips still pursed so tight she can hardly get out words, she manages, "Take me, baby, I'm yours."

———

They're into the same week as the circled due date on the calendar Marn nailed to the kitchen wall, decorating it up with different felt-tips—stars, fireworks—when Taz barges in with what looks like a couple sections of fence. Marnie raises an eyebrow, and Taz says, "Crib."

"Where did you find it?"

"I'll make her a good one," he says. "I'm just, you know, running out of time."

"Salvation Army?" she asks.

He says, "Sort of," and carries the pieces through to the nursery before she can say a thing. So she yells it. "Clean it. With bleach. Twice."

He shouts back, "I know," and a while later, "Directions. Directions would have been nice."

He hears her walk to their bedroom, come back down the hallway, stand in the nursery door. She doesn't say a word, so Taz turns, holding some big metal rod he can't quite figure the use of, and sees her with this big, white wicker-basket thing. "Mom's way ahead of both of us."

"What is it?"

"A bassinet."

"Isn't that something they play in band?"

She laughs. "It's what she'll sleep in first. In our room. Then, eventually, your crib, in here. You might have the time to build one yet."

Taz nods, as if none of this is news. "Then the big-girl bed."

"Matter of fact," Marnie says, "you might want to, you know, set your crib up in our room. We can put the bassinet in it to begin with."

Taz glances to the mattress frame, the door, guesses it'll fit through without taking it apart, starting over. He hoists it up, pulls it in against his chest. "Make a hole," he says, and Marn steps back just in time to let him bash his knuckles against the new casing. He hasn't let her lift anything heavier than a hammer in a month.

When he gets the mattress in, realizes they have no sheets for it, she says, "We can wrap it up in something. Cut down one of our old sheets."

He stands there looking into the crib. "Your mother will bring everything. All pinky and girly and gross."

Marnie laughs. "You think I just came all princess?" which makes Taz laugh, too.

"You know," she says, "there really isn't anything left to do."

Taz stands nodding, not quite believing that could ever be true.

"Sooo," Marnie says, "I was thinking. Maybe one last trip? Give the girl one more swimming lesson?"

"The North Fork?" he says. He gives a wave toward her belly. "That road'll probably shake her right out of you."

"I'm ready."

"You and me, going all homesteader? Delivering a kid on our own, in the swimming hole? What do you want to do, bury the placenta thing under a tree?"

"Okay, now that's just gross."

"Well, come on, if anything happens …"

"We'd be an hour away, tops."

"Which could get to seem like light-years."

"Taz, just once more."

"We'll go a gazillion times. Duh. But right now?"

She stares at him until Taz starts looking for his keys. It is, after all, her favorite place in the world. One last time, just the two of them.

ZERO

A week later, they strip the bed, replace the mattress pad with a vinyl shower liner, something she'd read, saving the mattress if the water breaks at an inconvenient time. "When would be a convenient time?" Taz asks, but she levels him with a look, flops the sheet in the air and he grabs a corner, tucks it in.

They make it about a minute before they start to laugh. It's like sleeping on butcher paper, just less comfortable. "Feel like a fish," Taz says, and Marnie does her fish-lip thing, and they're both gulping for air laughing as they peel it out from under the sheet, crumple it onto the floor, spoon in again, breathless. She laughs once more, says, "This is what it's all going to be like, trying to do all this shit we don't know a single thing about. Being complete idiots."

He says, "We were made for it," and she answers, "You were, anyway," scooching back against him.

The water breaks the next night.

She lumbers up, says, "I'm fine. I think I'll shower first. But, Taz, it's showtime."

He hears the shower start, asks once more if she's okay, and strips the sheets, bundles them back into the laundry bag beside the washer crammed into the kitchen. When she comes out of the bathroom, towel around her hair, sees the dark blotch on the mattress, she says only, "What's a mattress?" As in costs, the greater scheme of things. Her mother's gift, but Marnie trying.

"Exactly," Taz says. "We pretty much wore this bad boy out anyway, getting here."

She smiles, then bites her lip, bracing for another contraction. "Pick up another," she says, panting a little. "It won't stand a chance either."

They leave the house before dawn, the light easing into the darkness beyond the mountains hemming in the east side of the valley, turning the sky so red it looks on fire itself. It's their favorite time, they've always said, except for the waking up and all, the whole getting out of bed thing, and Taz has told her about the fire sunrises after he shuffles out to the shop every morning, asked her to get up and see, but he's never coaxed her beyond the front door, a stare down the street.

Marnie takes his hand and squeezes, and he squeezes back, says, "Bad?" and she pants, says, "Ha." The streets around them stretch empty, the stoplights blinking yellow all the way down, as if they've got a whole motorcade thing going on.

Only a few minutes later she clenches her fists, her eyes, grabs his hand off the wheel, begins to huff and puff. When it lets up, she turns, her smile shaky. "Phew," she says. "This kid is not messing around."

He takes the last turn into the hospital, and Marnie says, "You'll have to call Mom."

"Me!"

"You want me panting into the phone again? Moaning? Like it's a birthday call?"

Taz smiles, just the idea of going after her, trying to make her crack while on the phone with her mother.

She slaps at him. "Call her," she says.

"As soon as the eagle has landed," he promises. "FaceTime. The works."

DAY 1

He sits rocking beside the hospital bed with his pocket full of bubble gum cigars. One real one, for Rudy, wedged in with all these pink and blue Double Bubbles. Because, you know, who knows? No matter what Marnie said.

He holds his temples, squeezing, trying to remember. Acronyms, of course. Everything here is. But it was two words. He knows that. Or maybe three. He just can't bring them up out of that sudden rush and flurry. Holding the baby, grinning so wide, Marn's panting, after that last great push, not easing, but getting harder, her eyes going wide, trying to get out his name through the gasping. "Taz? Taz? Taz?" All question. He'd held the baby up, for her to see, still not catching on. He stood to set it on her chest, but the doctor and the nurse were already scrambling, others rushing into the room. Someone, he can't even say who, or how, took the baby, and Marn clutched his emptied hand like it was the last thing holding her to the planet.

Cardio. But that wasn't it. Pulmonary. Maybe.

Pulmonary, pulmonary. He runs through his medical vocabulary, the few TV shows they'd watched, before the TV gave out. Hematoma. Contusion. Embo—

Pulmonary embolism. PE.

Still rocking, head clutched in his hands, he whispers it again and again, wondering what it is.

Balloons tremble around him every time the AC kicks in, and someone finally reaches into the room and switches off the glaring lights, Rudy's gigantic stuffed bear looking bewildered in the gloaming.

DAY 2

DAY 3

Rudy brings them home, driving Taz's truck, and when they unload in the front yard, Taz feels Rudy follow him up onto the porch, like Taz might lose his way if left on his own. He touches Taz's back at the door, says, "Want me to ..." and Taz shakes his head and Rudy eases the door shut between them before Taz has to say another thing.

In the living room, Taz turns a circle, as if he's never been here before, the gleaming maple boards creaking beneath his feet, Marn's giant smiley face grinning from the kitchen. He cannot say now where the nursery is. Not to save his life.

He closes his eyes. Takes a breath. Another. A shift of weight in the car seat. A slight tug through his fingers, traveling to his shoulder. He opens his eyes and the baby's eyes are open too, blinking. It cannot focus this far away yet, the nurse told him. No more than a forearm's length.

"So, here we are," he says. He manages a wave around the room. "It's small, but it's half demolished." He edges one of the cigars out of his pocket, a pink one, and peels off the wrapper.

His fingers shake, but he gets it into the corner of his mouth. The baby watches whatever it sees. He pretends a puff, pulls the cigar out, wags it toward the car seat. "From here on out," he says, "it's you and me, Baby."

He rubs at his eyes, the cigar pinched between his fingers. Breathes.

The car seat trembles. A kick maybe. An arm waved. He bends, sets it on the floor. Pulls a chair from Marnie's gigantic table and falls into it. "Okay," he says. "Okay."

They'd read *Operating Instructions. What to Expect.* Her mother told them, *The baby will teach you everything you need to know.* How on earth could anyone—

God, her mother. He'd have to, to ... Make the bed? Put out towels? Had they done all that already? Before? Had that been the plan? That she'd be staying? Had he even called her?

Had they had a plan? Ever?

The baby whimpers.

He shuts his eyes, could not be more tied to the chair if ropes had been used. Chains.

He looks at his hands. Nothing but the pretend cigar. The bag, he guesses, is still in the truck. The nippled bottles. The three cans of formula the hospital gave him, something Marn had sworn they'd never use. He does know that. No formula. No way. Not even as a joke. And not just to save the money, she said. She'd pump so he could hold a bottle, see what it was like, his tits as useless as men in general. He sees her exact smile as she says it, and has to remember again to breathe. How to.

The baby squawks. Something avian. Head tipped back, mouth open, searching. A plea from a nest. Next, the nurse said, would be the squall. Then the scream. The progression of the *S*'s, she called it, trying the first small smile anyone had. After all the extraordinary measures, that smile seemed like maybe the most extraordinary of all. He'd tried one back, lisped, "All the *S*'s." But the smile cracked, and he felt it might carry through his whole body, leave him a piled jumble of broken bits on the floor. She touched his arm, said, "It's best not to let things go to the end," then almost flinched. "The *S*'s, I mean."

He said, "Will you come home with me?" and she smiled, kept her hand on his arm, whispered, "You'll be okay."

Now he forces himself to stand, whispers, "Okay," and looks away from the seat in the middle of the floor. The maple, grain so tight it's hard to see, so shiny and blonde and hard, is the color of Marnie's hair. All of it hidden when they'd bought the house, a surprise underneath the plywood, the mangy carpet. He walks across it to the kitchen's worn linoleum tiles, and, passing, tears the calendar from its nail, frisbeeing it and its hallowed due date toward the trash barrel. His hand scuffs the horsehair plaster as he braces himself along the wall to the window. They'd never gotten to the kitchen, he thinks, as if it's news.

The backyard wavers through the old glass. The gigantic apple tree. The fruit litters the ground, shriveled in the heat. Plans for the tree house already drawn out on the kitchen wall. Branches straight through the floor. The roof. A witch's hideaway, she'd said, tapping him on the chest. "You shall build us our coven's lair, or I shall turn you into a toad."

In the living room, the squawk reaches squall, a storm rolling in. He sees his life stretch out. Hiding in other rooms. Staring out windows at everything they'd planned.

"Hungry?" he calls. "Can I get you a sandwich? Or, you know, you just want to go out, throw a ball around? Get after that tree house?" His voice trails off as if he himself is vanishing.

The baby wails.

He squeezes the rough plaster until his fingertips bleed, his eyes shut until he wonders if blood will leak from them, too.

And then, suddenly, the baby is silent. Taz starts, knee bending toward a dash as he turns, but Rudy's standing in the kitchen doorway, the car seat swinging in one hand, diaper bag slung over his shoulder.

"I think," he says, "we're going to have to figure out how to feed this thing."

Which is what they're doing, the two of them, mixing formula straight in the bottle, fitting on the cap, touching the nipple to her lips, smiling at the way she latches on, Rudy whispering, "She's got Marn's way around a cheeseburger, that's for sure," when there's a knock on the door. They glance up, then at each other. Rudy says, "Momma H," and Taz says, "Really?"

They both stand, and Rudy says, "She got in on the midnighter. She's been at the hospital pretty much ever since, dealing with all their shit." He starts for the kitchen, the back door, and Taz says, "Rude, one favor."

Rudy stops, turns.

Holding the baby, Taz says, "Could you, like, the crib. It's in Marn's room. It's, I, that's where—"

"Want me to haul it out? Put it in the nursery?"

Rudy's already on his way, a moment later bashing down the hallway with it, calling, "What about this white basket thing?"

Taz stands anchored in the living room. He sees the bassinet in the crib, all of it pinched to Rudy's chest. "Yeah," he says.

There's a little crash from the baby's room, and then Rudy's out, moving fast for the back door. "Call," he says, "if you need anything."

"You're leaving me here?" Taz says, but he gives Rudy a wave, lets him dodge out before he crosses over to the front door, swings it open.

Marnie's mother stands on the porch, clutching the handle of a roller suitcase the size of a stamp. Under her other arm is a paper grocery bag, bulging. Food. Marnie used to say her mother's answer to any disaster—tornado, tsunami, nuclear holocaust—would be to put on some potatoes.

Taz takes one look at the reddened holes of her eyes, her trembling lip, so far from the cartoon he and Marnie had always made of her, and they both look away. She manages, "Ted, I, I don't, I—" and then only stutters in a breath. From somewhere she conjures a tiny laugh. "I picked up some things," she says, and Taz swings the baby away in one arm, takes the bag in the other. "Marnie would just kill me for that," she says.

Taz walks her into the living room, their show room, but she barely makes it a few steps. "Oh how she must have loved this," she says, and puts a hand to her mouth, all but cracking. "I, I don't know what to do, Ted."

He swallows, clears his throat, no idea if any sound will come out. "I'm with you there," he croaks, and she says, "I haven't slept since I, since she, since you called."

He says, "With you there, too," but he can't for the life of

him remember calling, how awful that must have been. Could he
have gotten Rudy to do it? Would he have sunk so low?

"Well," he says, "maybe we could start there. Sleeping, you
know?"

He shows her to their bedroom, the first room they'd finished, but the varnish still gleaming, paint smooth and hard as
china. With his hands full, she can only clutch at his arm for a
moment at the door, her eyes so scorched-looking that Taz asks,
"Lauren?"

She pulls up a shaky smile, and says, "Can I see her?"

If his hands weren't full, he'd slap himself on the forehead.
He turns, offering the arm cradling the baby, and she lifts her
up, almost wrapping around her. She tilts her head to the room,
says, "Could I?" and he says, "Of course," and without another
word she leaves her suitcase at the door and slips into their room,
and all Taz can do is walk down the hall to the other room, the
nursery, clutching the bag of groceries with undue care, feeling
something cold inside, smelling onions. He settles the groceries into the crib and starts out, but at the door stops, wondering
where he'll go, what he could possibly do. He reaches for the
knob and slowly pushes the door shut, steps back and sits on their
big-girl bed, and through the polished fir of the door, five raised
panels, a century of paints peeled off with a heat gun, Marnie
finishing it off with steel wool, he hears Lauren break down.

DAY 4

It is sometime in the middle of the night he guesses. The baby lies on the bathroom counter, on a towel he's folded over the leprous Formica. The diaper is off, in his hand, and he stares down at the baby's smooth nakedness. There is a plastic clip over the nubbin of umbilical cord that looks like it could fall off, though at the checkup that morning they'd said it all looked good. He doesn't know which of the S's the baby is on. How far past three they go.

From the doorway, Marnie's mother says, "Ted? Is there anything I can do?" She nearly has to shout.

He's in his underwear. His hair sticks every which way. He hasn't slept in four days. He says, "Why do you ask?"

She tips her head, gives him her own version of the look.

"Needing some shades," he says.

She's blank.

"You know, 'Future's so bright I gotta wear shades?' It's a song."

"I know," she says, and steps into the bathroom.

"You do?" he asks, like he might not have heard. The baby's screams echo off the old tile, ricochet around the room.

She sings, barely a murmur, "Things are going great, and they're only getting better."

He glances around the bathroom, as if their crate of records might be sitting right there. "Marn's got it on vinyl somewhere."

"I know," she says. "She stole it from me."

He looks back to her, surprised, and she smiles, waves it away, says, "It's okay. I haven't missed it."

The three of them crowded into the shotgun bath; one sink, double faucet, one hot, one cold, the skiff of delaminated countertop. The leaky throne, the rusted claw-foot. Tiny hex tile, white gone to gray. Along with the kitchen, one of the bigger reasons they could even pretend to afford the place. On the towel, the baby wails, staring into light he's sure should be blinding.

He blinks, finishes taking a new, factory-folded diaper off the stack in the corner. Pulls it open, lifts the baby by the ankles, her rear off the towel by an inch, slides the diaper underneath, works the Velcro.

Her mother tightens the sash of her robe, preparing for business. She says, "I'll take her. Really, you need to sleep."

He buttons the onesie around the legs and picks her up, holds her squalling against his ear, drowning out all else. "I've been sleeping like a baby," he says, then, to sound less like an asshole, adds, "I have to learn how to do this."

He waits for her to step into the hallway, then slips past to the baby's room, the bassinet in the crib, the big-girl bed, leaves Lauren standing abandoned in the hallway, and stands alone himself, rocking the baby until, at last, she takes a staggered, deep sigh of a breath and stops, eyelids fluttering down. Sleep. A moment later he hears steps, shuffling in the darkness to their room, his and Marnie's, the cherry double bed, the stained mattress.

In the dark, he puts the baby in the basket, settling her in like she's nitro. On her side. Moves the rolled blanket against her back. To keep her from tipping over, something the nurse showed him. Or a book they'd read. Something.

He hears, down the hallway, her weight settle onto the mattress, the slight crush of springs, the creak of a slat, and then nothing. She just sitting there, as awake as he is, as alone without Marn. He sits, too, his hands weighing down the ends of his arms, the same way his head weighs at his neck. Eventually, no noise coming from the crib, or from down the hall, he sets his elbows on his knees, and lets his head sink into his hands, too lost to dare close his eyes, afraid of what he'll find there in the dark, in his head.

DAY 5

He wakes sitting in the rocker, alone, tilts away from its spindles. Each spindle has left a groove in his back. He opens and closes his eyes. Looks first for Marnie. He is still in the nursery, in his boxers, a baby blanket stretched across his lap. Folded over. Pinched beneath his legs. A little hammock he remembers making for her. Tiny flowers, a web of vines. Rocking the only thing that put her back to sleep. But there is no baby.

He rubs at his eyes. His neck. Flexes his back. Wonders if he's still asleep, if he'll finally, at last, wake back up, right next to Marn, huge, the mattress as clean as the day they brought it home.

He takes in the whole room. Morning, the windows not yet shut against the heat, a breeze easing in. More than a hint of smoke now, the air palled with it. The September fires scorching everything in their path.

He grips the arms of the rocker, glances down, checks the floor, under the bed. "Come out, come out," he says, his voice like a stick against concrete.

He stands slowly, shakily, and from height can see into the

empty bassinet. "My god, Marn," he whispers, "she's walking already."

He turns, sees the single bed, still made, never yet slept in. Turtles swim on the turned-back sheets. Not cartoon turtles, no Yertles, just blocky prints of sea turtles, blue-black but mottled with sunlight, sailing through their silence.

Her mother, he thinks. She must have taken her from his lap. Something he'd never felt. World's worst guard dog. The baby Lindberghed from underneath his very nose.

He eases down the hallway, peeks around the corner into the living room. The two of them sound asleep. The baby in her lap, Lauren is half curled around her on the mangy couch he has yet to throw out. For a moment he can't take his eyes away. The blond's frosted in, not quite hiding traces of gray, and her mouth's slack, a gold crown glinting, but, still, he sees Marn there, just like that, giving him a break, taking her turn. Out like a light.

He slides back to the bedroom and sits on the edge of the second bed he'd ever built, the big-girl bed he'd made as much for Marnie as for their baby; walnut he hadn't scrounged, that they couldn't afford, fitted mortise to tenon. A blind fox joint he'd brought in from the shop to show Marn, explaining the bevels, the wedges, how you had to trust it would fit, how, once joined, it was impossible to take apart. One try and done. His first one. Getting way ahead of himself, she'd told him. But she'd bought the sheets, matching, kind of, her stencils, finished it that way; the bugs in the sky, the turtles in the sea. Their whole world ready.

He fingers the hem of the sheet, edges it back and slides between them, slips underwater with the turtles, still hoping to wake up.

DAY 6

His dresser is in his and Marnie's room, her mother's room now. He pulls the same shorts and T-shirt from the floor beside the bed, puts them on again.

The bathroom door is open, a new towel folded beside the sink. He reaches and touches it. There are more diapers on the stack. The diaper pail beneath the sink is empty, smelling of bleach.

At the end of the hall, their bedroom door is also open. He stands in front of it, says her mother's name, clears his throat, tries again. "Lauren?" He leans in, but can't make himself go any further.

In the living room, on top of Marn's old hoop rug, yet another blanket has been folded and the baby lies on it, blinking at the ceiling. He wonders how long since he has seen her. The ceiling fan whirls at its lowest setting. The baby seems enthralled. Maybe it can focus now.

He stands in the hallway door, a hand up on each side of the jamb, watching the baby watching the fan. The sleep, however long it was, has cleared some fog, the baby coming more into focus, and he forgets about his search for her mother, until, from the kitchen doorway, she says, "Ted?"

He turns, sees her holding a spatula, her right hip canted out, a ghost stance that staggers him.

"Did you get some sleep?"

He tilts his head toward the baby. "I must have."

"Your friend's out on the porch. Rudy. He won't come in. He says he's fine, but he never leaves."

Taz blinks, glances through the window, Rudy hunched out there like a gargoyle. Now and then he's heard him talk to someone, a friendly murmur, sometimes a 'Thanks,' or a 'No, not yet,' drifting through the open window, occasionally a 'Fine,' and once a 'Well, how do you think?'—Hagrid's Fluffy barring the door. "That's Rude for you," he says.

She shakes her head. "You people and your names." But she tries a smile, says, "I'm making eggs."

He turns for the shower. "He'll eat as many as you can make."

She says, "I'll scramble the whole dozen. Don't be long."

He stays under the showerhead until the hot gives out. Finds himself standing there shivering.

He steals into his room, slips fresh clothes from the dresser she'd refinished, does not glance anywhere else, take a chance of even a glimpse of anything of Marn's.

Her mother lets him get dressed before she tells him to come to the table. She does not ask.

The eggs are already on the plates. Mountains of them. Bacon. She is holding the baby. She says, "You need to eat as much as you needed that sleep. And then we need to talk."

He looks down at the table, rubs at his face. "I'm sorry, but I, I don't really remember anything, not since . . . Do we have a plan?"

She dips a shoulder, maybe a shrug, maybe just rocking the baby. "Who would have planned anything like this?" she says, but quickly adds, "I came one-way. That was the plan. Just staying as long as Marnie needed."

He can't imagine Marnie ever making any such plan. He picks up his fork, takes a bite, feels guilty for it. The mindless body, insisting on going on.

"Ted?" she says, as soon as his mouth is full. "There's the funeral to think about."

He pushes back his chair.

"You can't," she says. "You can't just not."

"After breakfast, okay?" he says, picking up his plate. "I better feed the beast out there," he says, heading for the door, even as she calls out that she's already taken a plate to him, that he still wouldn't come inside.

He drops down on the porch steps beside Rudy, who does have his own plate, is busy shoveling it in. Beside him sits a full ham, wrapped in clear plastic. "Hards and Dan dropped it off a while ago," he says. "Your third ham." He waves his fork toward what is suddenly a kind of garden. "I just started planting the flowers."

Taz looks, sees some actual plants holed into the weeds, more just bouquets, cut flowers, ribbons hanging limp, the card holders stuck into the ground along with the flowers. Rudy gardening, nothing hard to believe anymore. Taz says, "She ask you in?"

Rudy pushes in bacon along with the eggs. "I opted for the

company out here." He uses a knuckle to push in a bit of egg. "But, man, she can cook."

"They're eggs," Taz says, and watches Rudy eat, the flurry of it. He cannot muster another bite himself. "Anybody can scramble an egg."

Rudy shoots him a glance, trial-runs a smile. "You couldn't scramble an egg like this if you lived in a henhouse."

"You crack them, you whip them around."

"There's all sorts of other goodness in here."

"It's called cheese, Rude."

"And onions, the green kind."

Rudy picks through the eggs, and Taz looks down the block. "Mushrooms, maybe," Rudy says. "Some sort of fungi."

"Only fungi around here is whatever's growing on you," Taz manages.

"Cold, man," Rudy says, polishing his plate with his toast. "So?" he asks.

Still looking down the street, Taz says, "So what?"

"How's the little one?"

"She's asleep."

"The big one?"

"I don't even know when she's leaving."

"Okay," Rudy says.

"How about you? You planning on staying out here forever?"

"Nah. Just keeping down the riffraff. You know. The first few days."

"Thinned out yet?"

"Pretty much. You got a week's worth of casseroles in your freezer."

"Thanks," Taz says.

Rudy shrugs, glances down at Taz's plate. "You going to—" he starts, and Taz hands it over. Watches the frenzy resume.

Taking a breather, Rudy says, "Everybody coming over, Taz, they're, they're just doing what they can, you know? We're all busted up. Don't know anything else to do."

"I know, I just—"

"And," Rudy says, raising his voice just enough to interrupt. "Her, in there"—he jerks a thumb back—"she's just doing the same."

Taz sucks in his cheeks.

"She's been feeding me every day." He grabs his waist, gives it a shake.

Taz looks away from that. Like feeding a stray dog, winning him over.

"So, anyway, I figure, once you get your feet under you, we're going to have to, you know, do something. All these people coming over, they're all in shock. They need, I don't know, like a party or something. For Marn."

Taz stares. "A party?"

"For Marn."

Taz feels like he should laugh.

Rudy pushes himself to his feet, holding out the second empty plate. "You let me know when?" he says.

"What, you're leaving?"

Rudy smiles, nods toward the front door. "I think my work here is done."

Taz watches him amble off down the block, lifting his arm in a wave. Taz waves back, then turns, takes a breath, picks up the ham, and goes inside.

Lauren's still at the table, the baby up on her shoulder now, facedown against the burp towel. She pats the baby's back as she studies him, a look he remembers, as if he's from an alien species, something she'd love to understand.

"Rudy," he says, "loves your cooking."

"Rudy," she answers, "is a piece of work."

He gives a little smile. "No doubt."

"So," she says. "This funeral neither of us want to face." She keeps her hand going, the tapping on the baby's back as gentle as raindrops.

Taz looks around the room, as if for exits. "I don't know if I—"

The baby lets loose a burp that would make Rudy proud. Lauren almost laughs. "You know, this whole time, you've never even told me her name."

Taz blinks, still thinking funeral.

"On the birth certificate it only says, *Davis, girl.* I haven't even known what to call her."

"It's Midge," he says.

"What?"

"Her name."

"Madge?"

"No. Midge." He can barely say it. "It's a kind of fly."

"Honestly?" she says, starting the shake of her head. "A fly?"

Standing there holding a ham, he sees Marn singing it to the swell of her belly. Her pushed-out belly button. "It was Marnie's idea."

She says, "All right then. Midge it is."

DAY 7

He drives over with Rudy, plucking the pink bow from Midge's head, sits looking at it in his hand. He glances around the truck, out the open window, as if Marnie watches, wondering, waiting. He has never even dreamt of littering before, but he flicks the bow out the window, watches it flutter in their wake, whispers, "I know, Marn, but, seriously. Pink? The whole slippery slope."

"What's that?" Rudy says, and Taz just looks down at Midge, wonders if he shouldn't have hired somebody, day care or something, not put her through this no matter what she could know.

There's no clergy, no prayers, nothing like that, just a microphone, her friends getting up and saying some things. A few laughs, a lot of sniffling and choking up, and though whoever rented the place, put it all together, did him a huge favor, Taz can't help but think it should have been outdoors. Up on the North Fork maybe. She'd have loved to hear the aspen leaves rustling, gold up against the smoky blue, the water hustling through it all. He puts himself there, lets the stories become the rush of the river, nothing that will lay him low.

He holds Midge the whole time, his hands occupied. No hugging. No handshaking. He looks at the floor, over people's shoulders. She had so many friends.

People ask, and he says, Midge. The only explanation he gives is, "It's a little bug. Tiny." Hards, her college roommate, smiles. "What if she was a boy?"

"Midge," he says again. "Or maybe Pike." Almost like a conversation. "It was Marn's idea."

There's a food spread, sandwich makings, some salads, but Taz still can't muster a single bite and at the end, Rudy sidles up, says, "You need to go home with Lauren. Can't let her drive away from this alone."

Taz looks at him, and Rudy says, "Marn would skin you alive if you did."

He drives her rental, the urn tight beside him. The car seat in the back, because it's supposed to be. Her mother rides there with Midge and weeps.

———

People come to the house. He hadn't expected that. Her mother tells him as they approach, she'd had it arranged, that it was necessary. She says Rudy helped. That he'd get through it. That they all would. She admits she'd rented the hall for the funeral, hired the caterer, he mumbles something about paying her back, and she just shushes him, says again that Rudy was so helpful.

As their friends trickle in, Taz moves out back with Midge, hides on the porch swing. When Lauren comes looking, tells him he has to do this, has to come inside, he stands and says, "I'll be right back."

He retrieves the car seat, dodges back out, stops, looks at his truck, Marnie's disintegrating Karmann Ghia. Neither one with a backseat. The truck at least has a top.

Windows down, her wispy hair lifts and falls, waves, and he has to remember to keep his eyes on the road, catch the turn up the Blackfoot. At the Clearwater, the sky, already murky, closes down completely, air as gray as a sock, a campfire gone feral, half the Scapegoat on fire. He leaves the pavement for the two track, slows way down, tries to lessen the pounding, same way as he had for Marn, jesus, a week and a half ago. He parks at the rocks, the ponderosa, the scrub of chokecherry and willow hiding their little scrap of beach.

"Remember this?" he whispers. "Your swim lessons?" But Midge is asleep until he unbuckles the car seat, her eyes snapping open at the click. "Midge," he says, lifting her and turning toward the river. "Our favorite place." He has to reach back in for the urn. "She'd kill me for waiting this long to bring you here."

Cutting through the willows, he stops at the ancient ponderosa, dips his face toward the channeled jigsaw bark, breathes deep, the smell of butterscotch, one of Marn's favorite things. He puts Midge's nose close, too.

He walks to the water's edge. "We swam here with you," he tells Midge. "The whole time."

He looks up and down the little stretch of hidden water. No tracks, people or grizzly, the water low. "You weren't even the knot in the rope at first," he says. "Man, it was cold. But it was something she wanted to do. And you know how she gets then."

He squats down. "She was teaching you to swim," he goes on, and dips her toes into the water. "I didn't think it was quite necessary, what with you living in water at the time."

He kneels in the river, waves her feet back and forth, making ripples. She kicks, waves her arms. "But the last time," he says, "just before." He can't go on, but he can't help a smile either. "Christ, she was ginormous," he whispers. "Tight as a melon."

He takes a breath.

He can't remember when the nurse said to first expect a smile, but knows it is not yet.

"You will swim like an otter. She promised me that."

With one hand he works the lid off the urn, tosses it back to the whitened cobble.

This low, this late, the river edges toward bathtub warm, and he stands and wades deeper, in his funeral clothes, up to his waist, beyond, turns and sinks in, rolling onto his back, holding her up against his chest, easing her into the water. She kicks and waves, makes a squawk, which is not a cry, not even close.

"Check her out, Marn," he says. "Half amphibian already."

He tips the urn little by little. The lightest ash drifts some on what breeze there is, but mostly it just sifts down into the water. Together, they wash around the eddy, the gray streaks sinking and dispersing, fading. He lets the urn sink away.

Still floating, holding Midge up, he tips his head back. Water over his forehead, then in his eyes, up his nose. It would be fast. For both of them. He'd have to hold her. Find some way to keep himself under. Wedge himself into a logjam.

He jerks his head up as if yanked by his hair, floats blinking in the brightness. He swears he heard her, his name shouted, that total no-nonsense pull-your-shit-together tone he'd only ever heard from her maybe once or twice before. He can't help but look around for her.

The baby splashes her arms, makes that excited squawk, over and over.

"She's swimming, Marn," he says, "I mean, would you just look at her?"

You look at her, Marnie says. *Don't you dare take your eyes off of her.*

Breathing hard, he kicks to hold their faces above the water, out in the heat of the day. He smiles, and whispers in Midge's ear. "Don't let her scare you," he says, "all bark, no bite," then ducks under the swat that would bring.

He drifts back into the quiet water and still whispering to Midge, says, "The first time I ever saw your mom was at the river. Just me and Rudy tubing after work. And here came the college girls, bobbing around the bend. Just that one look and Rudy damn near drowned. Me, I was hooked, too. Fish on." He smiles, circling around the eddy, Midge on his chest. "The only word that came to mind was mermaid. Nothing else fit. Not even close."

They drift round and round, Taz telling her everything he can think of about Marnie. He could go on forever.

————

When at last he returns, the house looks empty. But people stand up from chairs when he opens the door, only their truest friends left. He glances around, her mother nowhere to be seen. Hards's boyfriend, Dan, tilts his head toward the bedroom. "She kind of gave out after a while," he says. "How are you holding up?"

The heat, the rush of parched air, has dried his clothes, but his suit still looks swum in. "Where've you been?" Dan asks.

Hards touches him, her hand on his arm. "Taz, what can we do?"

Forcing what might be a smile, at best not frightening, he says, "Find me a beer?"

Hards slides his jacket off his shoulders. He has to set the car seat on the table. "Seriously," she says. "It's like a hundred out there."

With the doors open all day, it's not that far off inside. She fits his jacket across the back of a chair, and he sees the gray streaks sketched across it, water lines. "I," he says. "I. We. You guys," he looks around at all their friends. "Thanks for coming. Really."

If the ceiling caved in, the walls toppled, he would not blink. He glances around for cracks, the first fissures opening in the sheetrock, listens for the splintering of the rough-cut studs. "I was," he says. "I was … christ on a bike, I was going for beer. You guys must be dying."

They look around him, near him. Not one of them has reached thirty. No one here is dying. Every one of them holds a beer. "I'll be right back," he says. "There's some booze under the stairs in the basement."

Rudy follows him to the door, takes his elbow in his hand before he can get past the porch. Turns him back. He leans in, whispers, "You really think I'd throw a party without beer?" They're all standing there, looking at him, and Hards, Midge in one arm, puts a beer into his hand, folds his fingers around it. Her three other college roommates, part of that first-ever tubing trip, who Rudy still calls the Sirens, lift their bottles, raise them like closed fists, and say, in unison, "For Marn, forever." Taz's arm goes up, too, as if controlled by strings. "See," Rudy says, "that wasn't so hard." He gives him a little push from behind and says, "Now go get Moms out of her room, and let's get this thing rolling."

Someone cranks the music, a playlist so close to Marn's he can't imagine where they got it, and Rudy keeps the pressure on his back until he's standing in the hallway, their bedroom door gleaming a few steps away.

He knocks, then turns the knob, pushes it in just far enough to see her feet at the end of the bed, and says, "Lauren?"

Her feet move, toward the edge of the bed, and he barely hears her say, "Ted?"

"It's me," he says, and he takes one step in.

She sits up, wipes at her eyes, rearranges her hair.

"You okay?" he asks.

She glances toward the mirror, away. "May have to borrow your shades," she says.

He feels for them against his chest, starts to swing the Croakie strap over his head, but she smiles, kind of, says, "No, 'the future's so bright,' you know?"

"Oh," he says, tries to smile back, drops his shades.

"But," Lauren says, "these eyes, they might actually be a good idea."

He lifts them off again, holds them out to her. She puts them on, his Ray-Bans, and looks at the mirror again. "Jackie fricking O," she says.

"They said—" he starts, but stops, holds the beer out to her instead. She takes it from him, takes a pull, gives an exaggerated "Aah," just like Marnie.

"If I can do this," Taz says, "you can."

She reaches back with the beer, but he says, "It's yours. There's no shortage."

She holds her other hand out, and before he can think, he takes it, gives her the pull up off the bed, again, the same as Marn, as she got bigger and bigger.

"We can do this," she says. "We have to."

When they step out, everyone raises their glasses and bottles again, as if they're the stars of the show. Another bottle's slipped into Taz's hand. The music gets turned up, Rudy starts to tell about the Sirens, how they came round the bend in the river, a paradise of bikinis. They toast Marnie. Then Midge, her eyes barely open in Hards's arms. Taz can't take his eyes from his ash-streaked jacket.

Rudy puts his arm around Taz's shoulders. Squeezes. Twists him away from the jacket. Hards, like it's nothing, lifts the jacket from the chair and drops it behind the couch, out of sight. The Sirens beg to hold Midge, even as she fusses, headed for the crib. Rudy watches, mesmerized.

Later, standing in the doorway, Lauren calling it a night having opened the floodgates, a round of hugging and a few more tears, he watches them all leave. Even Rudy, walking down the sidewalk, his over-the-shoulder wave. After the last taillights disappear beyond the end of the block, he stands watching the darkness, the empty street, a beer bottle still dangling from his hand. He turns back inside, looks at Midge, asleep on the couch, somehow now on top of his jacket.

Marnie gives her big *Whew,* and says, *You made it. And even Mom, in your shades.*

Taz nods.

And, really, it was a pretty good party. But, well, you know, let's not do that again.

He can see her looking around the room, the after-party wreckage, though, really, the place is pretty well cleaned up, and she blows out her breath, starts the first tug toward the bedroom, says, *We'll get all this later.*

Later, he thinks. Later.

DAY 8

Taz dozes through the morning feed in the rocker, never quite going out, but surprised to find Midge asleep, mouth hanging open around the nipple. He settles her into the bassinet, used to the little jerk she gives when separated from his chest.

He can smell the bacon, the coffee, and steps into the clothes he finds on the floor.

She sets his plate down before he's reached the table. Pancakes this morning. Blueberries. The cup of coffee. No cream. No sugar.

"Good morning," he says, and pulls back his chair.

She stands behind hers, both hands around her cup. Cream. Sugar. Two spoons. He knows it by heart.

She gives him a minute, just watching, then takes a breath and says, "That was nice last night. Being included. Thank you."

Taz can't think what to say.

"But, boy, it hurts this morning." She smiles, sips her coffee.

He wonders if it'll ever stop hurting.

She sets her coffee down. "You think I don't like you."

Taz takes his own breath, lets it out. "Lauren, there's no—"

"At first, I'll admit." She taps her fingers against her cup. "Well, let's just say I thought Marnie could do better."

"Marnie could do anything she wanted."

"And what she wanted was you."

Taz looks at his plate, the perfectly crisped bacon.

"It just took me a little longer to see why," she goes on. "To see how the two of you worked together. Both of you always thought I hated this house, and you whined to her about how I thought you were dragging her down."

Taz looks up, starts to say "Lauren" again, but she says, "You were so wrong. I looked at you here, saw neither one of you the least bit afraid, not a doubt in your lives." She shakes her head. "If her father," she starts, "if he had half the—" She almost laughs. "Well, let's just say that Marnie picked way better than I did."

Taz hears Marnie whisper, *Who is this person?* and Taz manages to say, "Lauren, stop."

"No," she says. "It's time for you to listen now. No matter what you said, or thought, I never went after you behind your back. I respected what you were doing. Hell, I even admired it."

"You don't have to say—"

"But you've got to find that again, Ted. Even if it was Marnie who brought it out, or the two of you together, whatever. Grieve, of course—god, we'll be doing that for the rest of our lives—but ..." She lifts her arm, points straight toward Midge in the bassinet, as if she can see through walls. "It's about her now. Everything is."

"I—"

"And I know a thing or two about being a single parent, so if there's anything, at all, you call. No matter what you think, I'll do every single thing in my power to help."

"Lauren," he finally squeezes in. "Are you done?"

She smiles. "Just one more thing."

He sits back, gives her the floor.

"I've got my ticket. This afternoon. It's time for you now."

He blinks, looks back down at his plate, then all around the room, and finally up at her.

"There's at least a month's worth of diapers in the bathroom," she says. "And your friends have brought more formula than four babies could ever go through. It's all stacked in the kitchen cupboards. The refrigerator's packed, the freezer full, the laundry done." She stops, looks straight at him. "It's your life now."

Taz lifts his hands, lets them fall. "Thank you," he says. "And, I'm sorry, you know, for being an ass."

She sits down. Lets go of her coffee. She smiles. Tiny. Waves her hand between them as if clearing smoke. "It's okay," she says. "I don't know anyone who would be good at this."

He sees again the first hint of graying hair, the skin starting to slacken, just some lines, not jowls or anything. All a Marnie he'll never see. "Wouldn't want to know them if they were."

She gives a nod, then sighs. "You know, I ..." She tries to keep her smile going. "I've been working on that speech all morning. And now I have no idea what I'm going to do."

"Me either."

"You have more to do than you'll ever know."

Taz looks at the bacon plate, eight slices left on the paper towel. For the two of them. He wonders how many more pancakes are in the oven, keeping warm.

He takes a piece of bacon. Then holds the plate out to her. "Thank you," he says again. "For everything."

———

Sitting alone after she leaves, Taz sees Rudy back out on the porch, the same kind of radar he's had since he was five, six. Elbows on knees, hands dangling. Like he could wait forever. All the time in the world.

Midge is asleep in the car seat, his kind of portable bassinet, and Taz opens the door, and sits down beside Rudy on the steps, facing out toward the street, the maples shading them, the heat still fierce, the air itself singed, smoked.

"Would not want to be fighting fire today," Rudy says.

Taz nods, and they look out at the street.

"So," Rudy says. "I was sort of wondering if you, you know, like need a hand or anything?"

"A hand?"

"Babysitting? Or work, if you've got any."

Taz glances toward him. "Babysitting? There's laws, Rude. Protective services."

Rudy smiles. "And you just know how jazzed they've got to be looking over your resume."

Rudy reaches his finger toward Midge's hand, his favorite trick, the reflex grab, but stops short of touching. "She's asleep," he says.

"I know."

"See," he says, "we're experts."

"No doubt," Taz says. "The basics, the bottles and stuff, the diapers. Even we can do that. And Lauren left us enough to get through the apocalypse. Cabinets look like we're Mormons."

"What else is there?"

"Sleeping."

"You don't look like you've *ever* slept."

"Yeah, that one's been tougher." Behind him the house yawns empty.

"Well," Rudy says, "I'm going to miss her cooking."

"Right," Taz says.

"And she's not bad-looking, either."

"Rude!"

"You know, for an older gal."

"Just flat creepy, Rude."

"The Rude cannot be choosy. Guy could do worse than those meals."

"She's Marn's *mom*."

Rudy rubs his belly. "Like I said, miss her already."

Taz stands and Rudy follows him up. "So, where do we start?" he asks.

Taz turns toward the door. "Rude," he says. "She's actually sleeping. I better try to get me some of that, too. While I've got the chance."

Rudy looks down the street, says something not loud enough to be heard.

"Rudy," Taz says. "We're going to be fine."

Rudy pushes up to his feet. He reaches out, touches Taz on the arm as he drops down off the porch, then walks off, giving his wave.

Taz watches until Rudy's out of sight down the block, then lifts the car seat, Midge's eyes opening at the first touch. He glances down, Midge watching him steadily. He pushes open the front door, the car seat in one hand, and swivels through. He carries Midge over the threshold, something he can't keep from narrating to himself, "He carries her over the threshold." The first time they set foot in the house, the mortgage all theirs, he and Marnie'd been laughing so hard he'd nearly dropped her.

He puts the car seat on the table and undoes the buckle, the house emptier than outer space, even the mother's ghost whisking around now, too, stepping out of the kitchen, something cooking. He bites his lips, squints, gives his head a quick shake, a rush of bile and desolation so fierce he's afraid he'll throw up.

"Well, here we are," he says.

It's what Marnie had said that first time, when they'd slid to the floor, barely making it over the threshold, her fingers working at his buckle, the house a wreck just waiting for them.

DAY 9

Taz stands in the kitchen, two in the morning, awake since the last feeding, Midge quiet in her room at last. His eyes scratch as if bedded in gravel. The car seat's on the table, empty and ready, as if they've someplace to go. Yesterday's coffee sits cold in his cup, but he thinks about it, looking around, the light from the bare bulb dangling from the last of the knob and tube, scalding. The computer sits open on the table, waiting, the screen gone blank. She'll be awake, hungry, in another few hours.

He does the math. Ten o'clock at night, still the same day. New Zealand, land of his father's dreams, twenty hours ahead. He sits. Taps the mouse. The screen lights up, Skype still sitting there waiting. They're online. He takes a breath and makes the connection. He has no idea anymore what hours they keep.

But his father answers, his face pixilated on the cheap screen. He grins, calls, "Serena!" and his mother dodges in over his shoulder. They're both still dressed, so.

His mother says, "A girl?" Her smile so wide. Their first grandchild. Their only. "Come on," she urges. "We've got money on this."

Taz says, "It's a girl."

She whoops and, even as the loser, his father cries, "Good on ya'!" as if he's lived there all his life. Taz has seen neither of them since his father packed it in, his original escape to Montana—a career building log homes he'd pretended were for the back-to-nature crowd, not just the impossibly wealthy—no longer far enough, not, as he said, with a second Bush junta. He'd abdicate, he declared, and by god, he did, dragging his wife with him, landing on the same Tasman Sea beach Taz had been nicknamed for, a place his father had seen forty years before, a seed finally taken root, building one last cabin. If Taz lets him get going, like a broken record he'll get into the conspiracies, how ICE will stop him at the borders, his name on some blacklist, an adversary too dangerous to ever let back in. His mother, if she gets a chance, would only say something quietly about the astronomical airfares.

Now she has to say, "Taz?" twice, bringing him back, and when he looks, she smiles, asks if he can hold her up to the screen. So she can see.

"She's sleeping," he says, and he can see them start in on their own calculations, realizing it's the middle of his night. His mother leans closer, studying him. He should have at least patted down his hair. She says, "How's Marnie?"

They've never met her. Were waiting for them to make the expedition to the antipodes, those plane tickets light-years further away from him than his parents.

They'd only ever, he realizes, seen this jerky, grainy image of her. Like she'd never even been real.

Under the interrogation light hanging overhead, he takes a catastrophic breath, lets it out. "Dad," he says. "Mom."

DAY 30

Taz leaves the clinic, Midge strapped into the car seat. He walks out beside the emergency doors, still getting used to the floating feel of pure exhaustion, a fever kind of thing. The doctor had greeted him like a cheerleader, told him how great it was to see the two of them again, to see them doing so well. Taz had no recollection of her whatsoever, even when she showed the marks on her charts from the two-week checkup. She showed him her new marks, told him what a great, great job he was doing. "Job?" Taz said. She assured him the nights would improve, that her tummy was too small to hold eight hours of nourishment. "Each day will bring a little progress," she promised, and pointed again at her ballpoint dots; height and weight both on the overachiever's side of the bell curve. Midge's eyes followed the doctor's finger. She blinked at her light. Milestones toppling like dominoes. Simple things, Taz tells himself, but he smiles as he wrestles the belt around the car seat, runs the back of his finger down her cheek. "Can you believe it, Marn?" he says.

He turns the key, works the gas, five quick pumps to get it

to fire, the roar almost hiding the phone's beep. Her mother. Clairvoyant, checking in for the first time. But she'd given him the time, weeks, a chance to catch his breath, maybe get his feet under him. He cranks down the windows, puts her on speaker so he can get rolling, pour some air through the cab, the heat wave and fires hanging into October, longer than anyone could have guessed, the sunrises still blazing, Taz and Midge, on their schedule, catching almost every single one.

He tells her mother the doctor's assessment, says, "I'd let you talk to her, but she's doing another sudoku right now."

Her mother gives a short, staticky laugh, hard to say how forced, then says, quietly, "You sound better."

"Better?" Taz says, a word he can barely recognize. "I don't think," he says, "I mean," and he manages, just barely, to switch his *I* to *we*. "Do you think we'll ever really be that?"

"Ever is a dangerous word, Taz," she says, and realizing just how hard she's trying, he almost has to pull over.

"Has she let you sleep yet?" she asks, more clairvoyance.

"The doc said she will. Eventually."

"She will," Lauren says. "There isn't a teenager on the planet waking every two hours."

She tries that little laugh again, and he pictures her alone, her phone pressed to her head. For the first time ever, he wonders if she has friends. People she sees every day. Who call now and then, check in on her this way. At least sit on her porch.

"Lauren," he forces himself to say. "How have you been?"

There's silence, then she says, "Oh, you know, just following the headlights."

He does pull over, wonders if it had been passed down, or up,

Marnie's line in the dark patches, her promise that even if they couldn't see past the headlights right now, they could still make the whole trip that way. *Hell, Taz, we are the headlights.*

A car zips past, and he looks up, wonders where he is. A maple-lined street, trim old bungalows. Almost home.

He thinks how many more years Marnie had following those lights with her mother than with him, how much more experience Lauren has as the single parent, how much more prepared Marnie would have been for this than he is.

"Yeah," Taz says. "We'll make the whole trip."

There's a noise, a muffled bark. A laugh? A sob? He hears the draw of breath. "Are you back to work?" she manages to ask.

"Soon," he says. "Marko's trying to give me time, but they're starting to get houses closed in, and, well, pretty soon we'll be starving." He trails off, remembering Marnie poring over plans with him, laughing at people's tastes, or saying, "Hmm," tapping her finger against her chin, her lips. "Maybe we steal this?"

"And?" her mother says.

Taz edges back into the street, makes the last corner, almost home. "I've been looking around," he says. "Day cares. Nannies." All lies. Just the word nanny almost cracks him up. Mary Poppins floating down, saving the day.

"Taz," she says, "You know I ..." She leaves it at that.

He does know. She'd move. In a minute. Would be happy to. Is dying to. To have this new Marnie to raise, some reason for each next day. Same as him. "I'll let you know," he says, and pulls into his drive. Tells her he has to go.

DAY 35

Taz lies under the apple tree, Midge on his chest as he explains the tree house plans. He points into the branches, the blue stronger beyond them than through the smoke haze at the horizons. He hears the crunch of footsteps in the drive and slows the rattle of terms he's been rolling off: balcony, French doors, louvered cupola, widow's walk. Anything he can think of, like a conversation. Maybe, he admits, just white noise, something she might drift off on.

He listens to the steps come closer, up the side of the house, toward the shop, the two of them. "I wanted eyebrow dormers," he whispers, "but your mom says that's just showing off."

Then he's quiet, not looking, hand still pointing up into the air, until he hears, "Taz?"

It's not Rudy, or any of the others who keep dropping by, Hards, the Sirens, even Marko. Just checking in. "Just passing by, you know, so ..." He turns his head, lowers his hand to shield his eyes.

"It's Ron," the silhouette says. "Ron Berquist."

Taz sits up a bit, shifting Midge to his lap. Big house on a corner lot, a real renovation, not a remodel, ten-inch mahogany crown molding, Ron one of the good ones, wanting it saved. Marn wanted to steal *all* his plans.

"I tried calling," Ron says.

"Phone's been on the fritz," Taz says.

"Well, Nicole and I, we were wondering if you're available for a little more work."

There's just the slightest edge of uncertainty, a note Taz can pick out anywhere now. So, he knows. Taz raises an eyebrow, waits.

"Just a pair of doors, front and back," he says, rushing a little. "To match the others. They look so good, we can't really hang on to the last two old ones."

Vertical panels, oak, quarter-sawn. "Usually they jazzed up the exterior doors a little," Taz says. "The front anyway. A mantel maybe. Glass. Sometimes sidelights."

Ron says, "We've got an old stained-glass window we'd like for the front door."

Taz says, "Of course you do," and Ron smiles. "When are you looking for them?"

"There's no rush." Ron steps closer, looks at Midge. "She's beautiful," he says.

"We've been discussing tree house plans."

"She's got big ideas?"

"Well," Taz says. "She's particular. Gets it from her mother."

He and Marn had barely started on their own house when Marko sent Ron and Nicole over to discuss their renovation plans. They'd looked around the wreck of Taz and Marn's place, maybe wondering if Taz was really the guy they wanted working on theirs, but smiling at them, like they knew what it was like to be just starting out, when tearing down plaster could be like a date.

"Taz," Ron says, struggling for a name, and Taz says, "Marnie," and Ron puts a hand up to his cheek. "We just feel horrible, it's just not, we're so sorry, we—"

Taz pushes himself up the rest of the way. "Thanks," he says. "I'm on child duty this afternoon, but I could come by tomorrow, take some measurements."

Ron says, "Really?" then, as if he can't risk letting Taz get away, adds, "You can just follow me straight home now if you want. I'm heading there for lunch."

Taz looks around the yard, cannot spy an excuse. "Okay," he says. "We'll be right behind."

Nicole is home, caught off guard, sputtering through more of the same condolences, but she's more than happy to take Midge for a minute, talk about their granddaughter, who is maybe just a bit older, almost a year now, and the measurements take only a few minutes, and then Taz is back home, opening the door to his shop, Midge cradled against his chest. He doesn't even turn on the lights. The tools, all honed and oiled and ready to cut, gleam dully in their places. He doesn't have a chance, everything *set up* to be within reach. And even if he just put her in her car seat, set it on the workbench, the planer's roar, making a rocket launch sound like a sweet nothing, would leave her deaf before she could shape her first word. Lungs too clogged with sawdust to draw the breath for it.

He imagines calling Lauren, saying, "Got a job. Come on

out." Pictures her standing waiting for him every morning with her coffee and cream and two sugars. Such a well-intentioned intruder in the nest they'd built for only the two of them. He brushes the top of Midge's head with his cheek. "The three of us, I mean. Of course."

He steps back out of the shop, locks up the door, but still takes Midge out to the hardwoods place. Something will come to mind.

At the yard, he takes Midge out of the car seat, walks her through the recycled lumber piles, mulling through their old, old, oak, real two-inch, all quarter-sawn, the grain hidden beneath the gray and the dust, but still stuff that even rough will cost more than a finished Home Depot pre-hung. He could pull enough extra for a door for their place, too, he thinks. Pad the bill a little. It was Marnie's idea long before it was his, but still he hears her calling him a criminal, a shady character, someone to watch out for. Punching at his arm, smiling, already fitting the ill-gotten wood into all their plans.

He gets the lot kid to help him load the wood into his truck. Does all he can while still holding Midge, who, truth be told, has had about enough of the sun, the lumber, all of Taz's plans.

At home, he backs down the drive to the shop, sits behind the wheel, Midge out hard in her seat, mouth sprawled, head down at an angle so severe he wants to tip it up right, though the fear of waking her keeps him from moving a single muscle. Only his heart and lungs, things he can't control.

He glances in the rearview, the shop looming just as deadly and impossible as it had before, now his pickup loaded with old-growth oak, this ancient wood felled a hundred years ago on the

other side of the country, beautiful stuff he loves to touch, run
his hands over, his eyes, even as he imagines it standing, arms
reaching into the sky, branches waving in breezes that won't
reach the ground.

He looks back down to Midge, her lip downed with sweat,
one hand clasping and unclasping in some dream he can't begin
to imagine or decipher. He closes his eyes, still seeing the lumber, the shop, those tiny fingers, the carbide steel tipping each
tooth of every blade.

Easing his head back onto the rest, he drifts off laboring over
math. Sixty-five hundred rpm, somewhere north of a hundred
revolutions a second, an eighty-tooth blade ripping eight, nine
hundred teeth into whatever it might touch. Every second.

Jesus, Marnie says, *knock it off. She doesn't go into the shop. Ever.
Plain and simple. You'll be fine.*

He wakes to Rudy tapping a knuckle against the side of the
truck's door. Appeared as if by magic, nodding toward the wood
in the back, whispering, "Looks like we got work to do."

DAY 40

Another night from hell behind them, Taz and Midge lie side by side on the floor. Wondering if she'll ever sleep, he watches the ceiling fan with her. He thinks about dimmer switches. Making the fan rotate even more slowly, each individual blade visible as more than a blur.

He looks over. Her eyes always open, deeper than cenotes, a thing Marnie had always wanted to see. And, in the light of day, she looks so harmless, so peaceful. Really, the sweetest thing he has ever seen. He might even say that if she weren't his. But, man, nights? Horns sprout. Fangs. Fire-breathing. He'd even called the doc, gotten the nurse, gotten assured that sometimes it's just an adjustment period, the baby getting used to the world. He looked up colic, closed the computer in horror.

He reaches up, spins the rattle wheel on the mobile bridge above her, a gift left inside the front door one day, a tag, Susan, *the woman at the plans exchange*, written in after the name, in parentheses, a name he never could have come up with on his own. A never-ending flood. One morning he'd found Rudy sitting on a stack of Enfamil cases. He'd just handed the card back over his shoulder, said, "You remember Mr. Brown?"

"Our math teacher? Hellgate High?"

"Apparently he's not liking the statistical probability of you feeding her on your own."

It's a moment before he hears the delicate tapping at the front door. A pause, then repeat, just a touch harder. Midge's arms jerk. She blinks. Taz, too. He glances at his watch, stunned to see it's well beyond dawn, the day waiting out there, Rudy ready to start. Or maybe just another gift.

But Taz can't imagine moving a muscle, can nearly feel them wrench clear of the bone with the first attempt at rising.

He listens to Rudy mull around, call his name once, too wary of Midge's sleep situation to dare ring the bell. Taz hears him sit, resuming his vigil. He should become a monk, Taz thinks, something that requires the patience of Job.

Yesterday Taz called Ron, let him know the doors might take longer than he thought. Maybe he should let him and Nicole watch Midge, a surrogate granddaughter. Even if just long enough to rip the stiles and rails, glue up the panels, get it to the assembly stage, which Midge could watch.

It's pushing an hour, maybe more, Taz anchored to the floor, before he hears a truck pull in, a door creak. Rudy says, "Nobody home."

There's more talking. Marko. Then a knock. Once, twice. Once more. Midge blinks each time, and he prays she doesn't cry.

She blinks again when the big truck cranks over. Marko and his headers. Before he backs out of his drive, Taz's phone rings, but he's already pulled it from the tool pocket of his Carhartts and pressed the silencer. Marko's name there.

He lowers his arm. Sets the phone on the floor. Nudges it away with the back of his fingers.

Without rolling over, he reaches across and touches her chest. His arms ache, his back, from doing nothing more than not sleeping. He runs his fingers down her side, over the diaper and down her legs, around her ankles, the bottoms of her bare feet, like he used to with Marnie, barely touching. Midge wriggles head to foot. Waves her arms. Kicks.

She about pops out of her skin when the front door swooshes open and Rudy says, "Hey, just, you know, welfare check."

Taz puts an arm up over his eyes. "Privacy?" he says.

"You alive?"

"Breathing, anyway."

He feels Rudy step closer, feels Midge squirm under his touch, too.

"Guess you didn't hear Marko," Rudy says.

"Who?"

"Yeah, that's what I thought."

Taz lets his arm flop to the side, looks over at Rudy.

"You retired now, too?" Rudy asks.

"Maternity leave."

"And I bet Marko's all set up for that. Those benefits you must be raking in."

"Yeah."

"The kid's gonna have to eat," Rudy says. "Once Hellgate's formula's gone. Or you've done something miraculous with your tits?"

Taz sits up, elbows on knees, blows out a breath. "What do you want, Rude?"

"I thought we were working today."

"Soon," Taz says. "Soon. It's just, man, she never sleeps, and who's going to look after her while we're out there slicing and dicing?"

"You okay?" Rudy asks.

"Yes," Taz says. "We're okay. I wish people would stop asking that."

Rudy walks into the kitchen. Taz hears the refrigerator open. "Rudy," he calls.

But Rudy walks back through the living room, and heads out without a word, leaving the door open to the heat.

They're both asleep, still on the floor, a changing and a feeding behind them, when Rudy walks back in, trundling in armloads of groceries.

Taz hears the whoosh of the gas, a pan dropped onto the burner. "Rude," he shouts. "You? Cooking?" He looks at Midge, says, "The earth's revolving backwards."

"Get your party clothes on," Rudy yells from the kitchen. "You might even consider a shower. We're going out."

He fries burgers, watches after Midge, makes Taz put on clean clothes.

"I'm guessing you've got a plan," Taz finally says, pushing back from the table, dropping the plates onto the drainboard.

"Just the Club, nothing earth-shattering."

"And what? We just leave her in front of the TV?"

"You don't have a TV."

Taz looks around. "So, she's coming with?"

"She needs to get out some."

"You want to take her to a bar?"

"She doesn't *have* to order anything, but staying in here all the time, she's going to grow up looking like one of those cave fish."

Taz looks around the room as if there are options squatting in every corner.

"You might want to change her clothes, too, that shirt or whatever it is," Rudy says. He gets up, opens the lid of the washer, peers in as if the inside is a brand-new wonder, but he twists the controls, says, "Soap?" and starts to pile in Taz's laundry, Midge's onesie going in on top. It's all Taz can do not to stare.

The washer rumbling into its cycle, Rudy sweeps up Midge, and Taz follows out the door, pausing just long enough to grab the car seat. Rudy's already headed around back for Taz's truck. "I walked," he calls.

"So, I'm driving? This explain your dating life?"

"It's a work in progress," Rudy says, then, "Heard anything from Mrs. H? She ask about me at all?" and Taz pushes him away from the truck an instant before he can climb in. He belts in Midge's car seat, then belts her in, Rudy riveted, as if observing brain surgery.

Taz pulls out. "How long did it take you to come up with this plan?"

"Well, you know, sitting on your porch all month, I've had some time to cogitate."

Taz takes his eyes off the road for a glance. "Did you just say cogitate?"

Rudy touches Midge's palm, getting her to grab his finger. "But, you not finding enough reason to open the door, answer the phone, I figured I had to take action."

As he parks, Rudy undoes the car seat, and Taz says, "We're not staying long."

"That a boy," Rudy says, and pushes open the door.

They find a place, sit Midge in her seat on the table, her eyes wide, transported to this new universe, taking it all in. Rudy turns the car seat so she faces the bar. "This, Midge," he says, "is the world."

Taz looks. "What? Where?"

"Don't listen to him. There's more to it than your ceiling fan."

"You're killing me."

Rudy pets Midge's head, flattening, for a moment, the golden wisps. "Well, she's already growing out her hair, planning on going all Rapunzel."

Taz pinches the bridge of his nose. "How about the river, Rude? Any one of them. Or just a drive down south, the Bitterroots? Or north, the Missions. Bust it all out, we can take her to Glacier."

Rudy turns back to him. "With the grizzlies?"

"They might be more *Parenting* magazine than the Club."

"It's not quite Sodom and Gomorrah," Rudy says, but he's looking around, scanning the place. "Service like this, I might as well go get us a couple."

But, before he musters the energy, a girl starts toward the table, and Rudy holds up two fingers, not a word exchanged.

"Humor me, okay?" Rudy says. "Just a beer. Maybe it'll clear your head. The cobwebs, whatever."

The pint glasses clonk on the wooden table; salvage wood, rough-cut buried under layers of acrylic. The car seat rocks as Midge kicks, squawks something. Taz watches frost slide down the side of his glass, pool on the plastic, barely hears the "Cute kid" the girl says as she turns away.

Before even reaching for his beer, Rudy says, "Oh my god."

Taz looks up.

"She speaks."

Taz slides his finger along the glass, squeegeeing away the frost.

Rudy nods toward the bartender. "It's not quite the first time, but, close enough."

Taz follows Rudy's gaze. She dips pint glasses like she's been doing it her whole life, brings them up soapy, back down into the rinse.

"But, the Rude has patience," Rudy says. "As evidenced by my sojourn on your porch."

"Sojourn?"

"Not to say that it hasn't been a thrill ride," Rudy says, reaching for his glass. He lifts it to clink, says, "But now that I've got you out, let's try it just a bit more often. You know, open the door, walk down the steps?" Taz gives a whatever, but just before looking away from the bar, he catches the bartender peek over, straight to Midge, the tiny crack of a tinier smile, and he gets it, Rudy's plan to get some girl's attention. He touches his glass to Rudy's. "You're a genius, Rude. Don't let anyone tell you any different."

"So, tomorrow," Rudy says, and he plans out a whole new life, rejoining the world, and Taz sips, thinking how Marnie would love this, Rudy his life advisor. He waits and waits, but she has nothing to say, and the next morning Rudy, as planned, watches Midge long enough for Taz to get the door pieces cut, planed, milled.

DAY 44

The screen swings open, as quiet as Rudy can get, and then he's in, whispering Taz's name, plodding across the living room, down the hallway, as if he owns the place. He glances into their bedroom, then steps down toward Midge's, maybe kind of trying to tiptoe. Taz watches from the rocker, Midge across his legs, arms sprawled to her sides. He gives a tiny shake of his head, and Rudy reels himself in, backstrokes down the hallway, stopping just before sliding into the living room.

Taz keeps up his rocking, slow and easy, a metronome. He tries to remember the night, wonders if she's not due up any second anyway. He slows the rocking, decelerating, hoping the heat shields hold through reentry. Trying to stay with the rocking, he rolls forward, lifting her from his lap, his forearms scooping in between her and his legs. He gets her into the air, rocking just a little as she starts, eyes still closed.

Down into the crib, the touchdown fraught with danger, but she stays down, out. He edges the blanket over, steps back once, twice. Starts to turn, keeping his feet on the floor, minimizing the squeaks. He makes the bedroom door and steps through, just one tiny glance back, nearly awestruck that she's still there, eyes still closed, breathing just as quick and steady.

Rudy stands in the living room, halfway to the front door. He raises his finger to his lips.

"You know," Taz says, "maybe knocking isn't such a terrible idea."

"You never answer."

"Then I guess I'm busy, or she's asleep, or—"

"Or you're just not answering."

"Yeah, or that."

"Well, how'm I going to know if you're home?"

"We don't really go a lot of places. Remember?"

Rudy dips a whatever shoulder. "Well, I had to see if you were really here."

"Why?"

"No reason, really. Just, you know..."

"But you just said, you had to see."

"Well, not *had* so much."

Then he hears Marko, the headers, blatting his way up the street, pulling into his drive. Rudy doesn't look at him. Taz says, "You know about this?"

Rudy says, "I might have kind of called him, yeah."

The truck shuts off, the door slams.

Taz says, "So this is what, some kind of intervention?"

A second later, Marko's at the door. He taps a knuckle instead of ringing, then pushes the door open a few inches, peers in, just the one eye in the crack of the door.

Rudy jumps, swings the door the rest of the way in. "Hey, Marko. Was just heading out. Good seeing you." He's by him like he's greased, like he was never there at all.

Marko watches him a second, then turns back to Taz. "So, you're here." He steps in, one clomp of his boots on the hardwood. "You okay?" he says.

People will never stop asking. "It's just—" he starts, but can't come up with another word. "Just been busy. Taking care of her. Figuring out how to."

Marko walks to the couch, the crunch of the couch springs, the bristle of old mohair against canvas pants.

"I got a little tired calling," Marko says.

"I know. Lost the phone. It's—"

Marko points with one thick finger. "Might try your pocket."

Taz pats it. "Damn," he says. "No guess why you're the boss."

"I'm holding on for you," Marko says. "But, I'm starting to ask around. These people can't wait forever. Won't."

"I know. I'm just, it's a time thing."

"People get day care, Taz. Almost every day. We did it." He stares him down for a moment, then looks away. "I need you back, or I need someone else. No other way I can say it."

Taz, finally looking right at him, sees the roll of plans pinched in Marko's ham of a fist. Marko gives it a shake.

"We'll see," Taz says. And though she never liked Marko, Marn gives him a nudge. *You can do this*, she says.

Marko rolls the first set of plans open on the table. "These folks don't want somebody else. They want you." He points. "When did you build your last Murphy bed?"

"I've never built a Murphy bed."

"I found a place I can get the hardware. Already got it ordered."

Taz listens for Midge, who isn't awake, just when he needs her to be. He takes a step toward the plans.

DAY 47

Taz puts Midge into the car seat, lifts it up onto the saw table. He lowered the blade first, then took it off completely, knowing he'd edged beyond ridiculous. But he narrates his every move as he assembles the door pieces; the dry fit, making sure, then the glue, the clamping, checking and rechecking for square, for flat. She watches, he thinks, and he says, "So, you'll have a trade, at least, if maybe not some huge trust fund."

Rudy goes missing for days after siccing Marko on him. So Taz does the finishing with Midge, too, outside, setting her up-wind for every step of it, the wood filler, the stain, the poly. He's got to break off once or twice for feeding, changing, naps, but it works, pretty much, and he calls Ron, lets him know he can do the install, but he'll have to bring the baby. Ron says his wife will love it.

And she does, except for the screaming every time Taz steps out of sight. She says, "Separation anxiety," and they learn, working with it, Nancy following Taz as he moves from door to door to outside, where he's set up the sawhorses, mortises in the hinges. But by the end of it, as much as they love the doors, as much as they pad the check, Taz can tell she's done, that half a day of tending the feral child clinging to her more feral dad has taken the charm off having a stand-in grandchild.

It's another few days before Rudy creeps back up onto the porch, stalling at the edge of the step. He turns when Taz cracks open the screen, scraping at the corners of his eyes, patting down his hair a little. Scratching at it more like.

"Am I a dead man?" Rudy asks.

"Thought that was me," Taz says, and walks back in. "I'll get coffee going."

Rudy follows him. "No, I'm okay," he whispers, then, "Where's herself?"

Taz reaches the kitchen, and slumps into the chair, rubbing at his face. He waves toward the bedroom. "Asleep."

Rudy stops dead. "Midge?"

"Only up once last night. Wasn't even shrieking. Ate, conked. I kept checking to see if she was still breathing. To see if she was still Midge."

"And you? You just woke up? This isn't the awake-all-night you?"

"Not really sure."

"Hmm. Doesn't seem much different."

Taz extends his middle finger, leans back in his chair, starts picking at a splinter. Rudy sets about building coffee.

Once it starts perking, Rudy nods toward his splinter work. "So, you back in the world of the employed?"

"Finished those doors, got them in," Taz says, and Rudy says, "Well, check you out. All on your own?"

Taz eyeballs him. "And there's Marko now, too," he says. "So, yeah, a working man again."

Rudy pours coffee, sets a cup in front of Taz. "This might help you join the world of the living, too." He pulls out his own chair, sits down with the cup he always uses. He takes one sip, swears, spits into his hands, then shakes them, the coffee flying. Leaning back in his chair, putting distance between himself and the cup, he says, "Hot," and wipes at his mouth, huffing air out over his tongue. "Why the hell do you use that thing? I mean, you steal it from some museum?"

Taz starts to smile, and suddenly Rudy breaks into his huge grin, says, "So, work."

"Marko was pretty persuasive."

"And it's Nanny Rude time."

Taz shakes his head. "Can't do that to you, Rude."

Rudy drops his chair legs back to the floor. "For real?"

"I called some day care places. This woman. She seemed nice."

"Some stranger? You know, right, that I can do it? Not a problem."

Taz blows across his coffee, takes a tentative sip, then looks over at Rudy. "I got to get things straightened out, Rude. Like for real, not just a fallback position."

"Fallback?"

"What, you're going into day care full time?"

"Maybe it's just the opportunity that's been waiting for me. Think of all the moms."

"Rudy, you can't—"

"She at least *knows* me."

"She loves you, Rude, but still."

Rudy stands up, dumps his coffee into the sink. "So when's this all start?"

Taz glances at his watch.

"You can't be serious."

"Meeting Marko at eight. Up at the site. Drop her at seven thirty."

"Today?"

Taz says, "I should probably get into the shower."

"Man, back to work. Feel like I should pack you a lunch, an apple, first-day-of-school pictures."

Taz stands up. "Maybe that coffee's cooled down enough for you by now."

"Still be poisonous," he mutters.

———

Midge is awake when Taz comes out of the shower, Rudy sitting with her, still on the construction-zone, throwaway couch. She finishes her bottle, and Rudy stands up, goes by Taz to the bathroom, says, "She needs changing."

Taz reaches, but Rudy's already past. Over his shoulder, he says, "Get your tools. I got her."

Taz stands a second, watches Rudy lay Midge down on the counter, whispering something to her, and then stands there longer, watching history in the making, until finally Rudy glances over his shoulder, says, "You're going to be late."

DAY 48

Day care, the drop-off, is like being drawn and quartered. He's shaking when he leaves, listening to her scream, the woman assuring him it's okay, totally natural, when he can think of nothing in the world less natural. Marnie walks him back to the truck, keeps whispering, *She's going to be okay. You're going to be okay.*

He staggers through work, not knowing if it's the time off, or exhaustion. He can barely stand by the end of it, everything hurting, but when he picks Midge up she's asleep and she sleeps through being put in the car seat, being put into the truck, being carried back inside her own home. He takes the chance and does laundry, everything in the house, the first loads since her mother left, or Rudy's one load, or did he just dream that? She sleeps through his Hamburger Helper, though he wolfs it anyway, getting ready, and he's wondering what they've done to her, what they've given her to make her sleep as she never has in her life.

She sleeps almost all the way until dark. And then, the sleeping is over. Till one, or two, Taz can't say for sure. He wonders about torture. Sleep deprivation. If last night was just a teaser, a reminder of what his life had been, if, long enough in, he will lose his mind.

At last she gives out, stays out when he lays her into the crib, even when he steps back to her big-girl bed. He lies there, eyes open, strung tight as a guywire, listening to the magic of her tiny breaths. He's not even sure if he's fallen asleep when she cries out again, but just once, a whimper, some odd burbling noise, then she settles, on her own. Already up on an elbow, Taz stares at the ceiling. Hardly daring to believe, he sinks back down, raises an arm up over his eyes. Dreams of sleeping.

No three *S*'s, when she wakes next she launches straight to infinity. Taz jerks up, adrenaline kicked in, heart racing. The nightlight flashes on, and he looks at this watch, the clock. He can no longer say when he's last been up, last warmed the bottle, rocked her back down. He says, "You *can't* be hungry."

He'd tossed even the boxers he was wearing into the laundry and now he stands naked before the crib, her screwed-up, shrieking face. "What?" he says.

He touches her head. She twists away. Not hot.

He slips a finger inside the leg of the diaper. Soaking. The rash. She'd been bone-dry when he checked before. He thinks he checked.

He lifts her up. The bathroom. The towel. The smear of zinc oxide. Lights off. Back to the crib, but still she screams. He sits in the rocker, wonders if he'll eventually wear through the floor, crash into the basement. He should have peed while he was up.

She goes quiet, but every time he peeks, her eyes are still open.

When he stands, as if carrying pure nitro, her eyes widen.

At the first hint of separation, her face begins its crunch. Her lip curls down. "I got to pee," he says, nearly begging.

She starts up. He puts her down. Moves the rolled towel. She raises the decibel level.

"Pee," he says again. "As if you don't know what that's about."

He leaves her. She screams as if he's falling into the abyss.

The light off, he sits on the toilet, holds his head, knows for certain that it is possible to go insane. That he's close already.

When he stands, forgets to flush, she is only screaming harder. At the door he turns left instead of right. Goes into their room instead of Midge's, lies down on the unmade bed, the stained mattress only flipped over. He pulls the crumpled pile of cleaned sheets and blankets over himself, clamps a naked pillow over his head, and whispers, "I'm sorry, Marn, I'm sorry."

———

He wakes just before six, automatically. The next feeding. But the house sits deathly still around him, dawn not quite there. His breathing jerks and he sits up, remembers. His feet hit the floor and he's up before he knows it, staggering with vertigo, but still driving down the hall, a punch-drunk has-been.

The nightlight flashes on. And she is there, asleep. Her mouth just barely slack around her thumb. He has to hold on to the side rail. Even in the gray light, half covered in a tangle of blanket, she is the most beautiful thing he has ever seen. "Okay, second," he whispers to Marn.

No, she says, *the most.*

He slide-steps back to the door, turns, retreats down the hallway, then goes back, just to make sure, before finally letting himself crawl back under his nest of blankets and pillows in his own room. He will only wait, arise at the first sound, bottle ready. He will do everything right. Marnie will not be afraid of him. For her.

And then he smiles, thinking of Midge in her crib, getting over the hump, settling herself, thinks of Marnie in this bed, with him, marveling over the genius of their child, thinks even of the Murphy bed he'd started on, how he'd laughed over it, wondering how he and Marn had never thought of one for their house. "Your mother," he whispers. "Make it all up, turn the sheets down, let her slide in, tiptoe over, tip it up, swoosh, gone."

Marnie laughs, says, *It would have been so perfect*, and, falling asleep, Taz dreams of her, as he has not since the day sliding nude into the North Fork, that first time, before they'd even thought of Midge.

Midge's first squawk brings him almost back, and he rolls in his blankets and pillows, looking for Marn, reaching to find her hip, to spoon in, cup a breast.

He opens his eyes. He is only in a pile of bedding. Alone. He listens for Midge, but she's gone quiet. Even the air waits as he holds his breath.

He sinks back toward the dream, the skin of her. He reaches down, the stupid, useless strain of his own skin and blood and desire. He runs his fingers over it the way she did, seeing if he was ready. Around the ridge, the entire head. It jumps in his hand as if his fingers have become hers. "Oh boy!" she would say, almost a giggle.

He tries, as he would have as a teenager, to picture her breasts, the surge and sway of them as they drive into each other, or the gentle prickle of her shaved mound, her ass cupped in his hands, lifted from the bed. But, as he runs her fingers up and back, all he can see is her face, her smile, her lower lip caught between her teeth, as if amazed at their boldness together. The dimple in her left cheek, a toddler's fall into a table corner, a place he has fitted his tongue into, just as he has her ears, the corner of her jaw, the hollow between her collarbones. Every inch of her.

Flat on his back, as lost in her as ever, he comes over himself with a groan, her name pulled from him as if he's tied to her by his sinews. "Marnie," he cries, choking back a sob, then unable to as they wrack him, pulling at his insides as if they will empty him, turn him inside out. His ribs strain, his sternum cracking. He rolls onto his stomach, curls onto his elbows and knees, face pressed into the mattress, the pillow, huge gulping choking wails, soaking the sheet pile. He feels her arms around him, clutching, the way she did sometimes, as if they could never be close enough. "Oh fuck," he moans. "Oh, Marn," and she moves her hands, rubbing his back, patting him, whispering, *Shh, shh, you'll be all right, you'll be okay.*

From the other room Midge answers with her own wailing and he beats his fists against the sides of his head, and she takes hold of his wrists, stills his hands, pulls his head tight to her breast, and keeps whispering, *Shh, shh, shh.*

––––––

After she is fed, he lies with her beside the little mobile. He spins the rattle. He squeezes the round thing, not sure what it is. Saturn maybe. It quacks. Midge waves her arms. He can't help it. He smiles. "Marnie," he says. "You should see her. You did so good."

She struggles to roll over. Taz does too. There's a day ahead of him. Laundry to do again. Sheets. Blankets. Everything they own. He'll have to call Marko.

Instead, he pushes himself up, starts the washer, dumps in the pile from the bed, closes the lid. He makes himself a sandwich, fills the water bottle, a thermos with what's left of the coffee. Picks Midge up, blows a raspberry against her naked belly. Slips her into a onesie. Trusses her into the car seat. Off to face the debilitating drop-off, another day of work.

DAY 60

Hards stands in the living room, his list in her hand, a smile she can't quite hide. "You sure you didn't forget anything?" she asks.

"I know. It's just, god, it's, it's just, I mean, you wouldn't believe that day care."

She looks at him.

"I'm, she's ... We're not used to it, being apart."

"I know," Hards says.

"And, really? Dan is coming over later?"

"It's the weekend. A practice run. But don't you dare tell him I called it that."

Taz looks at her. Her best friend on the planet. "Are you two ..."

She nods shyly, something not nearly committed enough.

"Be careful," he says, as if care has anything to do with it at all.

He leans into the crib, gives Midge a kiss on the forehead, tells her not to light any more fires, to quit playing with the knives. At the door he picks up his tool belt, another new place today.

He snags the yellow pad from the table, touches Hards's elbow, says, "I've got my phone," and walks out into the world.

DAY 62

It is not going to work. At all.

Hards and Dan. They had their weekend. Their chance to play, to imagine, to fantasize. Probably went back home and rutted like stoats, an expression Taz's father used to use. He imagines it, though he doesn't want to, the two of them tearing it up in every room, pretending they're making their babies, their family, their happily fricking ever afters. It flips, as he knew it would, to Marnie clutching at the couch upholstery, trying to hang on, to stay off the floor, then failing, trying to avoid the rug burns, his knees already glazing, something that will burn like acid, but only later.

He sits on the half-collapsed couch, the house darkening around him, listens for Midge in her crib, but the house is silent. He rubs at his eyes, the two of them so hot, so sweat-slicked, so unable to stop, to imagine ever wanting to, ever being able to.

He stands, wipes at his eyes, walks around the living room, avoiding, as long as he can, the first step into the kitchen, spinning the computer toward him. He drops down into the chair, and, elbows to knees, he holds his head, closes his eyes, practices his breathing.

No matter the money situation, Marn was going to stay home. She was going to raise Midge. They'd talked about home-schooling, then worried about the religious freaks, the conspiracy kooks, social bonding.

To Hards, who couldn't make it after the weekend, was never thinking of a long-term thing, he'd said, "It's going to be mostly shop work anyway," as if that meant he'd need no help, as if he could just shift Midge from shaper table, to saw table, to jointer bed.

How did normal people do it? How did they even know how?

There was Rudy. And he'd do it.

Or her mother. Lauren.

He thought of Mary Poppins again. But he lived in Montana. People in New York had nannies. Hell, they imported them from Montana. And, for christ's sake, he was a broke, half-assed finish carpenter slash cabinetmaker. As far from log homes as he could get, yes, but still only what his father had left him. All he'd ever had.

He could afford a nanny like he could afford … He couldn't even finish the thought. Afford? He couldn't afford a single thing. They'd hardly ever been able to.

He pushes himself up straight, opens the computer, sees the green glow of the dot from down under, clicks in the call before he can stop himself, prays it's his mother who answers.

And, one prayer finally answered, her face appears before he'd have guessed the satellites, or whatever it is, could have traveled so far. She looks half frightened. He tells her quick that everything is fine. Midge is fine. Flustered, she tells him that his father is out, won't be back till dinner. "Fishing," she says.

"Good," Taz says, and she lets loose a tiny, shy smile, and says, "What is it, Ted?"

"I was wondering," he starts, but does not finish.

His mother waits, finally says, "Taz?"

"I'm—" he says, and rubs at his face. "I'm not quite, I'm not … I'm not really making it here."

She closes her eyes. "I'd come, Ted, you know that, months ago, but, your father, he—"

"I know, Mom," he says. "I know. But I was wondering, you know, about visas." He hadn't once thought about such a thing, but he goes on. "Work visas, you know? If there's any work down there for finish carpenters. If I'd be allowed."

She blinks. Stops looking around the room. Stares right at him. She says, "I don't know, Taz." Her lip, he can see, even with the lousy, shifting image, trembles. "But, Christchurch," she says, "I think, since the quake, they'll take anyone."

He says, "Okay."

"It's a long way from here," she says. "The South Island. But you'd love it. It's like Montana with oceans. Midge could …"

He chews his lip.

"I'll talk to your father," she says. "As soon as he gets back."

He only nods.

She asks, "Ted? What are you thinking?"

"I don't know," he says. "I'm just wondering, you know. Like if things might be any easier down there."

She says, "Are you serious about it?"

He blows out a breath he didn't know he'd been holding. "I don't have any idea, Mom. About anything."

She holds her hand up, fingers wide, presses it close, too

close for the camera. Like a prison-visit touch. "My god," she says. "To see you again. To finally see Midge."

He feels he might smother.

"It's been so hard," she says, all she can get out.

"Not exactly walking on cake here either," he says.

He lies, says he hears Midge, that he's got to go. She talks fast, rushing out promises to call after she's talked with his father. They'll look into things for him, she says.

"Great," he says. "That'd be good."

He closes the computer. Sell the house? His tools? Just flee? Some brand-new start? Leave every last scrap of Marnie behind? Him and Midge?

————

The next morning Rudy finds him still sitting at the kitchen table, the computer closed before him, no coffee on the stove. He lifts an eyebrow, and Taz says, "Called New Zealand last night."

Rudy stops folding the newspaper he'd been reading on the porch. "What's that like? Calling a whole country?"

Taz doesn't crack a smile and Rudy sets the paper on the table in a kind of wad. "Hards told me about their weekend," he admits, as if he'd been spying.

Taz reaches out, fiddles with the edge of the newspaper. "That's what you do now?" he asks. "Sit out there and read the newspaper?"

"You called your dad?" Rudy says.

"My mom," Taz says, then, "Do I get the paper?"

"Your neighbor's."

Taz works on sorting it, folding it back up. "Rubber band?"

Rudy holds it out.

Taz goes back out, pitches it across toward the neighbor's porch.

Back in the kitchen, Rudy's rocking on the chair's rear legs. He says, "Some serious long-distance day care. Would she stay, or just make the commute every day?"

"Travel'd probably go the other direction."

Rudy drops the chair back down with a thump, sits watching him until Taz finally says, "I know, I know."

"And what? Work with your dad again? How long'd that last before one of you killed the other?"

"I just called, Rude."

"You wouldn't last one second."

"I wasn't thinking of working *with* him."

"So, what, move down there for day care? What the hell planet are you on?"

"She is her grandmother, Rude."

"What about Marn's mother?"

"I don't know, she—"

"She raised Marnie," Rudy says.

Taz dips his head. "True," he says.

"And there's the cooking," Rudy says. But he can't quite keep it going. "Your mom? She wouldn't come back? Not even for a little bit? See the grandkid?"

"Can't see her getting it past my dad."

Rudy says, "I suppose not," but then lights up, snaps his fingers. "I've got it!"

Taz waits.

"A wet nurse!" Rudy says. "Do they still have those?"

Taz puts a hand up over his eyes, rubs at them.

"Well, you got to admit, it'd be pretty hot."

DAY 70

Rudy lays off for the next few days, off on one of his secret missions, and Taz does what he can without power tools, taking Midge with him once on a measurement job, Marko floored, but the owner delighted.

He calls Lauren, just to test the waters, but when he gets the voicemail he loses his nerve, clicks off without a word, though he knows she'll see his number there.

He's sitting at the table, putting together the numbers from the measurements, sketching out a buffet that might fit the pseudo-Craftsman Marko's building, when he stops, thinking he heard a tapping. He turns toward Midge's room, but it comes again, from the front door, and Taz gets up, steps over, wondering why Rudy's gotten so formal. But, instead of Rudy, it's hardly even a kid standing in his doorway, looking at him, her smile growing less certain by the second as Taz stares. He's thinking, *Girl Scout cookies?* when she says, "Rudy sent me."

He hears the formula water coming to a boil. "Rudy?"

"He says you call him Rude?" She dips her head toward her shoulder. "Which I totally get."

He turns toward the kitchen, the kettle, then back to her. "Sent you for what?"

She pulls at her lower lip with her teeth. "He said you have the most beautiful baby in the world."

He looks away. "Rudy talks a lot."

"I don't think he's far off," she says, and it comes to him, the girl in the bar, dipping the glasses, that one quick peek she'd shot at Midge.

"He said—" she starts, but then looks back out to the street, anywhere but at him. So, Rudy had told her everything. "He said that you might be looking for someone to watch her. That you could maybe use a hand. During the days. So you can work."

"That's what Rudy says?" She looks about fifteen.

She turns back to him.

"How old are you?" he says. He's not sure what he's expecting. Mrs. Doubtfire, maybe.

"Twenty-two, and, yes, I know, I'll be getting carded at fifty." She looks to the ceiling. "I've heard that one before."

"And you're looking for work?"

"I've got two sisters. Five, seven. A brother, too, eighteen." The slightest eye roll. "Yeah, there was round two. The new wifey, the second fam." She does almost a curtsy. "And guess who got to raise them."

"Doesn't sound like you wanted to."

She flashes a *duh* look, makes it disappear before he's quite sure he's seen it. "It's different, you know, if it's your choice. Or, you know, if you get paid."

Taz says, "I do know that," and they stand there, looking at each other, until he finally says, "You want to come in?"

She steps in about three feet. Takes in the floors, the stripped trim, the wavy-glassed double-hungs. "Rudy says you did this all yourself."

Taz says, "I didn't."

She looks once, quick, then away. "Yeah," she says. "That's what he really said."

"So, you're looking for work."

"I've got one more year of school. Then student teaching."

"Sounds busy."

"It's not exactly rocket science."

"It's all rocket science to me."

She smiles. "That just means you've got at least a clue."

"Is school on now?" he asks. He walks to the windows, looks for the cars jamming every parking space.

"Mr. Davis, Rudy told me—" she starts, but Taz interrupts, says, "It's Taz," and closes the window, the day getting hot. "Not Mr. Davis." For christ's sake, he's what, six years older? Seven?

Still, though, seven years. A quarter of his life. Exactly how long he'd known Marnie. His whole life.

"Taz?" she asks.

"After a sea," he says, "not the devil."

She nods, biting at her lip again.

"So," he says.

"Rudy said—"

"I know, that I could use some help. What about the Club?"

"What about it?"

"Two jobs? And school?"

"I know," she says. "I'd've dropped it a year ago, but you wouldn't believe the tips."

Taz pulls out a chair for her at Marn's monstrous dining room table. She'd made a tent under it, blankets, couch pillows, sheets. They'd slept under it. More. "Can you imagine?" she'd said in the underwater light beneath the new sea turtles, "how Midge is going to love this place?"

Can you imagine? God, how many times had he heard that, her eyes as big and wide as this teenaged pretender's. And here he was, left with a banquet table for kings, something he looked at ten times a day, crowded now with plans and unsigned contracts, receipts, medical bills he'd pay just as soon as fricking hell froze over, wondering if he'd ever be able to pull a single leaf, store a single chair. She'd wanted hooks, a place to hang the chairs they weren't using. He'd already started on them.

"Taz," she says.

He looks down, sees her seated there, craning around to see him, glancing away. He's holding the back of her chair in both hands, fingers knotted around the spindles, knuckles going white. "Oh good christ," he says, and wonders what to say next, when Midge cranks, just the first roll in the crib.

"Damn," he says. "The formula." He leaps toward the bedroom as if for a life ring.

When he comes out, Midge pushing halfway away from his chest, turning out to the world coming at her, wispy blond hairs a fray, a flight, the girl sucks in her breath and says, "OMG," and Taz just manages to breathe out, "You're hired."

She is smart enough not to hold her hands out for Midge, and once Taz deals with the formula, he settles in across from her, the two of them studying her. She says, "I'm not cheap."

"All those tips to replace."

She touches the tip of her nose with the tip of her finger. "Exactly," she says.

He says, "I'm guessing I might not *make* as much as your tips."

"Rudy says you've got friends who'll help. Who'll do anything for you." She looks away. "You know, till you're working again."

Taz blinks as if he's been slapped. "I—" he says. "It, it doesn't really work that way here."

She gives this kind of half shrug. "Maybe it will for a while. You know, if it has to."

He shakes his head, says, "I suppose I better know your name." Midge reaches, grabs a handful of his hair. He winces, works to free her fingers.

She smiles at his untangling. "Elmo," she says.

Taz rubs at his eyes, looks at her, tries to focus. A fricking Muppet. What next? "Elmo?" he says.

"Last name's Elmore," she says, studying the table. "And with the hair." She pushes a hand through the mass of her red hair. "Middle school, you know. It just kind of stuck." She tries another smile. "Sure as hell beats Ginger."

DAY 75

Half days Monday, Wednesday, and Friday. All day Tuesday and Thursday. They work it out. The details. Weekends as needed. He asks if she thinks she can handle the workload, with school and all. She stares at him a moment and says, "Weekends weren't really optional watching my dad's kids."

"For free?"

She touches her nose with her fingertip.

The first day he has to ask her in, like she's not sure if she should be there, if she might be interrupting something, maybe imposing. But when she sees Midge on her blanket, she goes down to her knees and talks to her as if they're lifelong besties, gentles her up. Midge reaches for Taz, begins an uncommitted whimper, and Elmo shifts her to a hip, rocking slightly, says, "Oh, please, you're not even trying."

Taz has already taken a step toward them, but Elmo holds up a hand, says, "We're fine."

He stands back, begins to tell her of their routine, the daily ins and outs, but Elmo hardly seems to listen, and he goes quiet, watching her bounce Midge, just lifting up to the balls of her feet and dropping back down, up, down, like she's been here since day one, and when Midge cracks into a wide, toothless grin, eyes alight, whimper forgotten, she twists around, turning her first smile toward this girl, and Taz's knees nearly give out. He tries to say something, anything, but she has no idea, thinks these grins have been flashing across Midge's face her whole life.

He manages, "I'll just be out back, in the shop."

She doesn't take her eyes off Midge, grins back, widening her eyes even more.

"You can get me anytime, anything you need."

Elmo gives him the slightest of glances, whispering something to Midge. He catches his name, and feels like he did in middle school, passing girls in the halls, catching their glances, snatches of their secret conversations. He closes his mouth over whatever else he might have said, all the rest of his directions, and walks away in freefall, retreating to his shop.

So that's what it would have been like, he thinks. Every day. He and Marn taking their turns. Marn and Midge whispering about him, making their jokes.

He steps into his shop, suddenly surrounded by the hardness of wood, the bite of steel, surfaces to be smoothed, angles to make sharp, everything precision and function. He starts to close himself in, but then leaves the door open, as if he could hear her calling for him. Then he just stands for a minute, trying to remember why he is there, what's to be built. He leans into his workbench, hands down on the maple as if it's all that holds him up.

Taz says, "Cabinets," and pushes himself up straight. "Marko's cabinets." He reaches for the clipboard, pulls it over, reacquaints himself with his drawings and measurements. Finally he picks out a piece of the reclaimed fir, the same bleacher boards he'd lifted for Marn, these bought and paid for, and pulls a tape down its length, and begins to calculate, avoiding the old bolt holes wherever possible. He will do all he can to make it shine, but knows that from the moment it's in place it will show its every nick and gouge, its every bit of wear and tear. Just like anything.

He gets all the cabinet doors plotted, each rail and stile of the face frame, too, which piece from which length of wood, has placed the extra boards into his wood rack, has even set up the table saw for his first rip—this ancient cast-iron monster he has kept running from the days his father tore his rough-cut planking through it—before he can no longer stand it, before he turns back toward the house, has to see how Midge is, how this whole sorry Muppet experiment is flaming out.

He stops himself halfway there, one foot stepped out into air. He sets it down, stands in the middle of his yard as if dropped down by Dorothy's cyclone, and forces himself to go back into the shop, double-check all his settings, hit the switch, listen to the saw whir up to speed. He finds his glasses, lines up the first board, and starts feeding it into the teeth, making something.

Taz finishes the first round of cuts, runs them through the jointer, sets up the planer to begin thinning the boards that will make up the panels, and only then does he brush off the sawdust, walk back to the house. He'll say he's only in for a drink, fill up a water bottle to back up his story.

But when he peeks around the back door, she's standing in the kitchen, fiddling with the stove, Midge nowhere in sight.

She's in satin basketball shorts, something he hadn't even noticed before. Jersey, too, tank top, number on the back: 00.

Taz, stopped dead in the doorway, wonders, what is she doing here, how did this happen? and she turns, as if he's said it out loud. He wonders if he did, but she smiles, does her half-shrug thing. "I kind of thought maybe I'd make us something to eat. You don't mind, do you?"

"Us?" he says, thinking he'll have to let her know Midge isn't quite on solids just yet.

She lifts her hands, waves them back and forth, the two of them. "But, um, you don't really have much in the way of, you know, food."

"Oh, yeah. I was going to do that with Midge later, after work."

"Okay," she says, and he remembers, says, "I just came in to get some water."

She holds his eye for a moment, her smile growing, then glances around for a clock. Finding none, she says, "You made it a lot longer than I thought you would."

He walks to the cabinet, reaches in for the water bottle. "Hot out there."

"Uh-huh," she says, still smiling.

He fills the bottle, caps it, starts back out.

"She's on the couch," she says. "Asleep."

"Who?" Taz says, and Elmo just smiles wider.

He closes the door behind him, will never come back inside as long as she's there.

DAY 85

A few raindrops sprinkle over Taz as he heads to his truck from Marko's latest trophy house, and he looks up and stares, as if it's manna raining down. It doesn't last more than a minute or two, but in the mountains it'll be snow, and the fires, when the smoke and the haze had come to seem a part of life, may finally die out, the world just a bit less apocalyptic.

He climbs in and starts up the river toward town, the water leaden under the overcast. He glances to his phone, rattling on the dash, needs to call Rudy, who he hasn't seen in a week, more, not since the first day the babysitter started.

Rudy, who could ever tell? The international man of mystery, Marnie had called him. Just nobody home, Taz had answered. Marnie had given him a look, and he said, "He gets calls for work. Sometimes he forgets to tell anybody."

"Work? Changing lightbulbs?"

"Tower technician," Taz answered, but she knew that. "He doesn't just change lightbulbs."

"So, a little height. But, really, how can he always be available to work with you?"

"First," Taz said, "fifteen hundred feet is not a little height. And it pays enough he can do whatever else he wants."

"Like?"

"Fish?" Taz said. "Tear down our walls?"

"Well, I can see the attraction. Maybe I should apply."

Guessing Rude's been pulled away to another tower job, or something glam like cleaning bird remains from wind turbines, Taz pulls onto his street, slows for the turn up the drive, and sees Rudy back in his old place on the porch, giving a wave, like he knew he was about to call, saved him the trouble.

"Oregon?" he asks.

"Just Judith Gap. Oil. Grease. The migration, too. Some feathers. Guts."

Taz pushes down the brake, climbs out, reaching back around for his tools. "They should be home," he says, and starts for the porch.

"They?" Rudy says.

"Midge," he says. "Your babysitter."

"Mo?" Rudy says. "Got a bone to pick with you there." Rudy swings open the door, leading the way in. "Honey, we're home!"

"Who?" Elmo says, coming out of the kitchen. "Oh, you," she says, and gives Rudy a nod. Midge watches from her blanket, reaches for Taz.

Rudy starts in, complaining about losing Elmo at the Club. "A little extra here," he says, "fine, whatever. But I never thought you'd *quit*."

Taz glances to Rudy. Quit?

Rudy pulls bottles from the fridge, pops caps, pushes one at Taz, another at Elmo, but she holds up a hand, says she's got a paper to write. She tells Taz when the last feeding was, the last nap, and heads straight for the door, says, "See you tomorrow."

Rudy watches her go, whistles when the door is closed. "You stole her fair and square," he says. "Just like you did the first one."

It's their old joke, Rudy's and Marnie's, this whole glorious life they could have had together if she'd picked more wisely on the river that first day, but Taz just puts his bottle on the table, pulls Midge up from her blanket.

Rudy stops, takes a drink. "So," he says. "You two getting along?"

Taz lifts Midge into the air, once, twice, mesmerized by her grin. "We're good."

"I mean you and Mo," Rudy says. "The whole babysitter thing."

"She's—" Taz starts, then shrugs. "Midge thinks she's found her long-lost sister."

Rudy cartwheels his bottle over to the kitchen trash can. "So," he says. "You tell your mom you found a younger model."

Taz picks up his beer. "See how this works out first."

Rudy looks to the floor. "You think it might? Work out? That you might let it?"

Taz pinches the bridge of his nose. "I'm giving her a chance, Rudy. I am."

"That's all I'm asking," he says, then, "If you want to strap in our little buckaroo, we could head to the Club. I could tell her stories about wind in the Gap, rocking through those turbines, that'll curl her toes."

DAY 98

Taz shuts down the power. Another row of rails and stiles line the bench, waiting to be cut to length, rabbeted, mortised, tenoned. Cherry this time. Whole banks of cabinets for Marko's latest. An imitation Craftsman, in a dubious wood selection. Doing what he's told, making ends meet.

When he looks up, Elmo's in the door, Midge struggling away from her, shrieking so loud Taz can't believe he didn't hear her over the rip of the saw. Another round of the separation thing. Elmo tilts her head away from it, says, "I'm sorry, but she won't stop."

Taz brushes the sawdust off his shirt, the thighs of his jeans, the hair of his forearms, and walks to the door, reaches for Midge. In his arms, she takes one more stuttering breath and lets it go, a sigh, done. For now.

"I'm sorry," Elmo says again.

"It's okay," Taz says, bounces Midge the way she does. He feels her reach, strain, and turns to see the attraction, that glittering, whirring blade. "Oh, jesus," he says, wrapping her fingers tight inside his fist and stepping around Elmo, out into the air, finally crisp, like fall will come after all.

Behind him, she says, "I was making soup, and then she was just so done."

Taz blinks. "You're cooking?"

"Well, just soup, but ..." she starts, then glances at him, away. "I kind of have been, you know."

He looks blank.

"That food you find, it's not some Rumpelstiltskin thing. Some gnome or whatever getting after the stove all night."

Taz looks toward the house, the kitchen just through the back door.

Midge leans toward her, her latest, wanting to be with who-ever doesn't have her. Elmo starts to hold out her hands, and Midge pulls back to Taz.

"You have noticed that there's been food in the house, right?" Elmo asks.

Taz thinks. "I was going—"

She lets her hands fall to her side. "You have been eating, right?"

"I, I just thought it was leftovers or something. I guess."

She tilts her head. "Leftovers from *what?*" she says, almost a whisper.

"You've been cooking, buying stuff, filling the fridge?"

"The cabinets, too."

Taz pats at his pockets, the wallet he never takes with him.

"Relax," she says. "It's part of the deal."

"What deal?"

"Just, you know, part of the job, what I'm supposed to do when I'm here."

"I'm hardly paying you enough for babysitting," Taz says. "You can't be buying my groceries."

"Well, Rudy, we've …"

"Rudy? Rudy's paying for my groceries?"

"Just for what I need to keep the place going."

Taz bounces Midge as she reaches again for Elmo. "That was never any plan."

"Just till you get your feet under you. He's keeping a tally. All on the up-and-up."

"This is just for a few hours here and there," Taz says. "So I can get some work done."

She gives him a glance, starts to reach for Midge again, then looks away, over at the Karmann Ghia.

"Nice car," she says eventually.

"That?" he says. It's covered in dust, half-yellow maple leaves.

"A classic."

The paint is oxidized, the bottoms of the doors rusted. If it starts, farting blue smoke, it shakes hard enough to rattle teeth. "Would be if it wasn't falling apart."

"Still, pretty sweet."

"Want to buy it?" he says, an old line, but Marn jumps. *I will kill you.* Her pride and joy, for christ's sake.

Taz clears his throat. "It's not really for sale," he says.

"I know somebody who'd die for it," she says. "Myself, I'm not exactly in the classic car market."

Taz swallows. "It's really not for sale."

Elmo sucks the corner of her lip between her teeth. Turns toward the shop. "It smells good in there," she says.

"Your soup?"

"No. In there. The wood."

"Cherry?" he says. "Beats oak, that's for sure. But, fir …"

"Fur?"

"The wood in the house. Douglas fir. That smells good."

"Really?" she says. She tilts her head toward the shop. "I just thought it was, you know, wood."

Taz's smile is maybe not completely forced. "Please," he says. But he lets her take Midge before Midge has a chance to pull back, and steps to the shop and pulls a scrap of fir from the rack. He shows her the grain, tight straight lines. "This is old stuff, from the giant trees, old growth. Miles of it without a knot, straight as an arrow."

She leans toward the board, takes a whiff, looks unconvinced, and making sure she's got a hold of Midge, Taz cranks the table saw, runs the wood through the blade, can't keep from smiling himself, the way Marn got after him for his love affair with fir.

Taz flips the saw's switch, listens to it ratchet down.

"Now I see what you mean," she says.

"Right?" he says. "You can't not like that. Once I got this old stuff salvaged from a distillery in Tennessee. Big six-by-three beams, racks that used to hold the bourbon barrels, all notched and mortised. A ton of work just to cut it up enough to make anything out of it. But, when you cut it, man, the whole shop, it just filled up—whisky sort of, and butterscotch, vanilla. Used to want to cut it just to make the shop smell that way."

He stops, standing there with the stick in his hand, sees her smiling like he's not sure he has before. "Well, soup's on," she says. "Maybe it'll smell okay, too."

Taz hangs back. "I should really, you know, keep after it, while I got you looking after Midge."

She walks toward the house as if he hasn't said a word, crooking two fingers over her shoulder for him to follow. He hesitates, but does as he's told.

The soup does smell good, and Taz asks where she learned. She closes one eye, looks at him from under the other brow. "Seriously?" she says.

"Dad?"

"Uh-huh."

"Cinderella?"

"Pre—glass slipper anyway." She nods, shrugs at the same time, a gesture Taz has yet to quite decipher.

"Hungry?" she asks.

"Not so much." He hasn't been hungry. Not once.

"Well, that's just what a cook wants to hear."

"I guess I should eat, though."

"Oh boy," she says. "Way better."

DAY 100

Taz sits at the bar. Where she used to work. He peels at a label. Glances over to Midge in her car seat.

"And you're pissed?" Rudy says. "That she's cooking?"

"No, that you're paying. Me and Midge, we're not quite a charity case yet."

Rudy waves it away with the neck of his beer bottle. "Can she cook?"

"Are you listening at all?" Taz says. "Even if you weren't paying, she's the babysitter, not like some nanny or something, some live-in caretaker."

"You want me to talk to her? Make her stop? Let you take care of that, too, the shopping, the cooking, the cleaning?"

"Talk to her?" Taz looks around. "I just want you to leave it alone. I'm making this work."

"Yeah, because she leaves you dinner. Because you have food." Rudy snorts, one sorry laugh. He lifts a hand, calls for two more. "You know, since you're almost done with that label."

Taz puts the bottle down.

"She said you didn't even know she was leaving you food. You want me to start telling you everything *else* you haven't been quite tracking on?"

"What?"

"Hards?"

Taz looks blank.

"They're moving. Anchorage. I told you that myself. We're having a party. My place, though yours would work better."

"You could have it at our house." It's what Marn always wanted, a place people could come to.

"And what, you're not going to be there?"

"I, no, I mean, yeah, I'll be there."

"Taz, I'll admit it, okay? We're worried about you."

Taz lays his hands flat on the table, spreads his fingers.

Rudy watches. Taps his bottle against Taz's finger. "Personally," he says, "I'm surprised you've got all those left. You're the last person who should be working with power tools."

"Who's worried?"

"All of us. Your friends. Remember us? We're worried you'll fall off the edge of the earth and not even notice. That maybe you already have."

"What?"

"Oh, come on, Taz! You never leave that house."

Taz looks at the bar. The ground-out divots in the walnut. People gouging away with their quarters. "You were gone. Nebraska or wherever."

"For two weeks. I didn't move."

Taz sits rubbing his thumb into a divot.

Rudy takes a drink. A long one. "Look," he says. "Elmo says

the place is a mess. That she cleans it for you. That the table's covered in bills. Stacks of them."

Taz stares across the bar. Marnie paid the bills. Nights, at the table. Her reading glasses on, hair falling down around her face. He couldn't take his eyes off her.

"We're afraid you'll lose the place. Of what happens to you then."

"Lose it?"

"The mortgage, Taz. Gas? Electric?"

He interrupted bill night. More than once. She'd leave her glasses on. Go all librarian on him.

"Taxes," Rudy says.

Marnie meeting him at the door with the letter. "You didn't pay the property taxes, did you?"

"Me?"

"Damn it, read this."

It wasn't easy. All legal mumbo jumbo. Bone-tired, he'd looked up at Marnie, blank.

She shook her head. "Some asshole paid our taxes."

"Sweet," he said. "Let's get him a beer."

"No, Einstein. Read the letter. They do it twice more and the house is theirs."

"What? They can't do that."

She snatched the letter from his hand, read it out loud. Shouted it at him. There were tears in her eyes. "You know how much we have in savings?"

He stood there, tape measure dragging down his pocket. He shook his head. She did the bills.

"Not enough," she said. "Not even close." She crumpled up the letter, threw it at him. "And you just bought that stupid stove.

Like we'll be able to touch that kitchen before we're eighty. Before we lose this place."

Taz had blinked. She loved the stove, this ginormous old double oven. A cookie-making machine, she'd called it. Didn't even need that much work. Probably.

She turned away, saying, "And you think we're ready for a baby. Good god."

Rudy snaps his fingers an inch from Taz's eyes. "See what I'm talking about? Do you see?"

"See what?" Taz says.

"She's worried about you."

"Who?"

"Elmo," Rudy says. "All of us."

"Marnie used to do the bills," Taz says.

Rudy rubs at his face. "Well, Taz, I hate to say it, but you're going to have to come around to 'used to' not quite cutting it anymore."

Taz looks up from the bar. "What isn't cutting it, Rude, is you paying for my food."

"Would you just—"

"I've got money," Taz says. "All I do is work." He takes a drink at last. "I don't even know why. Like it's all I can think to do every day. Robot motion."

"So, you need Elmo, right?"

"I need somebody to watch Midge," he says. "I don't need anybody worrying about me, anybody paying my way."

"Well, great then. So, what's for dinner? What are you whipping up for me and the Midge?"

Taz takes another sip, sets the bottle down. "Finish up," he says. "We've got shopping to do."

DAY 105

Taz comes in looking for the plans. A double-wall built-in bookcase this time, and he can't remember how many shelves. He goes through the kitchen and finds Midge standing, legs quaking, a foot on each of Elmo's thighs, Elmo's hands wrapped around her wrists. They smile at him. Both.

"Check her out," Elmo says.

Taz already is. "You'll have her walking soon."

"It's all her," Elmo says. "Supergirl."

Taz goes to the table, grabs the plans, says, "I forgot what I was doing out there."

He's halfway to the back door when she says, "Lunch?"

He hesitates, glances back. "I— Can it wait? Until I get these cut?"

"Of course," she says. "I know how you are on eating."

Taz smiles a little.

"But, you know what's coming up?"

He waits.

"Like, next week?"

He shakes his head.

"I was afraid of that," she says, not quite hiding a sigh. "Thanksgiving. You know, Pilgrims and all?"

Taz rolls the plans tighter.

"I was thinking," she says. "Wondering if you had plans or anything."

Taz says, "I, maybe Rudy ..." He trails off as she looks at him. "I don't really have any," he says. "Hadn't even really thought about it."

"Well," she says, drawing it out. "Instead of the joy of my whole family in Idaho, I was thinking maybe I could do a turkey at my house."

"You can take the day off," Taz says. "You know that. Whatever you need."

She rakes her fingers up through her hair, Midge collapsing to her lap. "I was asking if, you know, since you and I, that I, that you don't have ..."

Taz stands, the plans rolled solid in his fists.

"I could have some people over," she says. "My friends. Your friends, if you want. Get out of your house for a day."

He feels her watching.

"So?" she says.

Taz looks down at the maple they'd slaved over, knows she wanted their friends here for all the holidays, just as soon as they could finish the kitchen, the bathroom.

"I think, you know, that I better stay here. It'll give me a chance to catch up on the bills." He waves at the envelope pile on the table.

It's too long before she says anything, and then it's only, "Okay, just thought I'd ask."

"Thanks," Taz manages. "But, really, I'm so far behind."

She reaches down to Midge, pulls her back up onto her feet, facing Taz, her grin leading to a string of drool down her chin. "It's okay. It's just turkey."

Taz unrolls the plans. Rerolls them. "So you won't be here Thursday? Friday, too?"

She looks at him. "Yeah," she says. "Friday, too, if that's okay. All those leftovers and everything."

Marn walks with him out the door, all the way to the shop, before she says, *She was only asking so you won't be alone. So she won't be. It's kind of, you know, nice.*

Taz rolls the plans out on the workbench.

Like she says, it's just turkey. Nothing to be afraid of there.

DAY 112

Taz sits at the dining room table, bills scattered everywhere, a few even in the paid pile. The computer's on and open, his parents' green Skype dot glowing, all their missed calls counted up, too, a number Taz tries his best not to see. When the doorbell rings he leaps for it like somebody's thrown him a parachute.

Elmo stands there, foil-covered plates in both hands, some sort of Tupperware deal pinched under an arm. "I—" she says. "I just felt sort of lame, hogging all this for myself."

He steps back, lets her in. "Lame? It's like Meals on Wheels."

"Not sure what that makes you then," she says, and spreads her plates on the table, careful to avoid the bills. "There's dressing in this one," she says.

Taz watches. "I thought you were having dinner at your place."

"I am. Just a few friends. You'd probably like them." She sets down the last Tupperware. "Where's Midge?"

Taz says, "Asleep," and she walks back to the bedroom without another word.

When she comes back out, she's smiling, says, "I've never really watched her sleep before. You know, by nightlight? She's kind of gorgeous."

Taz smiles, almost tries to hide it, and she laughs. "Look at you, all proud Papa."

He looks away, and she says, "You know, it's not too late if you want to come over. Whenever Midge wakes up."

"Thanks," he says, "but I think I'll ride this mellow streak she's on as long as it lasts. Have ourselves our first holiday."

"Just the two of you and your bills?"

"I got the whole dinner now," he says, giving a wave to the table. "I'm guessing Rudy might drop by. He can sniff out this kind of thing."

"I don't doubt that," Elmo says.

She walks past the table, tapping the top of the computer. "You could bring up one of those fireplace logs on YouTube, you know? Get all in the spirit."

"I was thinking the same thing," Taz says.

"All right, then, back to my feast." She takes the last steps to the door, then turns, says, "I don't know, it feels kind of weird leaving you here."

Taz says, "We're fine." He taps the computer himself. "I was just about to call my parents. See how big a deal Thanksgiving is in New Zealand."

"They live there?"

Taz says, "About ten years now."

Elmo opens the door. "Good for you," she says, "calling home for the holidays. Wait until Midge is up, so nobody misses out."

He makes himself nod. "That's the plan."

"Okay." She swings the door back and forth. "Really, I wasn't going to bring that all over, but I've got tons, and I knew you would be, well, you know ..."

"Yeah. Pretty predictable."

She smiles. "Should still be hot," she says, and steps through the door. "Happy Thanksgiving," she calls.

Taz lifts the foil off a paper plate. Dark meat, his favorite.

This Muppet of yours, Marnie whispers, *is kind of growing on me.*

Taz tucks the foil back down, listens for Midge, then, before he can stop himself, pushes Call on the computer.

He's barely taken a breath before his dad is there, hair gone to Einstein, gray and frizzed. He glares, says, "Where in the hell have you been?" sweeping away Elmo and Midge and Marnie as if they'd never existed.

"Happy Thanksgiving," Taz says.

His father snorts. "If the Pilgrims came to America today, they'd turn straight back around."

"Uh-huh," Taz says.

His father stares at him. "Well, what? We didn't know if you'd died or what."

"Not dead yet," Taz manages.

"Well?"

"Just working. Trying to work things out."

His father says, "Well, anyway, your mother." He almost smiles. "She finally hounded me all the way down to Christchurch. Worked some old connections I had down there."

Taz nods, seeing his father finding a story he can be the hero of. He tries not to look like the chair he's sitting on is on fire, that he can barely keep himself from slapping the computer shut.

"Talked to a foreman there. He'd love to have you. Wants to Skype an interview with you. I gave him your number. He even said he'd give *me* a go."

Taz's childhood rears up; following his father around, listening to his rants and speeches, tools jerked from his hands, cursed for going too slow, being too careful, nothing but a goddamn piano maker. Every step he'd made away from it, every step he made with Marnie, poof, gone. Vanished. Never happened.

"You didn't have to go to Christchurch, Dad," he says.

"No worries. Your mother and I've been talking. We could maybe go halves on the airfare for you, if it'd help."

"I'd sell the house, Dad. I'd have enough."

His father's smile falters, as quick to pounce as ever. He just watches. Glances away once. Looking for his mother, Taz knows. "You *would* sell the house," he says, his voice going flat in a way Taz can't forget. "That's a little different than you *will* sell the house. Than *I've sold* the house."

"Yeah," Taz says. "A little."

"Your mother ..." he starts, but lets it slide away.

"I was only checking. Things were pretty grim here for a while."

"And now you're just on Easy Street, are you?" Like it'd be some sort of failure.

"I got this day care thing kind of going on."

"That's what you were looking for?" his father says. "Day care? Your mother said you were looking for *work*."

"I got work, too. Enough to maybe turns things around."

"They're saying there's decades of work in Christchurch. Whole careers."

Taz nods, a bobblehead, hardly aware he's doing it, why. "Yeah," he says. "Yeah. It's just, maybe things here are ... It'd be easier, you know, if—"

His father laughs. "Easy? Like that's ever mattered to you." He works up a sort of smile. "My goddamn piano maker."

Taz tries to smile, too. "Yeah, still building those."

His father's lips a pinched, straight line.

Taz says, "I just have to see if I can work things out here."

"Things," his father says.

"I'm maybe getting it turned around a little."

"I'll tell you what you got turned around," his father whispers, almost a hiss. He glances around once more, leans closer. "Your mother."

"I was only checking options, I—"

"Well, that's not what she thought. She hasn't been the same since you called."

Taz puts his chin in his hand to make himself stop nodding. "I know. I maybe got ahead of myself."

"Wouldn't be the first time," his father says, and Taz knows he is never going to New Zealand, no matter what works out here, or doesn't.

"Is she there?" he asks. "Can I talk to her?"

His father's face has gone blank, glacial. "I don't think that'd be for the best right now."

Taz says, "I'll call then, as soon as I know anything."

"Won't hold our breaths then," his father says, smiling the

way he does when he says something like that, more dare than anything friendly. And then he's gone, the connection cut.

Marn whispers, *Asshole*, and Taz is so glad she never met him, that Elmo didn't come in the middle of the call.

He sits back in his chair, pulls over one of her plates, peels back the foil. Has no appetite at all.

DAY 128

The day after Thanksgiving, she brings more leftovers, a whole breast, sliced, an old yogurt tub filled with mashed potatoes, another of stuffing, a sour cream container loaded with sweet potatoes, some marshmallow kind of topping, stuff he'd barely seen since his parents left the country. A pumpkin pie with one slice out of it.

She lays it all out, hooks Midge's high chair to the living room table, all special occasion, napkins, the works.

He says, "Didn't you guys eat anything last night?" and she says, "I got carried away," and he wonders if she'd ever really had anybody over at all, or had just made all this for the two of them.

She goes into the kitchen, sets plates and silverware for both of them. "I kept thinking of you and Midge alone here last night. So, you know, I just figured I'd bring the tradition over, get Midge started off right. Later I can draw hand turkeys with her."

Taz stands watching her dish it out, asking what he wants, holding her fork or spoon over every dish, loading her own plate at the same time. Finally she pulls back a chair, and says, "Bon appétit!"

"I wasn't alone," Taz says. "Midge was here, too."

She picks up a little potato, a shred of turkey, tilting it toward him like a toast. "Got me there."

Two weeks later, he's still shaking his head over it, can't quite get past exactly how nice it had been, though at first he'd hardly known what to do. Just sat there, listening to her tell about her life in Idaho, her asking how he'd learned to do all this wood stuff, coaxing a few stories out of him, his life chasing his dad around half-finished log palaces.

She came back the next day, and the next, working through the whole weekend, and then the weekend after that too, but today he's got an install. A couple of trips in the truck. Which Midge loves. Watching from the car seat while he carries the cabinets. Then some level work. Some screws. He'll bring their mobile bridge, a blanket for her. He'll have to bring the nail gun, though, the compressor. That damn roar. He packs extra hose so he can shut the compressor in another room.

She should have a day off. Good god, she's earned it.

He looks at his phone. Holds it in his hand. She'll come if he calls. He knows that. Bring her homework over. Probably cook something. Have it ready for when he gets home. After having it out with Rudy, going shopping, she'd stood in front of the fridge and stared, finally asked, "What's all this?" He told her and, fridge still hanging open, she'd looked back over her shoulder at him. "Um, maybe you should just give me the cash, and I'll do the shopping." She'd taken off as soon as he opened the wallet, took Midge with her, said, "Girl, we've got some skills to catch you up on." That night she'd left a pot of chili. Her specialty she called it, No-Biggie-Chili. He had no idea how to stop her.

Now he opens the fridge door, pulls out the formula bottles he keeps ready. "Midge," he calls, "we're going to work!"

He puts the bag together, gets her into the car seat. "Heigh ho, heigh ho," he sings, and she grins like it's a vacation.

————

She cranes her neck. Kicks. Does her squawk. Maybe because she's seen so few, new places excite her. Even an empty house. Just like her mother. They'd walked together through so many. Junkers mostly, the only thing they could try to afford. Fixer-uppers that would send the most hardened flippers screaming for the exits. Though now and then they'd walk through a showcase. Touring behind the realtor, Marnie whispering, "Okay, we don't have to rewire, just paint over the new paint, tear out the new carpet, sandblast the bricks. Who on earth even paints brick?" In the kitchen, the realtor stepping aside with a flourish at this knockout blow, she'd whispered, "What is it about stainless? And, granite? People really want *rock* counters? You think we're going to spend the rest of our lives wiping baby prints off all this stainless?" All this, years before any shadow of Midge had taken shape, had left Taz breathless.

Taz sets Midge on the screwed-down Durock, the tile guys just waiting for him to finish. Terra cotta, Taz guessed. Big squares. Glazed. Definitely granite up top. Stainless in the gaps for the dishwasher, the fridge. The cherry so obvious. Marnie'd hurl.

"Okay," he says, looking at Midge craning in her seat, the

belt holding her tight. "I've got to go get the cabs. I'll be right
back."

He walks backward to the door, bumping into the wall, the
door's uncased rough opening. Monday's work.

She watches, and as soon as he turns the corner, he dashes.
He'd backed up straight to the door, the landscapers no farther
than empty black pipe jutting from the broken ground. He'd already undone all the straps, had pulled the lower units to the
tailgate's end, all with Midge watching.

No screaming yet, he grabs the smaller cabinet, shoulders
the nailing strip, and teeters in, careful, slow, unable to afford any gouges in the new walls, the flawless paint. He calls,
"Where's Daddy?" and when he turns around the doorway, he
raises his face over the cabinet. "Peekaboo!"

Midge does her belly laugh. Like he's a magician.

Maybe this could work.

He pulls out his tape, makes space for the door trim—all
waiting in his shop, cut, sanded, stained, polyurethaned—and
pushes and nudges the cabinet into place. He unrolls the plans
across the top. Dishwasher next. The stubbed-out plumbing, the
sink unit. The last easy one.

He plays peekaboo back to the doorway, hustles back with
the sink unit. She laughs again, never weary of his one-trick act.
He picks up the seat, swings her. No way he is going to be able to
carry the uppers in himself. Even the long lower for the opposite
wall.

Touring Midge through the house, he pulls out his phone,
dials Rudy. He'll come up, Taz knows, help haul in the long unit,
go back for the uppers, help hold them up while he sets them.

He'll fight to pay him. Somehow, in the dark of the night, Taz had pictured himself doing this alone, elaborate blocking systems, temporary nailing strips. Maybe it was possible, in dreams.

Rudy's phone goes straight to voicemail. But Taz hears an engine's growl, the slam of a door, and he's putting his phone back into his pocket when Marko walks in.

"Figured you could do with some heavy lifting."

He stops when he sees Midge, who smiles at this new person. Marko rubs his jaw, unshaven, and Taz wonders what he's given up today. Hunting? Sleeping in? Some shopping with his wife? A list of honey-dos?

"I think I can get it," he says.

"I think what you're going to need to get is a hard hat," Marko says, trying to smile. "A really, really small one."

They walk back to the truck, each take one end of the first upper, start in. "A baby on-site. My insurance guy," Marko says, grunting it up the porch steps.

DAY 129

Rudy comes up the next day, back from the Columbia River wind farms. "The geese," he says. "It's like pâté everywhere."

"Like you'd know pâté."

"I know it now," Rudy says, holding the other end of an upper unit, adjusting till the level zeros. Taz shoots in a nail, shuffling across to Rudy's end, shooting in another. "Barely hanging," he says through the screws pinched between his lips. He sets down the nailer, rechecks the level, picks up the screw gun. He drives screws into each of his pre-marks, steps back, says, "You can let go."

Rudy steps back beside him. "Damn," he says. "I do good work."

Taz's smile falters. Marnie, every single step of the house, the demolition even, she'd stepped back and said the same thing. Trimming out the door casings. Hanging the picture rail. At the first ultrasound, the underwater thumping of that tiny heart, she'd smiled up at him, "Damn, I do good work."

"Next?" Rudy says.

Marnie rubbing her hands over the first visible bump. Her eyes widening at a kick Taz had seen from the other end of the couch. The mess of water in the bed. *Damn, I do good work.*

"Earth to Davis," Rudy says.

"Um," he says. "Just door hanging now. Thanks, Rude. I got it from here."

Rudy follows him out to the truck, grabs a door himself. As they're carrying them in, he says, "So, Midge strapping on the tool belt. Elmo on vacation or something?"

Taz sets his door on the cardboard he'd brought in for it. "Her first day off since you left town."

"Slave driver. But, no complaints?"

Taz says, "Who doesn't like a day off?"

"Soooo," Rudy says, not quite making eye contact. "Maybe I could keep the kid busy? You know, just till you get this place wrapped."

Taz looks between Rudy and Midge. She's wearing out, rubbing at her eyes with the back of her wrist, a chub of forearm, as close as she can get to a fist. "Yeah," he says. "You guys could maybe go break out the rods, get working on her casting."

"Exactly what I was thinking."

Taz looks at him, his wool shirt, his Osprey ball cap, wings of hair curling over the edges. "She might eat," he says. "But mostly, I think she's just going to fall asleep."

"Can I pick her up?" Rudy asks.

"Of course you can pick her up. Just not by the head or foot or anything."

"Got it," Rudy says. "So, you mind if, there's this new girl working the Club, and, well, I was thinking if the Midge and I—"

"Maybe you could just walk her around outside a little."

Rudy gives a low, sad whistle. "Such low ambitions. You got a blanket for her?"

"It's under her. Everything's all right there."

Rudy picks her up, Midge startled for a second, then pulling at his cap. He yanks it off, puts it on her head. It slops down over her ears, her eyes. He tips it back, says, "There you are!"

She laughs, throws the cap on the floor. Points immediately for him to pick it up. He puts it on his head, tips so she can throw it back to the floor.

He gets the cap and the blanket, wraps her up. "Okay," he says, "outside. Time to let Uncle Rude show you the wilderness."

DAY 130

Ceiling fan–watching with Midge, Taz stands at the first sound of Elmo's run up the porch. He'd left the door open for her, and calls for her to come in before she knocks, before she can reach for the screen.

She pulls it back, and before she's even in, he says, "We did it. She's getting her union card next week. You should have seen her, all weekend she—"

Elmo stands there. "Why didn't you call?" she says.

Taz blinks. "I think Rudy's in love," he says, his voice faltering as it registers, her look, like an old balloon, no longer quite afloat. "I, because..."

Elmo doesn't even give him a look, just steps around him. Hearing her voice, Midge has lifted her head, pushed her chest off the floor, craning. Elmo bends and scoops her off the blanket, lifts her high above her head, lowers her to her face. Midge laughs, squirms, grabs at the thick rope of her braid.

"I would have watched her," she says.

"But, it was Saturday."

She lets Midge tug at her braid. "I've done Saturdays before. Like, the last two."

"That's why ... I was giving you a break."

"Busy as you've been, I was hoping it'd be me and Midge all weekend."

"But—"

"And I could have pulled a Rude. I could have watched her *and* helped with the cabinets."

Taz says, "But it was just for the lifting. The heavy stuff."

"Oh, please," Elmo says. "I can lift things." Holding Midge against her chest, face out to the world, Elmo curls an arm, flexes, nothing visible through her sweatshirt.

"Wow," Taz says, "Serious guns."

She shoots him a look. "Rudy?"

"But you should have seen him, he—"

"I know he's your friend and everything, but, well, you can't pretend he knows Midge from a hole in the ground."

Taz looks at the floor. "He's known Midge since before she was born," he says.

She does the slightest flinch. "I'll see you at one, okay? A quarter to. I've got a test. You can't be late."

"I won't be late." Taz walks around her, to the door. "I'm sorry, El. I just thought, you know, that you've got your own life, and maybe I was ..."

She waves him out the door, says, "Next time, just call."

He stops on the walk, turns toward where she stands in the doorway, holding Midge to watch him leave. Exactly how he'd pictured years of his life. The leaving and coming home. The two of them there for him to come home to. Waiting for him to come home. When she lifts Midge's hand, waving bye-bye, he can barely take a step, barely stand.

―――――

Taz makes it back home on time, but still she flies out the door. "Test," she says. "She just ate. She's asleep." He watches her run, her courier pack slapping her hip.

He steps into Midge's room, sits on his little bed, looks through the rails of the crib.

She sucks her thumb in her sleep.

―――――

And the next time he's got an install, Elmo doesn't say a word, just looks at him until he asks if she wants to come along. Before he's picked up a tool, she's gathering Midge's stuff as if she's been doing it for years. And she *can* do the lifting, even hold the level, call for him to shoot. She loves it, acts like it's a vacation. A job.

The time after that, he calls Rudy to watch Midge while he puts in more cabinets, but when Rudy pulls up, sees Elmo helping load the cabinets, all four of them go up. Marko'd die, but Rudy acts like it's a picnic, brings bags of burgers, and they eat sitting on the subfloor in the kitchen, leaning back against Taz's new cabinets.

"What're we going to call us?" Rudy asks, his mouth full.

Taz waits for him to swallow.

"You know," Rudy says. "For the website. Your business cards."

Taz wonders if he'd hit his head. "What?" he says.

Without missing a beat, Elmo says, "Tazmo and Rude. It's a natural."

He looks from one to the other, sees them smile, his new company. His dad would laugh himself sick, and Taz can't help smiling himself.

DAY 135

The school winter break hits without a word of warning, just Elmo coming in, telling him she'll be gone the next week, that she's got to go home just to prove she's still alive. "Put in my appearance, you know. Let them know I haven't dropped off the edge of the earth. Gone all *Here Be Monsters.*"

Taz says, "Sure. Of course."

"Sorry about Tazmo and Rude."

"What?"

"Your new company?"

He smiles. They'd been out all of three times.

"Rudy will be here, though, right? Back from wherever?"

"Yeah, we'll be good." He's got no more idea when Rudy will reappear than he ever does. But he can call Marko if he has to, have him hold off whoever. He can't, right then, remember his schedules.

But the next morning, alone in the place, he can't quite bring himself to shuffle out back to the shop. He sips his coffee, counts only one more missed Skype from Down Under, and when

Midge wakes up he loads her into the truck, tells her he's got
a surprise for her, and she loves the ride as long as she always
does, most of the way out of town, before she drops off, out cold,
missing everything.

She even sleeps through the dirt road, even when Taz pulls
over at the one towering ponderosa, the final bank of chokecherries, the berries long since picked away by the birds, the bears
maybe. He wonders if he and Marnie had made the road themselves. Or if it had been a turnaround, the scrub wall hiding the
water, their beach.

Instead of undoing the seat belt, he just undoes the car seat's
chest belt, leaves the seat behind, buckled into the truck. "Swim
time," he says. He should have been out here every day. Marnie
would have been.

He holds Midge tight, safe from the lash of the willows.
Edges around to their hole. Stops at the sparkle of ice edging the
rocks. Only reaching out an inch or less, and thin, like glass, but
still, ice.

He stands staring. Looks back at the leafless willows. Up to
the empty cottonwoods. Notices, at last, the carpet of dying gold
and red under his boots. He looks at his watch. Studies the digi-
tal date. "December?" he says.

He goes back to the truck. Hauls the baby pack out of the
bed. Left on his porch one morning. Not even a note.

He yanks off the tag, figures out the straps. Hoists her up. As
soon as he's back to the river, she kicks against his shoulders like
she's doing sprints, leans so far over toward the water she nearly
topples him. She shrieks her whoop of ecstasy. Taz bites his lips
shut. She is Marn.

Only then, with her all loaded up, does he remember the emergency fly rod, tucked behind the truck seat in its half-smashed aluminum case. He bends in, flips the seat forward, twisting to keep from bashing Midge against the truck, and just manages to grab the rod, the reel and little fly box tucked into a Chivas Regal bag he'd found.

"You aren't going to believe this place, Midge," he says. "Mom's fave of all time. And you're about to see your first-ever brook trout. Maybe we'll warm up with a cutthroat or two."

Going past the swimming hole, Taz hikes upstream for the canyon. Breathing hard, he keeps up a monologue to Midge, all the times he and Marnie had been up here, camping under the stars, how many times he and Midge will make it themselves. He still can't help but smile over her kicking and squawking and reaching, as if the river is something she needs to be in, as if it's something she'll get to take home with her. She loves the dance and dart of it, he guesses, the glimmer and flash, and when he can, he stands in it, her feet pounding his sides as the water works through his boots, the cold stabbing into his bones.

At the cliff face, he stops, wonders. Midge still on his back, he sets up the rod, ties on something simple, easy to see, a humpy, as if Midge will follow the action. It's not an ideal setup for December, and with his first backcast he realizes, holy shit, that she's right there, on his back, craning around, that one low cast will sling the hook right past her head, and he shoots the line out and lets it fall on the water, wondering if he's ever had a dumber idea in his life, hears Marn say, *Scads of them*, but one cutthroat can't let it go, and he smiles, pulling it in. He squats beside the water and holds the six inches of surprised trout up over his shoulder for Midge to see. She grabs at it, hauling it toward her open mouth, and Taz pulls back, saying, "I was just *showing* it to you." Behind him Marnie laughs, barely getting out, S*weet pea, let Daddy cook it first!*

Midge leans even farther over his shoulder, watching the mystery of the fish swim down into the pool, and Taz sticks the hook of the fly into the cork butt of his rod and looks up at the cliff, the sketch of trail along its face. He could set her down at the beaver ponds. Cast without fear of hooking her, really show her a fish, let her hold it, just block it from her mouth. Maybe even build a fire. Much as she liked the water's tumble, the flames would put her into a trance.

He breaks the rod down, slides it back into the tube, shoves the tube under his belt so he'll have both hands free on the cliff, and then sweats through the stretch along its face, which really isn't more than ten yards, maybe fifteen, but he clings like never before, wondering how hard it would be to get the pack off, whip her around front, out of the water, if he were to take the plunge into the pool below. Marn whispers, *I know, Taz, our spot, but still. God, be careful. Don't step on that one rock, the loose one.* It just wobbles, has never fallen, but Taz steps around it, goes full gecko along the whole wall, and as the trail widens and the cliff eases back, he laughs, says, to Marn, "Easy peasy," what she'd said the first time they'd done it. Then to Midge, he says, "You've been here before, but it was kind of dark where you were hanging back then. We'll see if you recognize it," and like a magician revealing his greatest trick, he turns backward, sweeping the pack off and around front, undoing the harness and pulling her free, carrying her into the holy ground. The North Fork.

"Voilà!" he says, stepping around the last of the cliff, the end of the little canyon, the opening holding their ponds.

He stops, staggers back to keep from falling over. Instead of the ponderosas dotting the hillside, the cottonwoods and aspen pushing in on the pond, their leaves still gold beneath the water, dotting the beaver dam, only trunks of seared pine and fir jut into the chill blue like blackened spear points. Even the cottonwoods are just ghosts of themselves, clawed fingers holding nothing. The ground is black. The ponds look slicked, greased. There is nothing left.

Behind the beaver dam, beside the unscorched mud and stick hump of their lodge, a trout rings the surface, and Taz turns, stumbles away, manages to get Midge back into the pack, strap her in, ease it back onto his shoulders. The blood pounds so hard in his ears, he can't hear if she's squawking or crying. Ash puffs away from his steps.

DAY 136

He stares at her jerky image, seven thousand miles away. He had to answer sometime. "I never said I was coming down, Mom," he says. "I was just wondering."

"That's what he told me, that you'd never had a plan in your life."

"I had a plan. It just didn't turn out exactly like I'd planned."

Yeah, Marn says, on the other side of the table from the computer. *Sorry about that one.*

"So, you don't think you're ever coming down?"

He looks away, to Marnie. She raises her hands, like, *Don't look at me.* He closes his eyes.

"I can't, Mom. You know what he's like."

She starts and he says, "Not to you, Mom. Just with me."

She goes back to her defense of him, same as ever, and he says, "So, what about you? You ever think about coming back here?"

"You know he'd never—"

"You, Mom. I'm asking you."

He watches her, sees the way she grabs one hand with the other. "It's awfully hard," she says. She's not looking at him exactly. "You know, the airfare."

"I'll send you a ticket."

She jumps like she's been stung.

Taz looks around his kitchen. Three in the morning. Midge's been getting way better, but got up tonight, had to be fed. He wasn't sleeping anyway. He holds her in his lap, just under the lip of the table.

He doesn't want to. He holds her up. Turns her to the screen.

His mom starts to cry.

"She's your granddaughter," he says.

And suddenly his father is there, in his boxers, gut still tight and hard, chest hair as gray and wild as the hair on his head. He reaches toward the screen, says, "We'll call you back at a better time. When we can actually talk. Not the middle of the night."

"Dad," Taz starts, but his father lifts his arm, thrusts his finger at him, the shut-your-mouth point.

"Say good-bye, Serena," he says, and the screen goes blank.

DAY 137

He sits with Elmo's piece of notebook paper, the one she'd left the first day she came into his house. Name, address, phone. As if the number's not the only one speed-dialed. She'd done that herself, later, seeing how good he was with numbers. He pushes the paper away, starts clicking through his entire contact list, again and again, top to bottom. Over and over, not a name registering.

Until finally he sees *MARN*. He blinks. His heart skips. Breathing fails. He pushes. Straight to voicemail. "Hi, this is Marnie, you know what to do—" He snaps it off. Gasping.

He dials again. Listens to the whole message. Calls again as soon as the tone beeps. Her voice. His hands shake too hard to call a fourth time. He can't see the buttons anyway.

He wants to hurl the phone off a cliff. Into a mine. Leap in after it.

He rubs away the tears, but, blindsided, only cries harder as he fumbles. He drops the phone. Picks it up. Goes back to contacts. Is sick as he brings hers up. Just the four letters emptying him. He glances all around the kitchen, as if something can save him. Anything.

He chews his lip bloody. Scratches furiously at his head, squeezes his temples. Pounds them.

He'll call just one more time.

He can't.

He pushes Erase.

Erase contact? He wavers, pushes No.

He brings it back. Erase.

He pushes Yes.

He can never, ever go there again. Not ever.

He shoves away from the table, the chair tumbling.

He walks into the living room, beating fists on his thighs, biting his lips shut so he does not howl. He moans. Wounded-animal noises. He cannot believe this is him. Knows he cannot wake Midge. Cannot ever let her see him like this.

He lies down on the floor. Stares up. The blades still. No motion anywhere. He listens for Midge. Prays for her to wake. To bring him back.

The phone, that evening, is still like kryptonite. He can hardly hold it. But he finds the name, right under where *MARN* used to be. *M's M.* He taps.

She answers just as he's about to shut it off, give up. She says hello, then says it again.

"Lauren," he says.

"Ted?"

"It's me."

"Is everything okay?" she says. "Midge?"

"She's fine."

"Good. That's good."

"She smiles now. Laughs."

They both go silent. Listening. Taz fights not to pant. "I was just wondering," he says. "You know? How you've been holding up?"

She waits, then says, "I have no idea what to say. What to tell you."

"Well, I know, it might be hard for you to ask, you know. About coming out."

She says nothing.

"It's going to be her first Christmas next week," Taz says, hardly a whisper.

He can hear every molecule she breathes.

"Come for the holidays," he says.

DAY 140

Rudy calls, from California, on his way up, but still two days out. "You might be on tree duty on your own. Maybe Elmo'd help."

"She's in Idaho."

"Uh-oh."

He and Marnie had always gone with Rudy for the tree, but Taz bundles up Midge and heads out. Even before he gets close, he can smell the warming fire they always made, taste the hot chocolate, Rudy's bracing schnapps additive, smell Marnie's first cut into the trunk, down on her knees in the snow, nearly swallowed by the low branches, these huge grand firs, big around as the whole living room. Three times he starts out, and three times he turns around, just can't go without her.

He ends up at a lot, in town, Marn saying, *No way.* Saying, *Really?* Saying, *You're just going to* buy *it? Her first tree?* He feels the breath of each word against his ear.

He sneaks it in at midnight, as if Marnie might not notice that way. He winds the light strings that still work until after two. Replaces the fuse with a blinker. Midge sleeping through another night. Her very own Christmas gift.

But, once the lights are on, he can't not go in and get her. He hesitates, watching her sleep, then eases his hands in under her and slips her out of the crib without waking her, his own Christmas miracle, and then sits with her in the swivel rocker he'd found out by the curb, just down the block from the last job. He rocks and turns till dawn and when she wakes, she doesn't cry. She hardly moves. He thinks he can hear her blink. The ceiling fan spins forgotten. She can't take her eyes off the winking lights. Like a campfire in the living room, only maybe better.

The ornament boxes are scattered in the dungeon of a basement, but he doesn't know if he needs anything more than the lights.

Lauren knocks. Early. He wonders if she'd be bunking here. Then he remembers her insisting on the motel, saying she'd never interrupt his life that way again. Her words.

He looks around once more. Stands, Midge in his lap, wrapped in her blankie. He feels her twist as he moves, her gaze locked to the lights while he walks to the door.

When he opens it, they look at each other, their breaths making clouds in the cold, snow coming down in the big flakes he'd always loved, slow-drifting tongue-catchers. Taz says, "Merry Christmas," and Lauren doesn't take her eyes off Midge. Taz twists a little, and Midge turns, at last, from the lights, the blast of cold, maybe, drawing her attention. Though she smiles, she leans in tighter to Taz, something he hopes Lauren misses.

She's loaded down with packages and, of course, groceries,

but still she reaches, and Taz says, "Come in, come in. Before you freeze in place out there."

Taz follows her into the house, closes the door shut behind them, has to push on it, knows he should pop the hinges, run a plane over the top corner. Something to do while she's here.

He trades Midge for a grocery bag weighing a ton, and Lauren takes her in like oxygen. Hugs her. Smells her. Breathes deep.

Midge squirms and Taz retreats for the kitchen, sorting and shelving, giving them time. When he does step back out, Lauren is in his chair, his very position, Midge in her lap, unblinking gaze locked in on the tree lights.

Lauren smiles, says, "Nice tree. Very minimalist."

"Yeah," Taz says. "I'm getting kind of a late start."

She brushes her hand across the top of Midge's head. "I don't think she minds," she says.

"I think she's missed you," he says, nodding toward the bag of presents.

"She doesn't even remember who I am. So, I'll spoil her, win her that way."

"What grandmas do, right?"

"For generations now," she answers, and he watches them both go quiet, staring into the glow of the lights.

DAY 144

Taz works every day up until Christmas Eve, Marko riding him like he might vanish any second, Rude stuck in the Tri-Cities. Blizzards, he says, though Taz wonders if his old flame might still be living in Richland. "Feeding off toxic waste," Rudy'd once said, but the holidays, everything's forgiven, right? Even Elmo's one week off has stretched to two, without a word. He's just lucky Lauren's there to hold down the fort.

Nobody wants Taz poking around their house on Christmas Day, though, so he stays home, actually even sleeps in a little, then planes the front door, trying to stay out of Lauren's way. She's a dervish in the kitchen, making ham, she says, because it's just too close to Thanksgiving to do another turkey. She covers it with pineapple. Cloves. Those nuclear-red cherries. A festival all its own. She peels pounds of potatoes, cheesy casseroles full of them, scalloped. No tricks missed.

Taz checks in on her once, kind of has to if he wants to catch a peek at Midge. He lets Midge hold his finger as she rocks back and forth in the swing Lauren bought for her, the one Christmas present that just couldn't wait, and something Taz has to admit is maybe the best baby thing ever. In their new game, Taz sways back, then rushes forward as she hangs onto his finger, laughing. Lauren watches, smiles, says, "Yes?"

Taz turns her way, still swaying, trying to remember the excuse he made to come in. He can't, so he asks if there's anything she needs, anything he can do. She shakes her head, but then waves toward the fanged smiley face on the wall. "You know, it might be kind of nice not to have that watching me all day."

Taz nods, says, "I know, but, it's Marn's," and Lauren only says, "Okay then," and gets back to work, spinning lettuce in the giant old sink.

Rudy barges in in a cloud of snow and frost, Amundsen reaching the pole, dragging in more champagne than any of them could ever drink, or want to. Rolling out stories of death-defying road conditions, the Herculean efforts involved in getting over the passes, he walks back out to the truck, and staggers in again under the weight of an old box television, fiddles with it and converter boxes, a rabbit's ear, and finally gets some football. He pulls a ragged red bow the size of a watermelon from somewhere inside his jacket and sets it on top, says, "You're welcome," makes one more antenna adjustment, then drops into the swivel rocker, and pops the first bottle of champagne, shouts, "Merry Christmas!"

Lauren looks out from the kitchen, and Rudy jumps up, cries, "Mrs. H., I am smelling some magic in that kitchen!" She just looks at him, and he says, "The Christmas spirit looks good on you, too." He lifts his bottle, says, "May I pour?"

She rolls her eyes, a look she could have stripped straight off of Marn, and Taz blurts out a laugh, and Lauren turns back into the kitchen.

Rudy stares after her a moment, the look a little low for comfort, and Marnie says, *Taz, make him stop.*

Taz steps toward the kitchen himself, says, "Want a glass with that, Romeo?"

Rudy shrugs, and Taz comes back out with two pint glasses, stolen from the brewery. Rudy pours. In the kitchen, when Taz offers, Lauren says she's not ready just quite yet.

Taz doesn't realize anything's arranged until Marko and his wife ring the bell. An hour later the bell rings a third time, just as they are about to sit, Lauren putting the ham on the table, Rudy refilling glasses. Eyebrows go up. They don't have another place set. Closest, Marko opens the door.

Elmo steps in, a cloud of cold right behind her. Elf hat on. Cheeks as red as Santa's.

Rudy cries, "Mo!" and leaps up, giving her a huge hug. He spills champagne, gives her a kiss, says, "I knew you couldn't stay away!" Taz watches, and Lauren watches Taz.

Midge goes frantic, cawing in delight, heels drumming the hardwood of her highchair, arms thrown wide open, and to Lauren, Taz whispers, "The babysitter," and Lauren's eyebrow rises.

Rudy, still standing, with what Taz thinks might even have been a little bow, does the intros, pointing his champagne bottle at each in turn. "Marko, and, um, his, his ..."

"Jeannie," Marko's wife says.

"Exactly," Rudy says. "Just a pop quiz. And Taz you know, the radiant Miss Midge, and the ever-lovely Mrs. H. Everyone, the equally exquisite Elmo."

Elmo says, "What planet are you from?" and Marn almost shouts, *I know!*

"The Rude is universal," he says.

She takes the bottle from him, says, "The Rude might be over-lubed."

Lauren stands, reaches her hand across the table to shake Elmo's. "It's Lauren," she says. Turning to Rudy, she says, "And it's not Mrs. H. That was Marnie's father's name. I'm Mrs. J." Then she laughs. "No, no, it's not even Mrs., what am I saying?"

Elmo takes her hand, gives it a quick shake, says, "Nice to meet you," and circles the table far enough to get to Midge. Rather than pull her up from the chair, she kneels, puts her face against Midge's, lets Midge grab hold of her braid.

"Really," Lauren says. "You can't truly be called Elmo, can you? Or is that just more of Rudy's—"

"No, it's really Elmo."

She keeps smiling. "Don't any of you have a real name?"

Elmo smiles back. "Elmo's fine."

She stands up, Midge reaching after her, and holds up the bag in her hand, a big-bearded Santa bright on its side, cheeks and nose as red as her own. "I'm sorry to barge in like this. I just got back this second." She waves the excuses away. "It's a long story. But I wanted to drop this for Midge," she says, lifting the bag a bit higher. "A cap. Mittens." She drops the bag back down to her waist. "I've taken up knitting," she says. "You know, exiled to the thrill that is Idaho."

Lauren is already setting another place.

Elmo puts a hand over the glass Rudy gives her. "Honestly," she says. "Just saying Ho Ho Ho." She sets the glass back on the table, rubs her fingers back and forth across Midge's cheek. First one, then the other. "My brother's out in the car. Surprise, surprise."

"Your brother?" Taz says.

"The older one. First fam. My car's up at the pass. Sticking out of a snow drift." She slips her mittens back on. "He rescued me. Anyway, got to run," she says. "North Pole, all that."

The door, newly planed, whooshes shut behind her, and they sit again, begin passing plates, taking food. Midge rocks in the highchair between Taz and Lauren.

Lauren says, "Such a pretty girl."

"I know, right?" Rudy says, mouth already full of bread. He starts cutting his ham. "Not that she's got a thing on you, Mrs. H., or J."

Taz dips Midge's spoon into the mashed sweet potatoes.

Marko takes a scoop, passes the bowl.

————

When they sit around the tree after dinner, Taz realizes he hasn't gotten Lauren anything. Nothing under there for Grandma.

All the presents, though, are for Midge. Every one. Clothes mostly, and diapers even, baby food, another swing, a jogger, all stuff Rudy's hauled in, as if he'd been running a warehouse, a Toys for Tots, gifts from their friends, all off with their own families. Marko gives her a tiny tool belt, the baby hard hat. His wife, Jeannie, plush-feet pajamas, a teacup pattern, not hammers. Taz helps her unwrap each one. Lets her play with the paper.

Rudy, dying for his turn, unveils a gigantic stuffed Elmo. Nearly kills himself laughing. All wild red hair, cue ball eyes.

Midge grabs at it, and Rudy leans forward on his knees, in her face, pointing at the stuffed doll, saying, "Elmo, El-mo, Ell—mmoo."

Taz says, "I think she's got it, Rude," and picks out the last present, the flat one, the best wrapped. Lauren says, "You better open that one yourself. There's glass."

Even before the paper is off, he feels himself twisting, swaying. He stops. His hands drop limp on the paper, the hardness underneath. Nothing you'd give a baby.

Lauren says, "She should at least know what she looked like."

He sets the frame, shrouded in half-torn paper, down beside the couch. "Later," he says.

"There isn't a single picture of her in this house."

The group goes quiet. Even Rudy.

"She hated pictures of herself," Taz says.

"Well, this is for Midge."

"She hated them. Hated me taking them. Hated seeing them."

"Midge needs—"

"They creeped her out," he says, his voice as flat as the glass in the frame. "'Only good for when you're already dead,' she said, 'for people to remember how cool you used to be.'"

Rudy starts crumpling wrapping paper, pitching it toward the TV, making a pile.

Her mother clears her throat. "Well, she needs to remember her."

"Remember her?" Taz says. "How exactly is that supposed to work? She never knew her. Not for one second. You want her to remember a picture?"

Rudy tears off a little curl of paper, hands it to Midge. Lauren blocks it with a single finger when Midge lifts it to her mouth. Tears track her cheeks.

Marnie puts a hand on Taz's arm, whispers, *It's okay*, but it sounds as if she's about to break down herself. "Tomorrow," he says. "I'll hang it tomorrow. Above the crib." He'll come in at a different angle, face some other wall.

"It's from our trip to Hawaii," Lauren says, the words barely rising above the hush that's fallen over the room like a blanket of snow.

"From just before you were married," she continues.

"I remember. She always wanted to go back."

"Well, I don't have anything more recent."

"I'll find you some," Taz manages. "I've got loads." He can see each one; Marnie blurred, spinning her back to him and his camera. Marnie flipping him off, hiding behind her hand. Or, all the ones with her ball cap pulled low, Marn hiding behind the bill.

He looks up, realizes the air in the room has reached perfect vacuum. Marnie whispers, *Taz*.

"I'm sorry," he says. He'd gut himself with a broke-bladed utility knife before he'd scroll through their pictures, all of them, no matter how hard she tried to hide, with that smile, Marn's smile. Huge.

Marko stands up, holding out his hand for his wife. "Well," he says. "We better not keep Santa waiting."

Rudy, though he has nothing but his empty place, says the same thing. "Can I give you a lift, Lauren?" he asks.

She picks the almost-unwrapped picture up off the floor,

holds it in her lap. She pulls off the last of the paper, sits staring at it in her lap, tears dotting the glass.

Taz sees everyone to the door, then turns back to Lauren still sitting on the couch, the picture in her lap, the paper pulled away, her and Marn, beneath the tears, both smiling that way. He takes Midge and her Elmo puppet, which she hasn't let go of yet, and, sliding the picture out of Lauren's fingers, he puts Midge into her lap instead.

"I'm sorry," he says again. "You're right. She should know what she looked like. It's only me who'll never forget."

He reaches the nursery door before she says, "Not only you."

He closes the door behind him, wonders about twisting shut the privacy bolt, never once used, though when they'd redone the doors, Marnie had dismantled every one, scraped away the paint, oiled them, tested them. Wanting everything perfect. Even the locks they'd never use. He leaves it unlocked, waiting for Lauren to bring Midge, to say good night, to drive off in the dark.

DAY 159

Three weeks without a day off. Except that Christmas Day. The bench seats benched. The built-ins built in. He even found old window sashes, cracked out the ancient glazing, pried out the old pins, lifted the wavy glass, the built-ins looking more original than the rest of the house. Just like he and Marnie had gone at theirs. Or planned to.

And once he ran out of real work, panicky, he measured out his own bathroom, pulled wood from his hoarded stash, and started in on cabinets, a floor-to-ceiling job for the corner—a place for towels, TP, bathroom stuff—something that would be in his way in the shop forever, waiting on him to do the demo, the tiling, the plumbing, fixing the old claw-foot, replacing the toilet. He and Marnie had sketched out all the plans, and he wasn't sure he'd ever really be able to face it, bringing back all her ideas. But, it kept him out of the house.

Three weeks in the shop, more out of shame than anything else. He'd apologized to Lauren again, the morning after Christmas, said he'd hang the picture wherever she wanted, but Lauren had only said she hadn't realized what she'd been asking, that she was sorry. He never saw the picture again. Two weeks in, middle of the night, Lauren safely in her motel, he forced himself into their bedroom, into the closet, up high on the shelf, pulled down the shoebox with all their pictures, Marnie's retro 35-mm days. Without daring to open it, he set in on the table, where she sat with her coffee, would find it in the morning. She never said a word about it, but the box never stayed in quite the same place, shifted an inch this way, half an inch that way, the top not quite closed right.

He hardly knew Midge anymore, only caught glimpses, saw her take to Lauren almost like she had to Elmo, like they say with ducks, latching on to the first thing they see out of the shell, duck or dog or disaster. He tried not to think which one he'd been.

He wrestled the woodstove into his shop. The one that'd been rusting under the tarp for the last two years, next to the double oven cookie-making machine, the rest of the junk/treasure he'd saved for someday. And, with the heat, he worked out there every day until Lauren had to come get him, tell him she couldn't stay on her feet another minute, had to go back to her room.

Practically a month in a motel. It had to cost a fortune. That and her rental car. He told her their room was empty, she was welcome to it, that he'd never moved out of the nursery. But she said she liked the clean bed every night. Liked to be free to surf the channels, no matter that nothing was on.

He wondered how different it was from her life back home.

Only once did Lauren venture back to his shop. "His lair," she called it. And then only to tell him that the babysitter was at the door.

Taz hadn't been doing anything more than feeding scraps into the woodstove, and all he could come up with was, "Really?"

Lauren nodded, smiled at herself. "I've already forgotten what she calls herself. One of the Muppets." Taz followed her back to the house, their steps squeaking against the snow. Lauren stayed in the kitchen as Taz walked through, hoping she'd invited her in, but knowing he never should have doubted even before he saw Elmo sitting at the table, like she had the first day she came looking for work.

"Hi," she said, standing up as soon as she saw him. "Did I pull you away from something fabulous?"

"Fabulous?" Taz said. "No. Just burning scraps."

"Not making any great smells?"

He blinked, then remembered, smiled. "No, none of those."

She looked around, said, "Fir!" like she'd won a contest.

"That's right. That's the good one."

She smiled, too, said, "I got my car back."

"Your car?"

"From the pass? I got so stuck. Going too fast. Trying to get back."

"No damage?"

"None you'd recognize over anything else. Just lucky my brother was there to bail me out."

Taz nods.

"So, I was wondering, you know, if I might still have a job here? But, I met Grandma again, so I'm not guessing . . ."

"I don't know—" Taz started, but she cut him off, stepping closer.

"I know I said I'd only be gone a week, and I'm way sorry, but it hit the fan back home, big time, and—"

"No, I just meant I don't know how long Grandma's staying."

"And?"

Taz almost laughs. "If you want back in on this. If she hadn't come, I probably would have called you in Idaho. Begged."

She smiles so wide she turns away.

———

Like every morning, he wakes first, before even Midge. He fixes the coffee, waits, looks at his watch. Pours hers. Stirs in the two sugars, the cream. Sets her English muffin in the toaster. But she's started bringing her own Starbucks. Makes a point of it maybe. More money flushed down a hole. He guesses she pours his out as soon as he leaves.

She's late.

He looks again at his watch. No work, he won't have to make any calls

He brings Midge out at her first "Baa baa baa," feeds her, she turning the highchair into the usual Superfund site, rice mash everywhere. She paints more than eats.

He is halfway to plugging in the tree, sitting in the swivel with her, when he realizes it's gone. Not a twig. Not a needle. He'd wondered what she did all day.

Marnie's picture is on the wall. Next to the bookcase. Where the tree would have hidden it. The two of them on the beach, the water coiled around their calves a color water in Montana never was. Their arms over one another's shoulders, Taz wonders how she ever got Marnie to look straight at the camera, smile with her. They look more sisters than mother and daughter, and it's only then that he realizes how close to identical their smiles are. He stares and stares. Holds himself up against the wall.

He pictures Lauren sneaking out to his shop, looking through all the hardware drawers for a hanger, lifting a hammer from its hook. Maybe she'd just stopped at Ace, bought her own.

He looks around the room, almost surprised to find himself alone, not to see Marnie there smiling at him, saying how she was about to get married to him, how could she not smile?

But the room is as vacant as his and Marnie's. Lauren has not once been late.

Only a minute later she texts. From the airport. Didn't want to bother him. His phone pings once more, when she adds, "You can come in from your lair now."

He wonders again about keeping this going for life, Lauren's long visits, taking so much of the load, but not staying in the house. He texts back, "Thanks. For everything," and Marn gives him a shove, says, *Suck-up.*

He turns the phone off, and says, "She wasn't that bad," and Marnie says, *You didn't have to grow up with her.* Taz thinks the same, Marnie never meeting his father, but with Midge in one arm, he walks across the room, lifts the picture from the hanger, trying not to get lost in her face again. "Grandma," he says, to Midge. "And Mom." He bends, leans it against the wall, face-in. He pulls the hanger out with just his fingers, the metal edge creasing the ball of his thumb. He pushes the hanger into his pocket, nail and all.

Yeah, uh-huh, I see that, Marnie says. *She was just fab.*

He gives Marn the blah, blah, blah, and lies down with

Midge, something he hasn't done in a long while, the fan a pale replacement for all those blinking lights. But, left on his own, he probably would have forgotten to ever take the tree down. Would be lying under it when, parchment-dry, it finally spontaneously combusted. "She saved our lives," he tells Midge.

He looks over at Midge, the two of them exactly where they started, the emptied room echoey around them. As if they'd never left the floor.

But Midge rolls over, grabs his shirt, half drags, half crawls herself up against him, legs quaking, almost standing. A smile, half awe, half disbelief.

"There's your mother," he says, touching the corner of her mouth. "Right there." He reaches, lifts her the rest of the way, sits her on his chest, meets those eyes head on. "You'll never need anything more than a mirror to see her."

Without an ounce of thought, he says, "She sent you that walker, you know. Your mom. Said to be careful. She knows what a daredevil you are. She is so bummed she couldn't be here."

A picture is supposed to replace her?

"It's not an easy thing, being an explorer," he says. "Some of the expeditions she goes on? It's like they never end."

He runs his fingers down her sides, back again. Over her wispy hair, the same color as Marn's, across her cheeks. She shivers, smiles.

"We used to go together. Down rivers, through jungles. Over mountains. But this time she had to go by herself. The longest one ever."

Midge pushes against his chest, his collarbone, trying to

stand, to reach unattainable heights. "I got to stay behind with you," he says.

"But she can't wait to get home to you." He shakes his head, rolling it against the hardwood. "And, holy moly, when she does? You are just not going to believe your own eyes," he says. "As beautiful as you."

She blows a spit bubble, which bursts, slides down her chin. She laughs. Taz wipes with his thumb. "And exactly the same sense of humor. You guys are just going to crack each other up."

He takes her wrists, lifts as she struggles to her feet. "When she gets back? The two of you? The world won't stand a chance."

She wobbles, the grin all awe. She looks down, drools on him, squawks in delight.

He tries to remember where he's seen her like this before. Someone holding her up. Midge so proud of herself. Red hair aglow behind her.

DAY 161

On his way to Marko's next job, a single day installing doors he made last month, Midge sits beside him, gumming the paper he'd written Elmo's address on. He cruises past, peering through the half-frosted side window, and cannot believe it. It's a place he and Marnie had looked at. Too small, even if they weren't already thinking about Midge. Not a disaster, but close. The owner must have given up, kept on renting it out. He can still picture the layout, the living room running into the kitchen, a half wall, the single bedroom and bath off to the side. The floor sloped, the porch roof sagged. *The bathroom*, Marnie says. *Remember? Those pink fixtures.*

He drives on, taking it easy up the mountain, the doors stacked in back, cardboard separating each from the next, each made with wood they found who knows where. They'd told him. A river bottom? The Blackfoot? Salvage logs? Nicer wood than that, though. Old growth. Perfectly clear. Grain so straight it looks drawn with a ruler. Faded though, from a century beneath the waves. He'd messed with stains for days, not quite able to bring it all the way back.

He unloads Midge first. The walker. Does a go-through just to make sure. He puts the screen gate in over the basement stairs. Not a thing to fall into, to trip over. Empty houses; the child-proofer's dream. As soon as he fits her feet through the holes, settles her into the walker's saddle, she's off, her legs cartoon-windmilling until he lets go. It's like she's shot out of a cannon. The edges are cushioned. She can't even scrape paint. Even the soft, raw stuff.

He goes out for a door, checks the top, the Roman numeral he'd punched there, knows the countdown through the house by heart. Clockwise, starting with the coat closet in the front hall. The three hash marks here? First-floor bedroom. Office. Den. Whatever it's going to be when these people fill it up.

He checks Midge. Goes out for a second door, slides the cardboard separator out onto the snow.

He feeds her before lunch, then spreads out the porta-crib. Puts her down. Enough doors in this place to keep him going all day.

She wakes in the middle of his lunch, rolls around a little, finds her feet, her legs. Stands holding to the side of the crib. "Da," she says. "Dada." He's not quite claiming it's not just the next Ba ba, but, really, he is.

"Wait until she hears you said that before Mama," he says to her, pumping his fist, almost crowing. "Man, heads will roll. Mine, anyway."

She said Mama last month, Marn says, heaving a sigh, all dramatic.

He laughs, says, "She so did not." Then he looks around the

empty house, just a glance, says, "Once she starts talking, Marn. I don't know, we may have to knock off these little chats."

Taz goes out for the next door, head hunched down between his shoulders, as if expecting a blow.

In a near miracle, every door fits without planing. Not even a shim hidden behind a hinge. No stain touch-up. No polyure-thane. Just mortising the hinges, lifting the doors, fitting the hinges together, dropping in the pins. "Whoever put in these jambs is a genius," he tells Midge, who rolls down the hallway. "Oh, that's right. Your old man. Pure fricking genius."

Get over yourself, Marn says.

He gets through the day without a single cry.

On the drive home, he again swings by Elmo's house. No lights. Just his headlights, sparkling against the new snow. He wonders if school is back in session. He'll have to check for cars, the parking situation in front of his place.

He makes his dinner for one. Lets Midge play with a piece of spaghetti. She maybe eats some of it.

He sits down with her, rocking a little, listening to her quiet chatter.

He pulls his phone from the tool pocket of his Carhartts, brings up her number, just one touch to call her in, have her start the next day. Only the kitchen light on, his house dark around him, the phone seems almost blinding. He shuts it. "We should get used to this," he whispers to Midge. "Making it on our own." But she's out, curled into his lap.

The two of them, he thinks, sitting alone in the dark.

He settles her into the crib and sneaks into the bathroom to brush his teeth. Uses the tweezers to pull the day's sole sliver.

Does not look at himself in the mirror. Reaches under the sink, lifts out another handful of diapers. Stacks them beside the folded towel. Everything ready.

He shuts off the last light at nine. Climbs into the little bed, exhausted. The turtles swimming around him. Her breathing. "What more could we need?" he says, whispering.

DAY 162

He wakes at five. As if a klaxon's gone off. Jolts upright.

She was with him. Only an instant ago. Her skin.

Slowly the room fills in around him. The gray, gauzy light. Just his sitting up tripping the nightlight's hair trigger.

He puts his hands behind him, leans back. Locks his elbow. Breathes.

Midge snores gently. He wonders about a cold.

He slides his feet over the side of the bed. Touches the floor. He finds his shirt. Socks. Stands.

After the bathroom, he's halfway to the kitchen, the gas under the water, when someone says, "Well, there he is. In the fricking flesh."

Taz leaps sideways. Knocks into one of the giant table's chairs.

Without knowing it, he's spun one eighty. Stands crouched, facing the swivel rocker. "Rudy?" he says.

"Bingo, bright boy," he says. His voice deep, graveled with drinking.

"Couldn't find your way home?" Taz asks, easing upright again.

"No, I just, you know, wanted to see if you were still alive. Still," he raises his hands, waves them at the room. "You know, *sooo* busy."

"Damn, Rude," he says, still catching his breath. "Must have been a hell of a party."

"Oh, you got that. Shoulda been there."

"Where were you?"

"My house, asshole," he says. "I invited you myself." He snorts. "Me, inviting you. Like some kind of stranger."

Taz looks at him there in the dark. Glad he can't see any more than a shape. He waits a few, says, "I'll start some coffee."

It's only a few steps. He twists on the burner. No need for a light.

He hasn't gotten back to the living room before Rudy says, "You know what Hards said?"

Taz stops. The going-away party. "Rude," he says. "I hung doors all day. I forgot."

"She was crying. Couldn't believe you wouldn't come. Alaska, man. It's not like around the corner."

"I know. I'll get over there first thing."

"First thing? They're gone, man. Hours ago."

Taz slumps against the table.

Rudy stays slouched deep in the chair, watching him. "She said it's like you think you're the only one who loved her."

"Rudy," he says.

"Which is bullshit, you know. Total bullshit."

"I know, Rude."

"She says it's like you died, too. That maybe Marnie got out luckier than you."

"Rudy," he says. "I think maybe it's time I take you home."

Rudy snorts.

"Did you drive here?"

"Wow," Rudy says. "The dead man is, like, concerned?"

Taz walks to the window, sees Rudy's truck parked on his lawn. Tire tracks in the snow, climbing the curb.

"How long have you been here?"

"The fuck would I know?"

"There's a bed."

"A bed? Man, you got everything don't you?"

"Or you can sleep in the snow."

"Even Elmo asked about you."

"She was there?"

"I brought her, let her know you used to actually have friends."

"Rudy, I'd drive you home, but Midge—"

"Her take's a little different than Hards's," he says. "She thinks you wish you'd died instead."

"The bed or the snow. Your choice."

In the bedroom, Midge stirs. It's like the mattress springs are strung into his nervous system. He's on his way before she starts her morning call of Ba ba ba, or Da da da.

He comes back with her, her hair, as always, flying every which way. She's got her chimp grip locked into a fistful of his, steering him, saying, "Da da da," maybe changes it to, "Du, Du," when she spots Rudy in the chair, lunges for him. Taz holds on, goes for the fridge. Her bottle. He pours a cup of coffee, carries it out to Rudy, flips on the light.

He's asleep in the chair. Mouth pitched open. Passed out.

Midge says, "Da, da, da."

DAY 175

He knows his name must come up on her phone. She doesn't say hello. Just, "When?"

"When?" he says back.

"When do you want me to start?"

He swallows. Can feel his heart beat. "What's your schedule look like?"

"Today?"

Taz turns to Midge, barely daring to breathe. "That would be cool," he says.

"Be there in drive time."

"Great. It's a shop day."

"What this time?"

"Just more cabinets."

"Cherry again?"

"No, oak."

"How does that smell?"

"You can come out. Smell for yourself."

"Okay."

He can't think of another thing to say. He carries Midge over to the window.

"All right then." She draws a big breath. "I'll see you in about ten. Maybe fifteen."

"El," he says, fingering the big thumb push on the sash lock.

"Yeah?"

"I didn't want to die instead."

She's silent for a beat, then says, "Rudy talks too much."

"I mean, I did," Taz says. "But more *too* than *instead*. I mean, I would've done anything right then. I would have traded Midge for her in a second."

He waits, but there's only her breathing.

"You know? Midge was, she was just this thing then. I didn't know the first thing about her. About anything."

Not even breathing. He says, "I just wanted you to know. It wasn't like that. It wasn't like anything. It just, was. I didn't know which end was up."

"Taz?" she says, hardly a whisper. "I don't know, but I'm not sure this is the kind of thing you tell your babysitter."

Surprised, he smiles, as if they're face-to-face. "Yeah, probably not."

"See you in five," she says.

DAY 195

They figure it out. He works around her, not fleeing the way he did from Lauren, but getting as much work done as he can. Midge goes with him on some installs, but mostly they fall on school days, and if he needs help, he gets Rudy. He pays her every week. Extra if she cooks. Extra every time he catches her cleaning. Which, she says, isn't often enough. They even come to a bookkeeping arrangement, after she watches him lose another fight with the checkbook. "I can do that for you," she says. "A math whiz." She lines out the bills, prioritizes, lists out the checks he has to write, keeps an eye on the account. Time and a half. Every time she sits down to work over the money stuff, he's afraid she'll see he can't afford her. Though, really, the work's been steady, maybe even getting ahead.

On installs, he finds that if the customers come up to inspect, to imagine themselves already moved in, so close, find him working with Midge, he'll sometimes get a little bonus. He guesses they talk to Marko, get told about Marnie. Hating himself for it, he starts trying to take Midge up days he guesses he'll get a walk-through. On purpose.

She crawls, not exactly speed-of-sound stuff, but fast enough. The walker saves his bacon. Mobile, but restrained. He won't work in a house with naked wires poking from junction boxes. Wire nuts or not. Trust an electrician to have the breaker thrown? He's watched them wire boom boxes straight into live wires.

Midge sails by as he's shutting things down, coiling the air hose, folding his extension ladder. He pays no attention to the front door opening until he hears the timid "Hello?" echo down the hall, then the walker's pause, and then Midge kicking into high, the swish-slap of her traction-soled feet pajamas. No heat up here yet. He slips through the bedroom door, angling the ladder through.

"Why, hello there, beautiful." A woman's voice. The hello, he thinks, was a man's.

"Hello?" Taz calls, loud, before they can think abduction.

Down the hallway into the entryway. A man and woman barely older than he is. Dressed up. Flash suit. Black cocktail dress. Heels. He has a bottle of champagne, and, rolled in the other hand, a giant air mattress, the inflator pinched under his arm. She holds a carry-out bag. Another full of what looks like candles. Marn says, *Oh, spare me.*

She blushes, and they reintroduce themselves. The owners.

"We know you're not done, but we cleared it with Marko. Day off tomorrow. For everyone."

Taz pulls Midge out of the walker, reversing his usual breakdown order. "I'll be out of here by noon," he says. "Almost there."

"Not tomorrow," the owner says, chewing back a smile.

"It's Valentine's Day," she says. "We couldn't wait."

And neither can Taz. To get out. Away from them. He says, "I can clean up in there. Pack away the tools." But they're already rubbed against each other. She whispers something in his ear, and he smiles at Taz and says, "No. Thanks. We're fine." After that first hello they haven't even glanced at Midge.

"All right." Taz collapses the walker, pitches it over the side of his truck, in with the last of the trim boards, some cords. He opens the door, works Midge into her car seat, says, "Wave, bye-bye." She waves like her hand's on fire, but when he backs out the drive, the front of the house is already closed. All candlelight and champagne, the mattress inflating in the master bedroom he'd just trimmed out. The mountain view. City lights.

Valentine's Day. It'd made Marnie gag. But they celebrated every year. Like fools.

DAY 196

Elmo hasn't knocked in weeks. Just walks in, calls hello, sees Taz at the kitchen table.

"Hidy ho, neighbor," she says, and lobs something at him. It bounces. Skids across the table. Stops against his forearm. A little box. Candy hearts. With the lame sayings. BE MINE. BE TRUE. FOREVER. The same he'd scattered all over their bed. What, last year? The year before?

Taz looks at the box, like he's never seen such a thing before.

"Settle down," she says. "They're for Midge. But I thought I'd get the okay from you first."

"I don't know," he says. "Looks pretty choke-inducing. Even without the words."

"I kind of thought so, too. But, you know, all my admirers, this is just like recycling."

Elmo starts into the bedroom for Midge, who squawks, has slept late. A first. She says, clear as a bell, "Ma, ma, ma."

Candies still in his hand, Taz leaps for the shop before she can come out of the bedroom. Minimizing Midge's separation problems, he tells himself.

He opens the stove doors, pushes in the first crumpled paper, the sticks, short ends of moldings, scraps. Lights the match. When he's added the dimensional, the final log, he slips his hand into his pocket, throws the candies in before he can read one KISS ME. Closes the door as fast as he can.

He goes and sits at his bench. Turns the chair so he faces the stove. Waits for the first trace of warmth.

They'd thought they'd cleared all the hearts off the bed, but later, afterward, he found one stuck to Marn's hip, laughed, pulled it off, the FOREVER transferred to her skin, a sweet, crimson tattoo he'd licked away.

DAY 224

"It could have started with a cold," the doctor says. "But it's an ear infection now."

Taz looks at her. "What do I do?"

She writes, asks for their pharmacy. He tells her he doesn't have one. "Not really pharmacy people," he says.

"Well, you are now," she says. "You're a parent. Albertsons?" she asks.

"Eastgate, I suppose."

He goes and picks up the antibiotics, staggered by the price. The baby Tylenol. The baby Advil.

The night starts. Shrieking like he's never heard. Clawing at her ear, the whole side of her head. He sleeps, he thinks, an hour. Maybe not that much. None of it in a row.

He calls Elmo so early he's afraid he'll wake her. If he does, she lies.

"She's sick," he says. "Ear infection. We've been up all night."

"That blows."

"Huge," he says. "So, day off for you. I couldn't work on a dare."

She drops soup off on her way to school. Wakes them both on the couch. She swears. Apologizes. Tiptoes away.

Taz drifts off, seeing her going. Up on her toes.

The next morning he can barely get up. The doctor. Again. A sinus infection. "Probably not related, but . . ."

More antibiotics.

Elmo texts. Asks him to let her know when she won't be waking anyone up.

The room swims with his fever. He floats above it, in the rocker, the baby in his lap. The lines in the corner, wall meeting wall meeting ceiling, won't line up. Drift apart. She screams, pulls at her ear, wearing down, eventually, to whimpering exhaustion. He keeps up the Advil-Tylenol rotation, keeps her fever down. Does the same for himself. He writes it all out. Who. Which. When. No way he'd remember any other way.

Getting up the next time she wakes, he walks right out of the bedroom. Takes the wrong turn getting out of bed. Stands floating in the living room, wondering why. Hears her cry ratcheting up. Follows after it.

When Elmo comes over, she leads him straight to the bed she thinks is his. The big one. His and Marnie's. She pulls up the sheet, pushes him down. "I've got her," she says. "She'll be fine. You, though. You look like you're on your way out."

He's on fire. Burning up. She gets a wet cloth for his head. Double-doses him with ibuprofens.

As she leaves the bedroom, he calls her Marnie.

DAY 226

Taz is only just back up on his feet—sweats and a tee, the fever gone, but his head still wobbly, light—when Rudy and El show up at his door, worse shape than he'd ever been. He stands staring as they giggle, Rudy in a lime-green plastic bowler, the rim still mostly attached, El with a shamrock painted on each cheek. Her smile straight leprechaun. Lucky Charms. He should have known. The hair. The freckles. Too cliché not to be true.

Rudy holds her up in the doorway. His arm around her shoulders. Hers around his waist. "Happy St. Patrick's Day," Rudy says. "I brung you a pot of gold."

"Hey, Rudy," he says. "El."

"Kiss her," Rudy says, "She's Irish." The Irish one mushed syllable.

Elmo leans away from Taz, out toward the door, driving an elbow into Rudy he's well beyond feeling, but Rudy swings her back, bumping her into Taz, where she plants a kiss on Midge's head.

Midge turns, takes it on the temple, rubs there with the back of her hand.

"Thanks," Taz says.

She looks at him. Less than a foot away. "This was not my idea," she says.

"I see that," he starts, but Rudy has to haul her in before she goes down. They both stagger, and Rudy laughs, then pushes her at Taz, deposits her, weaving, for Taz to hold up.

"Rudy," he says. But Rudy is backing away, already half out the door, winking.

"Rudy!"

The door closes.

"Shit," she says. "There goes my ride."

"You'd be safer with flying monkeys."

She flops down on the couch. About three-quarters to straight up. The way Midge sits. "How you feeling, boss?" she says. "Any better?"

"Better than you're going to," he says. "How about some water?"

"Be fab."

He puts her to bed in their room. Throws the spread over her. Leaves a bucket. Midge cries when he closes the door, tells her she has to be alone for a while.

"Hush," he says. "Hush. She'll be here in the morning."

He rocks her to sleep in his lap. Stays that way for hours. Eyes wide open in the dark.

DAY 227

He sits with coffee. Midge in the Jump-Up, bouncing like a bean.

When he hears her, the swish-shut of the bathroom door, he doesn't know if he should turn his chair toward the bathroom, or away. He's still trying to decide when she comes out.

She looks like she's been through the spin cycle. Left wet in the washer. Nothing left of her shamrocks but green smears. Her hair every which way, like her head's on fire. She paws at it, waves him away with the back of her hand. "Don't look," she says, her voice raspy.

But he turns toward her anyway. She says, "You *want* to turn to stone?"

Taz smiles, though he feels like he might blow away. The house so normal around them. "Juice?" he says.

"Seriously?"

"Coffee?"

"God. I'm not even sure about *water.*" But she finds a glass, tries the tap, lets it run, stands there with her back to him, braced against the sink.

Marnie says, *Class act.*

He can see her shoulder blades, flared, pushing against her T-shirt like wings. They'd both, he and Marn, been there before, though it seems like another life now.

Elmo lifts the glass. Sips, he guesses, though it's hidden behind the hair. "Phew," she says. "So far, so good."

"You and Rudy together all day?" he asks.

"Um. I don't think so. I started with some friends from school. I think. Ran into Rudy later. There were shots involved."

She lifts the glass again. Puts it down. Goes back to bracing herself against the sink.

"You okay?"

He sees her head dip as she looks down at herself.

"Well, clothes on. That's a good sign."

Not one word, Marnie says.

"Babysitter rules," he says.

"Well, thank god for those, right?"

He pushes the handle of his cup to the side. Back. "Right," he says.

"I—" she starts. Brushes her fingers through her hair until they snag. "Jesus," she whispers.

She keeps her back to him. "Thanks," she says. "For letting me crash. I didn't mean for this to happen. Last night. None of it. I didn't even know we were headed here till he banged into the curb."

"No worries," he says. "I know what he's like."

"Install or shop today?" she says.

"Either."

She starts to breathe, deep, measured. "You think it'd maybe be possible for me to take a day off?"

"All yours. Paid. I'll give you a lift home." He stands up, rattles the keys out of his pocket.

She starts to say no, but he says, "In celebration. For the snakes being driven out."

They're quiet then. Her breathing filling the room.

"Um," she says. "Is it okay if I puke here?"

Taz doesn't quite keep in a laugh, but she's serious, off and running.

"It's fine," he says.

He tries not to listen. Wonders if he should help.

Holding Marnie's hair back for her in the first tri. Cleaning up.

He gives her a minute. Two.

"You okay?" he calls.

"Oh, good god," she says. "I do not do puking."

"You sound good at it."

"Ha, ha."

Taz puts his forehead against the table, holding in the laugh, listens to Midge bob, the grunt she makes pushing off in a new direction.

He hears the flush. A second one. The door opens, closes, the wobble-bladed wall fan whirring.

It's a second before he recognizes the other sound. Their bedroom door closing, the click of the latch. Silence.

He waits. And waits. Nothing more. The house quiet. Even Midge barely babbling. Humming more like it.

He is so tired. He closes his eyes.

———

He sleeps at the table for maybe an hour, he isn't really sure. Midge wakes him, not really crying, just tired of the Jump-Up, arms held up in the air, shouting. He pulls her out, does a finger check of the front of the diaper, a nose check to the rear. All good, he loads her into the car seat, takes off for the grocery store, rides Midge around in the cart, all those brightly lit, perfectly organized aisles.

He comes back with eggs, bread, butter; his old morning-after cure, fried-egg sandwich, lots of salt. He sets the bag on the counter, Midge on the floor, and she crawls straight off to the bedroom, calling, "Mama? Mama?"

"Elmo," Taz corrects, whispering it really, and he sees her note on the counter, an apology, an "I'm mortified," a, "HUGE babysitting violation." The *i*'s are dotted with little shamrocks, and he can't not smile.

"It won't happen again, ever!" she promises, her last line, the *ever* underlined, and he picks up the note, sticks it on the fridge, under the church key magnet. Then he hears Midge, pushed up against the closed bedroom door, and realizes he's hearing, too, the laundry going. The sheets, he's sure of it.

Midge calls, "Mama?" and Taz says, "No, Midge. Just Elmo."

DAY 255

Spring finally arrived, the day too gorgeous for anything else, Taz walks Midge through the park, her pointing from the stroller, at every single thing, like an untrained bird dog. He threads through the college kids, Midge narrating their every move, a constant string of babble. The girls bend into the stroller, coo, talk back to her. She points, calls them all Mama, and Taz can't help hear an upturn at the end of every line. Mama? Mama? The boys stand back, impatient, watch, wait.

He is no longer of their species.

The only of their gang to take the plunge, tie the knot, Taz and Marn pretended they'd changed nothing. But getting pregnant wiped even pretending away. Marnie said they'd taken the critical step up the evolutionary ladder. Rudy disagreed. At the Club, where Taz made his announcement, Rudy held up his hands as if framing a headline. "Wild Man Becomes Mild Man," he said. "Adios, amigo." Taz had smiled, denied it up one side, down the other, ordered shots. He'd loved it. Couldn't wait to be mild man, to withdraw further, him and Marnie and this new thing, their baby, their own world. Pull up the drawbridge. Flood the moat. Release the crocs.

And now he spends whatever downtime he gets at the park, all this urban stuff, the pock of tennis balls, the college kids winging the Frisbee, kids screeching in the freezing water in the spray pool. The lilacs are trying, the buds straining to burst, that fresh wet-dirt smell, and the swing chain, squealing with every back-and-forth, could use some WD, something Midge doesn't give a rip about, waving for more anytime he thinks of slowing down. Nine times out of ten, he's the only man there. If Rudy only knew.

He takes the long way home, a way they've never walked. New streets, houses, dogs. Taz pretending he has no idea where they'll end up.

They find Elmo sitting on her listing porch. Book in her lap. Reading glasses.

She smiles, says, "Now there's a surprise."

Midge hoots, kicks, pulls against the seat belt like the Hulk.

"Just walking," he says.

"Get lost?"

The stroller rocks. Midge shouting "Mama." Or maybe it's Momo.

"For christ's sake," Elmo says. "Release the beast."

"You're studying."

"Oh, please."

Struggling with the belt, trying to push Midge back to gain some slack, he hears the book hit the warped porch boards.

He sets Midge on the grass. She takes off. All hands and knees. It'll be cartwheels next.

Elmo steps down, sits on the grass splay-legged, lets Midge climb right in, haul herself upright on her chest. "This your way of telling me I don't have to come over today?"

"They're still framing."

"Finish your chairs?"

He nods. "I hate chairs. No way you can charge enough."

She nods, too. He guesses he's been over this. She takes Midge's hands, gets her own feet under her, starts walking her in a circle, so close to taking off on her own without the hand-holding. "We could," she says, "you know, take her out somewhere. Go up into the mountains or something." She is looking at Midge, not him.

Taz eyes the porch roof. He says, "You know, I looked at this house once. When it was for sale."

She rears back. "You've been inside my *house*?"

He smiles. "Every room. Those pink fixtures."

"What's not to love, right?"

"You know," he starts. "I've got nothing to do for a while. I could fix the porch. Maybe get some rent knocked off for you."

"Rent's for nitwits," she says. "No offense." She smiles. "I'm a homeowner."

Taz sees her there on the grass with his daughter. "How—"

"Tips," she says. "Babysitting money. Mortgage up the ass."

"Well, then, for sure I can work on it for you."

"I don't have the money."

He lifts his eyebrows, says, "Seriously?" trying to get her intonation right.

"I'm working on it," she says. "When I can." As Midge leads, Elmo's bent over her, a near ninety at the waist that makes Taz's back ache. She turns Midge toward the porch. "Come on in," she says. "I'll show you around."

She picks Midge up, carries her over the stairs, through the screen door. Taz follows.

She's painted the bricks, the fireplace. It's the first thing he sees. White. He hears Marnie; *Who the hell paints brick?* But the wall is rust, and he has to admit, it looks nice. All her work is paint, some stenciling. Surface stuff. She points and waves. Vanna White.

Taz follows along. She dodges the bedroom, swings the door shut. "Hazmat site," she says.

They glance in the bath. Taz says, "We could start here. New fixtures. Well, not new, but, you know, white anyway."

"You don't like the pink? The flowers?"

He'd forgotten the daisy stickers. *Not me*, Marnie says.

"Well," he says. "The kitchen. I could make some cabinets. Glass doors maybe."

"So people can see the crap I eat? I don't think so."

"Okay, raised panel. Go classic."

"No," she says. "I think I'm okay, really."

"I owe you," he says. "All that cleaning I failed to notice. I can start tomorrow."

"You don't owe me a thing," she says.

"All the sick stuff? That's not in your job description."

"The drunk drop-in/hangover ward? Not in yours."

"I owe you huge," he says. "Honestly."

She pulls at her lip, scans the old cabinets, the coats of paint thick enough to soften lines, pool in the corners of the panels. "Thanks," she says. "But it'll be a rental soon enough. It's not really worth it. Makes more sense to work on yours. Your own kitchen. Bath. I could even help." She pulls her muscle pose.

"Rental?" he says.

"You know. Finish school. Get a job. Start a life."

Taz stands, blindsided. "Oh yeah," he manages. "That."

She purses her lips, looks down at Midge as if surprised to find herself holding her. She walks her out of the kitchen. "If I set you down here, baby," she says, "who knows what disease you'd catch."

Midge storms the couch, pulls herself up. Slaps at the cushions.

"Watch the dust," Elmo says.

Taz doesn't hear the steps on the porch. Just Rudy's voice through the screen. "Hey, Mo, you home?"

"Yeah, Rudy," she says. "Just giving Taz the tour."

"Davis?" he says, swinging open the door, walking in. "I should have known," he says. "The stroller out there."

"You're a genius, Rude," Taz says.

Midge beats the cushion. Shuffles down to the end, eyes the abyss between the couch and the chair. Teeters. Shouts, "Du!"

"There's this concert at the park," Rudy says. "Like seventy-two tubas or something. I thought you might want to check it out."

"Given my oompah background?"

"Right."

"When?"

Rudy glances toward the watch he doesn't own. "Now, pretty much, I guess. It was in the paper. The bandstand."

"You still reading my neighbor's paper?" Taz says.

"My neighbor's. You in?"

Taz holds his hand down for Midge to grab. Just his thumb. She sets off, swinging like Tarzan and Cheeta. "I've got to get her home," he says. "Big day already, cruising the city. Nap time chugging down the line."

"She could sleep at the park," Elmo says.

"With seventy tubas?"

"Seventy-two," Rudy says.

Taz lifts Midge. She struggles away. Squawks. Not her happy one.

He carries her outside, sets her in the stroller, wrestles again, getting her strapped in. She yells. Elmo holds the handles for him. He sees her squeeze the bag. Feel the bottle in there. "Come on," she says. "Feed her, she'll sleep through the Second Coming."

"Think about it," he says. "Just the porch. Curbside appeal. Might get you more rent."

"Let you know," she says.

He leaves her there, gives Rudy the over-the-shoulder wave.

He turns right at the corner, instead of left, walks all the way back to the park though Midge truly is wearing out. Fussing. He unzips the bag, lets her hold the bottle herself, stops when it hits the sidewalk, Midge like a passed-out teenager slumped in the seat.

There's a little crowd starting to fill in around the bandshell, the oldsters with their camp chairs. Others pulling tubas out of their enormous cases. A couple tuning blurts from a horn here and there. It'd be a disaster, these guys cranking up, shocking Midge out of her nap.

At the corner behind the shell, he turns and heads for home, the empty house.

DAY 257

Monday after lunch, when her classes start. The truck loaded the night before. His dad's old log stuff. Jacks. Beams. He's down the block when she leaves. Watches her go. Rolls forward. Marn says only, *Creepy.*

He sets Midge up in the yard in the playpen. Drops in toys. She stands holding the edge. Watches him set up the ladders, walk the beam up under the porch roof. Post each end.

He turns the jack. Slowly. Judges the creaking. Watches layers of paint crack. Goes up the ladder with the level twice, a third time. Steps back down, tears out the existing posts, finds rotten wood. Not just the planking, but the deck joists. He picks at them with the claw of his hammer. Tears out chunks as if he's whacking Styrofoam.

"Shit."

He scrapes out the footing blocks. Finds what he knew he would, not much bigger than coffee cans.

Normally this is when he'd hire Rudy. But he can't really afford to be doing this at all. He calls anyway, guesses he'll volunteer. Guesses it might help even, if she finds the two of them here. He leaves a message.

He gets the shovel. Digs. The wheelbarrow. The premix sacks. Finds her water. Hose. Builds footings that won't budge. Looks over his shoulder for Rudy.

He's on his knees, troweling the concrete, Midge snoozing in the playpen in the shade, when he hears her behind him. "I suppose I should be all excited," she says.

He keeps working. "I'd hope so."

He raises up the last of the fines, smoothing, making it more finished than he normally would, a footing. Waiting.

"You can't just tear the front off somebody's house," Elmo says. "You know, without asking."

He smiles. "I did ask."

"You know," he says. "I am going to put it back."

"Well, yeah, I'd hope so."

He hears her walk to the playpen. "Looks like she's had fun."

"She loves installs," he says.

He can't even pretend there's more smoothing to be done. He sits back on his heels, stretches. Turns to look at her. Finds her with her back to the playpen, studying him.

"Once this sets, tomorrow, I can put in permanent posts. Treated ones. That won't rot. I'll wrap them. Tapered." He points across the street. "Kind of like that."

"And you never once thought to ask?"

He dips his head to one shoulder. "It's bugged me," he says. "Ever since we first looked at this place."

"*We* didn't look at this place." She is not smiling. "You did once. Then I did."

He's usually more careful with his pronouns. "I know," he says.

"It's not your house."

"I know."

"This is not cool."

Taz looks down at his concrete. "I just thought I could kind of repay everything—"

"You don't owe me a thing. I have a job. We have a deal."

He stands up. Hoses off his trowel, then keeps going, the wheelbarrow, the shovel. His water shuts off halfway through.

He looks up. She's standing, hose kinked in her hands.

He says, "I'll make it look exactly like it used to then. Except without the sag."

"Or you could ask me what I want."

He waits. "What do you want?"

"To be asked."

He drops the hose, wheels the barrow toward the truck.

"You know, this is something Tazmo and Rude should be knocking out."

He runs the barrow up the plank. Stands in the bed of the truck.

"Bring Midge over tomorrow. The three of us can take turns with her. You can show me how to make those pillars."

"Okay."

She lets go of the hose, the water cannoning, the nozzle whipping. She jumps out of its way, but, Taz notices, keeps herself between the spray and Midge. Once the surge dies out, the hose still, she moves out into the sun. She shields her eyes, looking up at him.

"Why don't you go home?" she says. "Take a shower, clean up. I'll bring Midge over later. You can make us dinner."

He's still standing in the bed of his truck. Hands desiccated from the concrete. He scrapes them against the thighs of his jeans. "Okay," he says, and Rudy pulls up, jumps out of his truck, pulls a cooler out of the back. "Am I late?" he says. He holds up the cooler. "Had to stop for beer."

He looks back and forth between Taz and Elmo, lowers the cooler. "Okay, I'll admit it, I've been parked down the block the whole time. Waiting." He glances at Taz. "You know I hate concrete."

Elmo says, "We're all done for the day. Dinner at Taz's, though."

"Perfect!" Rudy says.

DAY 263

It takes only a few days with the three of them. Then a few more in his shop, on his own. Rudy comes over to help babysit. He considers flat-paneling the posts, tells her, but it'd be too much, she says, wouldn't really fit the house. He goes back to look at it. At dusk. When she won't see. She's right.

With Elmo watching after class, Rudy out in the yard with Midge, Taz cuts the tapers, joins three sides in the shop. They drive it all over to Elmo's, and they biscuit and clamp the fourth on sight, wrapping the posts. She climbs the ladder, holds the other end of the fascia board, which is usually Rudy's job, but he's taken Midge to the park, experimenting with the baby-as-girl-magnet hypothesis.

Elmo lets him add some detail up high. No gingerbread, but just half-inch rectangular blocking, a pattern, some relief.

She does the painting. Careful. Drop cloths. Primer. Color, field, trim.

He realizes, halfway through, that his shoulders have been tensed, waiting, but as soon as Rudy's back, she tells Taz to go home, that she'll call him for the unveiling. She sends Rudy home, too, says she can't pay him, and that nobody works for free. Rudy glances to Taz, lifts an eyebrow, and says, "I do. All the time."

Taz straps Midge into the truck, heads home. She sleeps straight through the nights.

Elmo texts when she's done, and they stand on the sidewalk, admiring. Midge in the truck, asleep. He holds his breath, prays she won't say, "I do good work." *She does, though*, Marn says, all quiet.

"The paint's still a little wet," she says. "It won't be quite that shiny."

He lets his breath out. "It looks good."

"It does," she says. "Thanks."

They stand looking. "That bathroom next?" he says.

She shakes her head.

"Really?"

"We can't work for free. Either one of us."

"Wasn't much work. Didn't take me away from any paying jobs."

"We're not renovating this place."

He glances to her. Arms folded across her chest. Lip caught between her teeth. The freckles. "If anything," she says, "we do yours. Spare-time stuff only."

DAY 275

Another week without work, she won't let him get out of it, keeps hammering about his bathroom, claims she wants to learn, that she liked working on the porch, liked working for Tazmo and Rude, wants to be able to fix her own place, waving off toward some invisible future. And, almost before he knows it, his bathroom—Marnie's bathroom—is gutted. Studs. Nail holes. Plaster dust. A faded red rag plugging the waste hole. Tub plumbing sticking up, bent.

Elmo, at the very end, picks up one huge sliver from the old pine subfloor. Shoved up under her fingernail. He has to leave the room. It's not the finger. He's seen more slivers, more torn and beaten fingers, than he can count. But her face. Tears in her eyes. Shock. The disbelief.

Marnie. At the end.

He comes back, still shaking. Apologizes. Asks if she can afford the clinic. If she wants him to take it out himself.

She raises an eyebrow. "Health service," she says. "On campus. It's free."

He drives her over, just the three blocks. Wonders if he can enroll.

———————

Next day she's back, big white bandage the size of a plum on the end of her finger. She points it at him, croaks, "E.T. phone home."

He smiles, like he knows he should, and she says it doesn't even hurt, that she's good to go. She asks what's next.

"Work," he lies. "Marko called."

"Well, that's great and all," she says, "but, um, where's a girl going to take care of business around here?"

"What?"

"The toilet? The sink? You've got no bathroom."

"Oh. That."

"Well, yeah," she says, laughing. "I mean, hello? It's kind of like, a nice thing to have."

He starts toward the kitchen, waving her along. "Ever been to the basement?"

"The basement?"

"It's kind of through the broom closet."

"Seriously?"

"Yeah, like Hogwarts kind of."

He swings open the first door, wriggles through to the second, pulls the light chain, the bare bulb swinging, then the turn, the steep, open treads, another swinging lightbulb at the base.

"This is so not like Hogwarts," Elmo says, right behind him.

When they reach the bottom, she looks around, almost on top of him. "You know," she says, "there isn't a single person in a single horror movie who's ever made it out of this place."

"And nobody believes you just followed me down here. They were all screaming, 'Don't do it! Don't go down there!'"

She grins, her hair like blood in the dim, swaying light.

"So, anyway," Taz says. "The throne." He leads her around the stairs, an old American Standard plunked down on the dark concrete, a blackened floor drain nearby, a crusty six-inch-wide showerhead plumbed in above it, wiring and piping threaded through cross-braced joists.

"Are you serious? Just sit down here on that and wait for Jason to plant a cleaver in me?"

"I know it's not deluxe, but—"

"Deluxe?" She breaks out laughing. "You've got to promise me, right now, that you will never, ever take Midge down here. She won't potty-train till she's forty."

"It's just till we get—"

"Nope, me neither. No way I'm dropping my bonbon on that down here."

"Drop your *what?*" Taz says.

"You heard me. You get one of those porta-potty deals if you have to, or, I don't know, just bring the old toilet back in and hook it up, till you're ready to roll again."

"El, I've showered here before."

"Showered!" she says, all but shrieking. "Like, you took your *clothes* off down here! Are you out of your freaking mind?"

Laughing, Taz follows her to the stairs. "It's just a basement," he says.

Elmo's already on the stairs, climbing up. "Just a basement like Gitmo is just a beach resort."

Following her up the stairs, he says, quietly, "Your bonbon?"

She whips around, her finger an inch from his nose. "Total," she says, "violation."

When they step out of the broom closet, they hear Midge from her crib. "Mo? Mo? Mo?"

He brings the old toilet back in, some three-eighths ply to get it back up to height. She inspects, asks about the sink, about basic hygiene, and he says, "The one in the kitchen?"

"Why don't we just finish it? How much time would it take to put walls in?"

"And wire and plumb and tape and mud and tile and paint and trim and—"

She holds up her hand. "All right, all right. For now. But weekends, we finish this place."

"If I have weekends."

"Don't even pretend. And don't you dare mention that basement again." She gives a stage shiver, mutters about still not believing he actually took his clothes off down there, lived to tell about it.

———

A month passes with no more work in the bathroom, Taz avoiding it, Marn everywhere. Even those first weeks, crowding in with Lauren, trying to figure out Midge, feel like something he can't lose. Real work caught up to him, he says, though, in truth, there's been precious little of that, Marko still framing, any finishing long weeks away. But she's done with school. Only student teaching left. He pays her, every week, never forgets, wonders, sometimes, if that's the only reason he works, to pay her. But the little nest egg is turning into more of a goose egg.

He can hardly force himself to look at it. That gutted waiting. He and Marnie'd done their bedroom first, *Because, like, what else do we need?* Then the whole front room, Midge's room, all at once. "One fell swoop," she kept calling it. "Well, time to head into the swoop." They'd slept outside on an air mattress, away from the dust. Didn't set up anything permanent. "If we do, we'll never move back in," she said. Showering together in the grungy tub, its makeshift shower, scrubbing the dust and dirt out of each other's hair. Out of every single pore. Tended to scrapes, slivers. Aching muscles. Hours on the leaking mattress. Every single muscle and tendon, nerve and synapse.

Everything he and Elmo had torn out.

Pulling down the plaster in the bath, the lath, it hadn't hit. Only afterward. Their whole house like that, every morning when they'd creep into the kitchen, stand beneath the stare of her smiley face, pull back the Visqueen and stand with their coffee, surveying the swoop, what they'd done the day before, what still lay before them. Like adventurers, standing on the edge of a new continent. Same as they'd looked at her belly, trying to see if it showed yet. Later, when there was no denying. No wish to.

This was their place. Theirs.

He hadn't recognized that until he saw Elmo on her knees

with the sliver, eyes wide, holding one hand so tight with the other. Unable to believe what had just happened to her.

Marnie's eyes so wide. Clutching his hand like it would have to break. As sure as the rest of him was breaking. So unable to believe what was happening to her.

The day after Elmo's sliver, the toilet returned to its place on the subfloor, the dust vacuumed as much as it could be, he threw his tool belt into the truck bed, left Elmo and Midge waving on the porch. Took the right turn at the end of the block, but then, out of sight, cut out of town, climbing up onto the highway. Like he was having an affair.

It's only a bathroom, Taz, Marnie said. *Really. That's all.*

He veered onto the empty state road, again off onto the dirt, the two track, down to the river, the bank of their chokecherries. Peeled off his clothes. Carefully. Almost folding them. Stacking them. Slipped into the water.

He didn't think he'd ever go upstream again, the desolation around their pond. He wondered if the beavers survived, if they could just hole up in their lodge, wait it out in the darkness, the creep of smoke through the tangle of sticks their only clue as to what was taking place outside.

He worked his way around the eddy, pushing toward the true pull of the current. Wondered about building his own lodge. Mud and sticks, a hidden underwater entrance. He dove, looking for it, the light going dim, mottled, the sound cut to only a rushing gurgle. When his air gave out, he blew back up, into the world, the glaze of sun, the touch of breeze, the tumble of water.

What are you doing, Taz? Marnie asked.

He broke through the eddy line, and put his face down and

started to swim, as hard as he could, straight into the teeth of it, sprinting at first, gaining ground, then settling into a steady pull, finding his pace with the river, swimming against it until exhaustion took over and it nudged him away, back to their spot, and he rolled onto his back, the brightness biting, and took two more pulls, his arms slack, slapping against the surface, pulling himself through the line, into the quiet water, where they'd circled and circled.

Taz, she whispered. *It's okay. Go ahead and finish it.*

"I should have Midge here," he said.

Yes, you should.

His feet touched bottom, he squatted, stood, glanced down at his farmer's tan, his nakedness. "Jesus," he whispered. Here on earth without her.

DAY 365

He's come back ever since, whenever he gets a day. Never once leaves Midge behind. She squeals every time she sees the water. Pulling at her own clothes. Dying for it.

He calls Elmo, and he lies. Tells her he's giving her a day.

Then, one morning, even though he'd called the night before, he finds her at dawn standing on his porch, ready to start.

"But," he says, and she says, "What are you doing this for? These days off?"

"It's just another install," he says. "You know, teaching her a trade. So she can support me one day."

She watches him.

He's got a towel behind the seat of his truck now. A bag with fresh clothes for her. Diapers. Snacks. Where he used to carry a level. A tape. A hammer.

He's afraid she'll ask to come along, afraid she'll say, "Tazmo and Rude?," but she only says, "Don't be all day. Okay?"

"No," he says. "Of course not. It's only a few doors anyway."

Then he looks at her, catches it. As if he's leaving her here. As if she'll stay.

"El?" he says. He wonders if she'll work on the bathroom herself.

"Wherever it is you go," she says, looking out the window, "just don't stay there all day. Not today."

He swallows. Blushes, he's sure. How do people do it, he wonders. Lie. Cheat.

She purses her lips. Not in the good way. Disappointed? Disgusted?

"It's just—" she starts, then looks away, anywhere but at him. "Man, I don't know if you even know." She runs her hand up through her hair. Does look at him. "You've got a birthday today. And the kid's got to celebrate."

Taz does know. He doesn't. It's what's been creeping around the edges of his days, like something in his eye, that he can see, but not quite. He swallows. "I don't know if—"

"Yes, you do," Elmo says. "No matter how much you don't want to." She looks at him. "For her sake, you have to."

"I—"

"Yeah. You, Taz. You have to be happy. If only for her sake."

Taz holds Midge by the hand, ready to walk her out to the truck. He looks down at her.

"There are some people coming over," she says. "Five o'clock. I'm making the cake. She's going to make a mess of herself. She's going to be the center of attention."

Taz breathes in. Out. One year.

"And you are *not* going to be the black hole here."

He wants to throw something at her. Make her go away. Disappear. He wants Midge to eat her cake. Both hands.

"How," he manages.

"Rudy." She looks straight at him. "Remember him? Your best friend?"

Taz nods.

She waves him toward the door. The back of her hand. "And then, tomorrow, we start rebuilding. The bathroom. Everything. No more stalling."

"Aren't you the babysitter?" he says.

"Yeah," she says, "I am. And sometimes it feels like double fricking duty, okay?"

He takes a step backward, toward the door. Midge teeters, totters to catch up, free hand waving like a ropewalker's.

"And, for christ's sake, brush her hair when you're done swimming. You know the knots it gets into?"

Taz gets a hand on the door. Holds himself up.

"Someday maybe we can all go. You two can show me this secret spot of yours."

He just stands there, silent.

"Now go, and don't come back without your party hat on."

He steps onto the porch, lifts Midge over the stairs.

"I mean it," she calls out after him. "Girl's got her own place to cut in the world. Ghost-free."

Taz is shaking. He swings Midge up, all the way, into his arms, and has trouble making it down the stairs, as if he's carrying an anvil. He glances back, the gauze of her through the screen.

Elmo waves her hand, shooing him away.

"She's not a ghost," he manages. "She's, she's her mother, and she's ..."

"Gone," Elmo finishes, a whisper, almost a ghost herself.

Taz shakes his head, says, "Don't."

"I'm just—"

"The babysitter," he says, before she can say whatever it is she is going to say, and he can see the impact even through the screen. He's gone off the porch before he can see one more thing.

———

They float in their river. He tells more stories, new installments. "She's rounding the Cape of Great Hopes," he says. "Last I heard, anyway, before she went out of contact. She may already be in Neverland. But she made me promise to tell you how much she loves you. More than anything in the whole wide world. Misses you even more."

He rolls her over, so they're chest-to-chest. "She had all the sails on, hair flying, huge dark clouds. It's not an easy place to go." He looks her in the eyes, which have darkened, just like hers. "She sends you thirty-two million kisses, one for each second since you were born. Some extras to help you grow."

He tells her it's her birthday. Tells her, again, what a swimmer her mother is. "If her ship goes down, no worries there. She'll carry the whole crew with her." He holds her out in the water. Works on her kick. Her stroke. Lets her go. She swims like a frog. She squeals when he lifts her back out. No idea how she knows to hold her breath, that one medium is not the other. He tells her, "Your mother, she won't be one bit surprised to see how perfect you are." He touches her nose. "Not." Her chin. "One." Her belly button. "Bit."

They circle and circle together. Longer than they ever have. Pruned toes. Fingers.

As he dries her off on the truck seat, his phone lights up. Lauren. He doesn't pick up. She doesn't leave a message. He checks missed calls. Lauren. Twice. Elmo. Once. He does the diaper. Tickles her. Snaps the overalls.

He's late, but he drives back slowly. A hazard to what traffic there is, all the fisherman, the tubers. Marnie says, *Step on it, buster.* Then, more quietly, *She was right, you know. You have to do this for our Schmidge.*

There are no cars parked in the drive. Along the street. He says, "Midge, I'm sorry. I've ruined everything." Marnie says, *Unbelievable.*

He pulls into the empty drive. Midge just waking up in the car seat, dressed in her fresh, practically new Goodwill bibs. No tee. Ready to party.

His phone vibrates. He glances. Lauren. He presses the Silence button. Marn says, *You have to answer. I know, I know, but you have to. Midge is hers, too.*

He works Midge's seat belt. She yawns prodigiously.

He carries her up the walk. Swings back the screen. Pushes open the door. Steps through, swinging the baby seat in after him, clanking it against the screen.

They jump. They shout. Blow party things, those zipper deals.

Midge cries.

Everyone laughs, says, "Oh," says, "Baby," says, "Sorry," says,

"Beautiful." Elmo steps forward, takes the seat from his hand, takes Midge out, soothes her. She reaches up, puts a party hat on Taz's head, the elastic string catching in his hair. She says, "Haircut."

Rudy blows a party horn at him, the coil stopping just short of his nose. "You made it," he tells him. "One year."

"We did," he says. "We made it." He watches Elmo move through the people, holding Midge. He'd been so afraid she'd be gone. The babysitter.

Surrounded by people. Some he's sure he hasn't seen in a year. Since the funeral. That party. Someone puts a beer in his hand. Rude maybe. They all want to talk to him. Ask him. How it's been. How he is. All about Midge. Some he wonders if he's ever even seen before. Elmo never comes near until she bumps him in the back with a shoulder, says, "Candles."

She sits at the table, Midge in her lap before the cake.

Chocolate frosting so rich it looks nearly black. Knife-swirled peaks. The treacherous black waves off the Cape of Great Hopes.

Taz holds the flame close over the waves, gets the candles lit. They sing "Happy Birthday." He wonders why there's more than one candle.

Elmo pulls Midge's fingers back from the flames. Blows for her. Now lets Midge grab. Everyone claps. Chocolate everywhere. They clap harder. Blow the horns again.

As he starts to back away, Rudy, standing behind Elmo's chair, catches his eye. Taz bites his lip, shrugs, and opens the back door without looking, without turning around. Rudy nods, a little sideways dip, like he knows.

Nobody knows. Not a single thing.

He breathes in the dark on the porch swing. The world never emptier.

He pulls his phone from his pocket. Looks at the list of missed calls. Pictures her in Ohio, in her own darkness. Her day all about loss. Not even a candle about to go out. He punches Call.

She doesn't say hello. The ringing just stops. Then, "Has she blown out her candles?"

He says, "She had help."

The quiet stretches, just her breathing, a mirror of his own. "I would have given anything to see that."

"There's a lot of people here," he says. "Somebody must've, their phone or something. I'll send it."

"Is that what you'd want?"

He pushes the swing. Tilts his head back the way she used to. Stills it instantly. Foot on the ground. Her birthday present, the first year here. Teak. Only time he'd ever used it. His unveiling and her one word, "Teak?" A sudden blowup over, for christ's sake, tropical deforestation. His general ignorance about, you know, the whole world. "It's wood, you know?" she'd shouted. "I mean, I thought maybe you'd at least know about that."

Her mother says, "Is that how you'd want to see it? On some stranger's phone video?"

"No," he says.

She lets that sit.

He says, "As far as I know, the planes still land here."

He fingers a screw in the brass eye holding the rope. Backed out just enough to feel the edge. The pressure of the freezes and thaws.

"Was that an invitation?" she says.

"You don't need an invitation. You're her grandmother."

"Is *that* an invitation?"

"I just—" he starts, but lets it slide away. "You can come anytime you want. Stay here. Motel. Whatever you want. I'm working nonstop. You'd hardly even know I was here. You could watch her full days."

"What about your babysitter?"

He squeezes the phone. "She's going to be moving sometime," he says. "Getting a real job."

She asks, "How's Midge? Tell me about her."

He takes a breath. How on earth? "She's perfect," he says. "You'd see her every day. In everything she does. Everything."

She says, "Marnie?" like taking a blow.

He sits, swings just the slightest bit. "There's a party here I'm supposed to be at," he says.

"Can I talk to her?"

"She doesn't talk yet."

"Taz."

"She's in the middle of her cake. She won't know what's going on."

She makes a noise. Maybe some sort of laugh. "Marnie hated my birthday calls, too."

She did. Made vicious fun of them. The two of them in bed, the 6 a.m. call, insisting, always, that she be the first to wish her happy birthday. Taz doing everything to Marn he could to blow it wide open. Marnie having to jump up, run naked out of the room, trying to keep her voice level, bland. He says, "No, she didn't."

Lauren laughs, and Taz can't help a smile. He pushes the swing back. Tips his head. Closes his eyes. Pushes again.

"You better get back to your party," she says.

The world sways beneath him. He keeps his eyes closed. "It's just, you know, a party."

"It's about Midge now. Everything is."

"I know."

"You have to call, though," she says. "Before I come out. Tell me when it's a good time."

"I will," he says.

Then she's gone and he swings until the push is gone, the brass and rope and teak and his own dead weight pulled back straight toward the center of the planet.

He stands. Phone still in hand. Opens his eyes. Draws a breath. And steps back inside. Shields his eyes, looks at the floor.

Rudy bumps up against him. "You okay?"

Taz holds up his phone. "Had to call Grandma."

"Mrs. H?" Rudy says. "She ask about me?"

"Of course she did, Rude. They all do."

"I can't help it," Rudy says, and Taz asks if he filmed the candle deal, the dive into the cake.

Rudy says he did, says, "Crazy wasn't it? Just like Marn around a dessert."

Taz opens his phone, says, "Could you send the video to Mrs. H? She misses her pretty bad." He reads off the phone number.

Rudy taps it in, says, "Thanks, man. She will be forever in my debt."

Taz scans the party until he finds Elmo, carrying Midge

again. Still some chocolate cake on Midge's face. Icing between her fingers. A streak of it down Elmo's cheek, a little in her hair. They're laughing.

Every single thing Marnie wanted to be.

She catches his eye and smiles, and he smiles back, nods a thanks. There is no way to make it across the room. No way to make his house be empty. He steps backward through the door again. Sees her stop to watch him leave. He holds up his phone, an excuse. He doesn't know if, through the screen, she sees it.

At Midge's room, he works the screen's turn buttons, drops it down beside the house, pushes the window up. He jumps, hooks his belly over the sill. Crawls through. She will not like this. Who would? Marnie says, *Are you kidding me?*

He hasn't said a word to her all night. Never got the chance. Just that one bump in the back, like, Wake up.

He curls on the small bed. Punches his pillow. Buries his face in. Their baby's birthday.

―――――

She's quiet. Just whispering to Midge. Singing kind of. Hardly even breathing. The crib does its squeak. A sigh almost.

He pretends to be asleep.

She stands and waits beside the crib, making sure. The same way he does.

One step back. Another.

His every move.

Around the low foot of the bed. Maybe a finger drag across the post. The hand-rubbed walnut.

She stops.

He waits.

The mattress sags with her weight. Sinking him toward her. He leans a shoulder the other way. Opens his eyes. He is turned away from the door. Her. She won't see.

She pats him, on the shoulder. Leaves her hand there. In the same voice she used with Midge, she says, "You did okay tonight. You tried."

One year, he thinks. Not one step forward.

"I know," she says. "How hard."

He bites his lip.

"More than I could have done," she says.

He says nothing. Keeps pretending.

"The window thing, though," she says. "That one even surprised Rudy, who says he knows your every move."

She pats him again. Stands up. "I'll see you tomorrow?" she says. He hears her pause at the door, the touch of her hand on the knob.

She says, "Sleep tight, okay, Taz?" and he listens to her tiptoe out, ease the front door shut behind her, the house like a vacuum around him.

DAY 366

Elmo taps at the door. Says through the screen, "I know you're awake."

He rolls onto his side, faces the door. Midge just drifted off again beneath the mobile. But he's been spinning the hoop, around and around. She hardly pays attention anymore, even when she is awake. Just crawls off.

"Come in," he says.

She walks in. Stands watching him.

He should have put on a shirt.

"Do you ever sleep?" she says.

He sits up, ducks into the bedroom, comes back out pulling on a tee. "I suppose you want to start in on the bathroom," he says.

She sits, on the chair edge, keeps her head down, looking at Midge. "I didn't get a chance to talk to you at the party."

"I know."

She glances up. "You noticed?" she says, but digs at her back pocket. "There's something I wanted to tell you." It's an envelope. Creased and folded. "I thought the party'd be the perfect time." She pulls the paper out of the envelope. "But I changed my mind."

"What are you talking about?"

"I got my student teaching assignment."

He sits on the couch, facing her. "That's good. Right?"

She keeps looking at Midge. Her hair, almost caught behind her ear, falls forward. The crooked part line. Somewhere between red and brown. Mahogany. Not as flame as it had looked that first night, in the bar.

Marnie's hair, splayed around her on the bare floor, an almost perfect match for the maple.

"It's in Helena," she says. "Other side of the mountains."

He hitches. "I thought it was going to be here," he says.

More hair falls across her face as she nods. "I know. Me too."

Taz looks at Midge. The two of them watching her sleep.

"When?" he says.

"End of the month. But I'll have to go over, find a place to live."

"How long?"

"The whole semester. Till Christmas."

"Then?"

She blows out a sigh. "Put out apps. Wait."

Taz puts his fingertips together. He has no idea what to say, has not given this moment a second of thought. Has not thought a single day ahead ever. Not since. Only moving. Motion.

"For Midge," she says, "there's a couple people from school. I could ask for you."

"What about your house?" he says. "Students starting back. Rent it?"

She glances up at him.

He tries a smile. "I could watch it for you. Do anything that needs to be done."

"Like what, the manager?"

"I don't know, I'm just saying."

"Well, don't, okay? I think we can just leave it for a while, right? You know, wait and see where I get a job. If. Gives me some place to crash whenever I can get back over."

He looks down, sees he's still holding his fingertips together. Like some kind of asshole. A lawyer or something. He stands, his head doing a little spin, no idea where he's going. "You want," he says, "some coffee or something?"

He's in the kitchen before he knows he's started there. Finds the grinder in his hand, the tin in the other. He looks at the grinder. The coffee. Knows they go together. He just has to figure out how. Like the game he plays with Midge. Two of these things belong together.

When she touches him, barely, fingertips between his shoulder blades, he starts, the leap nothing he can pretend away.

"Jesus, Taz," she whispers.

"I, it's, just. I don't know, it's just, Midge. What she's going to do without you." He turns slightly toward her, tries again to smile. "I was, I'm making some coffee," he says. "It'll just be a minute."

She fills the whistler, turns on the flame. "I'll talk to these two girls I know," she says.

"Yeah," he says. "Thanks." He hits the grind button. The blades whirring.

DAY 390

They road-trip. The three of them. Under two hours on the interstate, but she says, "Who's in a rush?" and Taz turns up the Blackfoot, straight past the turn for the North Fork, their secret swimming spot, which he says not one word about. They cut through the mountains, up over Flesher, then down Canyon Creek, the longest way there is, the water low and slow, neither of them in any hurry. She works her phone, guiding them to three addresses in a row. They look from the street. Don't bother getting out of the car. Leave the owners waiting.

"Cutting it kind of close," he says. "Waiting until the last week."

"You wanted to do it earlier?"

He shakes his head. "Didn't even want to think about it."

She reaches over the car seat and touches his arm. Gives him this little pat. "She's going to be okay. She'll like Alisha."

The last apartment looks possible. She texts the owner, who is in his car, across the street. His first words, when they get out of the car, are, "No kids."

Taz wonders if it's even legal.

"It's only me," Elmo says. "They're just my ride."

Taz walks up the stairs behind her, carries Midge through the apartment with her. This old fourplex. The price more enticing than the rooms, the half-scabby furniture. "Like I give a rip?" she says. "I'll be gone before I'm out of the boxes."

Taz lets Midge down. Lets her walk through clinging to Elmo's finger. She signs a yearlong lease. Back in the truck, she says, "Let him try and find me."

"Rent and mortgage?"

"Nobody promised easy."

Taz guesses not.

They take Midge to a park, a swimming pool beside it. They sit on the grass. Elmo watches Midge tilt toward the sound of the water, says, "You ever going to show me her Aqua Girl skills?"

"No suits," he says.

She lifts an eyebrow. "No suits, huh?"

"I mean, we didn't bring any. It's kind of frowned on, in the city."

"Helena. So boring." She opens the cooler, peers in. "Chicken," she says, "or ham?"

It was her deal. If he drove, she'd do lunch. Rules.

DAY 400

Her last day. Her replacement all lined up. Alisha seems nice. Will move into Elmo's house for the duration. "Boyfriend troubles," Elmo explains. "As if they aren't all trouble."

Elmo gives her the walk-through, Taz barely a shadow in the background. "This is the dad," she says, a wave in his direction. "He can be useful."

Alisha can give him afternoons. Monday, Wednesday, Friday. Elmo trying to come back for a weekend when she can. "Keep marking my territory," she says.

From the porch they watch Alisha walk off, and Elmo says, "Okay, then. This big, secret thing you do with her."

Taz looks at her. "I can't," he says.

She looks at him, taps her foot. "It's me, Taz," she says. "Why do you keep me out of her life with this one thing?"

He looks out at the street.

"I know how to swim." She tries a smile. "I'll be all right." She drops off the porch, starts for the street. Midge takes off after her like there's a string between them.

Taz takes one step down. "El," he calls after her. "It's where I tell her about her mom."

She stops at his truck door. "Good," she says. "I'm glad you do that."

He stands, hands at his sides.

"It's the last chance I'll get to see her," she says. "You don't have to tell her stories today, if you don't want. But it's okay. I wouldn't mind hearing them myself."

"They're not that kind of story."

"What? That I can hear?"

He looks at the sky. Not as hot as a year ago. A whole fire season without smoke. "They're like bedtime stories," he says.

"I can take a nap. We both will, you talking us to sleep."

Taz pictures it. Midge on his chest. Marn's head on his shoulder. His arm around her back, the sweep of her blonde hair, wet from the pool, across his shoulder, his chest. He stops.

"We don't sleep," he says. "We're in the water."

"I'll stay awake then. Promise."

He watches her, then walks down the steps, around the front of the truck. She pops her door, hesitates, then fits Midge into the car seat, looks to him once more before snapping the buckle. Midge says, "Da da da," as she waits for Taz, and Elmo climbs in, smiles the tiniest bit when he starts the truck. Her lips open, just the trace of teeth. A gleam.

"Your door," he whispers.

She reaches out, brings it in.

"I'll keep my eyes closed the whole way," she says. "You won't have to blindfold me."

"Okay," he says.

He puts the truck into reverse.

She's true. Eyes never opening. Not on the first turn, not even on the gravel. He keeps glancing over. Her freckles. That glimpse of teeth. Her head tips to the side. She may really, he thinks, be asleep. As asleep as Midge, the ride working its narcotic magic on her.

He crawls over the two track, twice as slow as usual. Three times.

But still he gets there. Their wall of chokecherries, the giant ponderosa. His and Marn's secret spot. He lets the truck roll to a stop. Neither of them moving. He turns the key. A second of dieseling. Then silence. Even Marnie gone dead quiet.

Elmo cracks an eye. Stretches. "Here already?" she says. She sits up. Looks around. "I kind of thought there'd be water."

"There's water," he says.

"*Bueno*," she says.

Midge wakes when Elmo opens her door. She looks around, blinking, sees the tree.

She caws like a raven. He's got no choice.

He lets her down to the ground. She does her stiff-legged waddle, straight to Elmo. "Momo!"

Midge tries to push on, but Elmo waits for Taz, and he shows the way through, around the far end of the wall, over the rock, where they won't leave any marks, no telltale path crushed through the willows for others to follow.

Then it's there before the three of them. Their swimming hole.

Midge pulls down her pants, holds up her arms. Dances in place. "Wow," Elmo says. "You go, girl." She works Midge's arms through the sleeves, pulls off her shirt. Looks to Taz. "Diaper?"

He nods. Looks away.

"Yowzer," Elmo says. "The full Monty."

He hears the pull of Velcro. A moment later she says, "And you?"

"No," he says, only a whisper. "No diaper."

"Double yowzer," she whispers.

He closes his eyes. He's got a shirt with buttons. An old Hickory, sleeves cut off, something he wears in the shop for the pockets. His fingers fumble with the first button. He tries to listen only to the water.

"Are you going to tell stories," Elmo says, close.

"No," he says. "I don't think so." He works loose another button.

"Well," she says, "I wasn't quite ready for *this*." She touches him on the shoulder. "But, she's kind of going crazy waiting." He feels her walk away, hears the light clack of a stone beneath her foot.

He doesn't open his eyes until he hears the change in the river. Not splashing, but a new surge, something the water curls around. Midge, able to reach the water on her own if he's not right on her.

His eyes flash open, but Elmo's in the water with her. Bent, holding both of Midge's hands. They walk forward together. Midge's skin white. Hers nearly as. Freckles across her shoulders, but then none. Her back tapering. Spine, as she leans over Midge, like a chain tightened beneath her skin. He looks away from the rise of her ass, the slice of her legs entering the water.

Marnie says, *I don't think I need to see this.* But he knows she'll peek, and when she does, she says, *Okay, now that is just not fair.*

Taz laughs, and Elmo peeks back underneath her own arm. Smiles beside the slight fall of her breast. "It's warm," she says.

He manages, "I know."

"What do I do? With her? How does she swim?"

The sun dazzles off the riffle below them. "I'll show you."

He steps out of his clothes.

She looks upriver. Where he will never take her.

He wades in. Water coiling.

She's gone deeper, her back to him. Holds Midge high on a shoulder. The ends of her hair wet. Snaking along her shoulder, down her back.

"Here," he says.

He holds his hands out. They're within feet of the line, being swept downstream. The water low, glass clear, reaching only to his ribs.

Elmo lowers herself as she turns, the water up near her neck. He drops lower, too.

The river runs just below her collarbones. The hollow at the base of her throat. Midge kicks like she's an outboard. Elmo smiles. "She's, like, going crazy."

Duh, Marnie says, but he can feel her smile.

"She loves it." He reaches toward her. His hands. "Just let her go."

"Really?"

"Ready, Midge?" he says. "Put her flat, on her belly, on your arm." He extends his arm, his fingers only inches from her. "Like this."

Elmo shifts Midge, lays her out on her forearm, floating. Her legs whip.

"Swim," he says, softly.

Elmo lowers her, Midge straining, but Elmo still holds her up.

"You have to let go," Taz says. "All the way."

Elmo laughs. "I don't think ... God, really?" She keeps laughing. "I can't."

Taz reaches the last bit. Touches fingers with Elmo. Slides his hand down the inside of her arm. Working his arm between hers and Midge.

He lowers his arm, taking her down too until she has to tip back her head, only her face left above water, in the sun, still laughing.

And then Midge is swimming. He lets her frog, then gives her his hand. Eyes wide open beneath the water, she grabs tight. First to one finger, then another. He pulls her up, to the surface. She sucks in a long breath. Laughs. Kicks the water.

He says, "We came here when we first knew. About Midge." The only thing he can tell her.

God, it was cold, Marnie says.

Elmo bites her lip. Nods.

He turns Midge to face her. "Ready?" he says, and she holds out her hands.

He sends Midge off with a little push. She lets her swim, sink, then lunges and lifts her back into the air. She hauls her in, stands and kisses her. The two of them, water streaming down their faces, their sides, their arms. Skin to skin. Laughing.

Taz sinks under. So he can't see.

And the next day she's gone.

DAY 405

He never touches a tool. With no work to do, he sits out in the shop while Alisha is inside. Then can't stand it, goes back in to check on Midge. Like a yo-yo. Excuse after excuse. Midge crying each time he leaves. The whole week this way. Elmo starts texting the second day. "In or out. Not both." "Talk to her." "She's not me, but still." "TAZ!"

He reads them, clicks off. He brings the snail mail in to the workbench. Junk. Bills. He studies the bank statement in disbelief. Alisha, when he does bump into her, is jumpy. Frazzled. Friday he just tells her to go. Take the afternoon. Tells her it will take a while. For Midge to get used to her. He pays her, wonders about eating, where the food will come from.

He takes Midge outside, puts her in Marnie's car, the dust thicker, the ragtop more ragged. His spring ritual months late. He opens the hood, looks at the engine. He is not a motor guy. But he wriggles the plug wires, hooks up the jumpers, and climbs in with Midge, says, "Ready for nothing?"

Midge waits, no idea for what.

He cranks and there's something approaching life. On the third try it fires, puffs smoke, stinks. Marnie shouts, *Ha!* The whole car vibrates. Midge laughs as if it's almost as fun as peekaboo used to be. It dies, but starts again, and he keeps it revved until an idle settles in. He climbs up out of it, pulls the cables, shuts off his truck.

"This is Mommy's car," he tells Midge, setting her in his lap, behind the wheel, hardly room enough for him. His head scrapes the top, bulges it. She cranks at the wheel, hits the turn signal accidentally, is mesmerized by the blinking.

He squirts Armor All onto his rag. Wipes away a year's worth of dust, more. Hits the windshield with the glass cleaner. Leaves Midge on his lap to steer as he runs down the blocks to the gas station to air up the tires. The huge risks involved. She loves it.

He's just taken the pictures, uploaded them, is about to put the whole ad onto Craigslist, when Marko calls, like something from heaven. He's still telling him about all the work, this huge new job, "It's like the whole interior is finish work!" when Elmo texts again, says "I hand-picked Alisha, remember?"

A moment later it's "Give her a chance, or I'm coming back!" and Taz loses track of anything Marko's saying, tells him he's got to go.

"Got work," he texts back. "Huge job. A whole house."

"I'll talk to Alisha. See if she can fill in. Rudy?"

DAY 416

Rudy says he's good for the next few weeks, and though he can't afford the time, Taz calls crack of dawn one morning, wakes him up, asks if he can come over early, squeeze in a few minutes on his own place. Rudy's there in minutes, clutching his coffee keg, hair a fair imitation of Midge's morning do. He doesn't say a word as they manhandle the old claw-foot out from under the tarps in the backyard, pull it away from Taz's collection of pieces and parts scabbed out of rehabs over the years; a great old toilet, pedestal sink, the cookie stove, school lights and blackboards he thinks he might be able to turn into countertops, assorted lumber.

Alisha shows up while they're in the back, is sitting on the couch with a textbook in her lap when they come in, risking hernias with the tub. Rudy nearly drops his end, starts into introducing himself, and Taz staggers, grunts, says, "Rude!" and they shuffle on.

Once in the bathroom, Rudy looks back over his shoulder, doesn't mention, when they finally set the tub down, that there's nothing there but subfloor, studs—that this will all have to be hauled back out if he ever actually finishes the bathroom. He just, handing over wrenches and pliers as Taz jerry-rigs the old plumbing, says, "Nice. The rustic look."

"Thanks."

"Um, you just needed to stew? Feeling parched?"

"It's, she, she can't stand the basement."

Rudy looks at him, then back toward the living room. Then to the tub. Whispers, "So, you're thinking get her naked in here?" He gives a low whistle. "Maybe there's hope for you at last."

Still behind the head of the tub, Taz shakes his head. "I just let it go too long."

Midge starts calling for him from the crib, and Taz, jerking up, bumps his head against the rolled edge of the tub. Alisha calls, "On it."

Rudy steps to the door, swings it shut between them and the rest of the house. With the tub in place, there's hardly room for the two of them.

His voice still at a whisper, he jerks a thumb over his shoulder toward where Alisha sits talking to Midge. "So, who's the new wet nurse?"

Taz nearly winces. "You're still on that?"

"Well, yeah, but who is she?"

"Alisha. She's the friend who—"

"Who's on the *rebound*?" Rudy says. "Alisha," he says. "Lish Delish."

He puffs up a little as he slides around Taz, opens the door, and introduces himself to Alisha, tells her he's Midge's uncle. Uncle Rudy. Alisha holds Midge a little tighter.

They work like dogs, weeks' worth, Rudy even out in the shop, carrying, sorting, keeping Taz humming on the tools. They build face frames. Raise panels, groove the inside faces of the rails and stiles. All old-school. French casements he's never even seen before, has to take apart an old one to see how they're made. It's eleven before he looks at his watch. After. "Jesus," he says.

"I'll take the babysitter home," Rudy says. "Not a problem."

The house is nearly dark. One light maybe. The living room. No. It's over the stove. The tiny appliance bulb. They find Alisha asleep on the couch. Taz, giving one warning glare at Rudy, sneaks by, finds Midge in the crib. Thumb tucked in tight.

He pays Alisha extra, holds Rudy at bay, gives her a head start before setting him loose.

Then, alone again, he sits on the edge of the little bed. Can barely remember what to do besides shape wood, put together the pieces. His fingers tingle. Saw, jointer. Shaper, sander. Sawdust fills his hair. His pores.

He should shower. Maybe sneak down to the basement, not waking Midge. Or, the tub, soak it away.

Instead, elbows on knees, head sinking, he pulls out his phone. Turns it back and forth in his hands for minutes before texting, "How's school?"

She answers in a second, as if she'd been waiting. "Lesson plans suck." Then, "You?"

"Nonstop. Still behind."

There's nothing for a few seconds, and he texts, "Kids love you?"

"Of course. Finley, I'm not so sure about."

He should shower. She texts, "What are you doing up so late?"

"Just finished. You?"

"Lesson plans."

He pulls the blanket over himself. Doesn't undress. He still has the phone in his hand when she texts, "Sleep tight."

DAY 417

He steps out of his room. The light gray. Predawn.

He goes into the bathroom. Sits in the dark. Same as any morning. But, when he comes out, instead of heading into the kitchen for coffee, he stops in the hallway, looks down toward their bedroom.

He takes a step down the hall. A second. Stops at the doorway. Hand up on each side. Grips the casing. The room still breathes with her. That night sleeping on the shower curtain. Her lurch up the final morning. The spread of the water. He can't believe he never bought the new mattress. He begins tapping the side of his head against the doorjamb. The first wave of nausea in months.

Don't, Marnie says.

Taz stops, turns, walks to the kitchen. Stands there for minutes. Then turns on the burner, goes through the motions.

He chews a fingernail. Another. Draws blood. Just waiting for Rudy.

When Midge finally starts up, he flinches. He takes his cup.

Heads for Midge just as Rudy walks through the door. "I got her," Rude says, and Taz turns like a parade march about-face, swaps his coffee into the traveler and walks out to the shop. Gets started.

DAY 424

He texts. "What are you doing weekends?"

"That's your business how?" she answers, maybe an hour later. Then almost immediately. "JK."

"?"

"Just kidding."

"I was thinking."

"Must be so proud!"

He smiles. "Rude and I are going 24/7. Alisha can't keep up."

His phone rings. She sounds out of breath. "You want me to work weekends?"

He can't answer for a moment. "Only if—" he starts, but she says, "I can make it over Friday after school. Just one party I'll have to miss."

He has no idea if she's serious, but she dashes on, asking about Midge, about Alisha, if he's letting her do her work, and it seems she's practically still talking when she blows through his door Friday night, huffing and puffing as if she's run over the mountains. "Schmidge!" she crows, dropping to her knees, bracing for the collision, their reunion something that should take place on Russian steppes.

Taz can only stand and stare.

"Oh," Elmo says, looking over to him only after Midge struggles away, runs off to her room. "Shouldn't you be working?"

"Right," Taz says, and turns for the kitchen, the back door, the shop.

"JK," she says.

He turns back, not quite hiding a smile. "Really," he says, "you're right. More work out there than I can keep straight."

"Can I see?"

"Not quite at install yet, but maybe next weekend they'll have the library ready for it. It got so crowded half of it's stashed at Rude's, all the glass doors."

She stands up. "Next weekend, too? Tazmo and Rude?"

Midge trots back in with her stuffed Elmo, considerably bedraggled since Christmas. Sometimes Taz talks to her with it. As Marnie. She brings it to him, but Elmo intercepts her. Wriggling her hand into the pocket at the back of the head, she works the jaw. "What do you think, Midge. Can you take two weekends in a row? Think your dad can?"

"I think we'll bear up," Taz says, and she waves him away.

"Girl time here."

He watches a moment more, the two of them, and goes out, back into the grind. He barely sees her again for the rest of the weekend, just stands by her car as she climbs in for the ride back to Helena. She says, "Thanks, I missed me some Midge," and he says, "Next weekend?" and she says, "Give a shout near the end of the week. Let me know where you are." Then she backs up,

Midge waving fiercely, Elmo rolling her window down to blow her a kiss.

———

She does come back the next weekend too, but there are no installs yet, the flooring guys holding everybody up. She seems disappointed, and Taz walks her through the shop, shows her what he can, and she asks about maybe taking a break. "You know, before you break down yourself," she says, and he says, "I'd love it, but..."

"Like, even a walk. Though it's maybe warm enough for one more swim before the season's over."

He pictures it instantly, nearly shakes with it. "I'm just too jammed—"

She turns and walks away, taking Midge back in, and, later, when he comes in for coffee, she's gone with her somewhere, again when he comes in for lunch.

She knocks at the shop door that evening, tells him dinner is ready. He can hardly stand. Another cabinet set nearly done. He asks, "Midge?"

"It's almost eight," she says. "She ate an hour ago. So did I."

"Could have told me," he says, starting to smile.

But she says, "I did," and turns back for the house.

Midge is in the Jump-Up. Hardly notices he's back. There's a meal. A bowl of something. On the table. Stew, maybe.

He looks around, Elmo in the swivel chair. "I'm heading back over tonight," she says.

"Tonight?"

She looks away. Chews on her lip.

"But—" he starts.

She looks back to him, holds him in her gaze for a moment or two, waves him toward the bathroom. "Go wash your hands."

He does what he's told, forgetting there's no sink in the bathroom, and when he opens the door he's greeted with a wave of steam. He steps back, then in. The tub is full, the air fogged. "Bubbles?" he says.

"We went shopping," she calls from the living room.

"I'll just be a second," he says.

"It's for you."

"The tub?"

"Even the bubbles."

He closes the door. Looks at the twist latch. Every flake of paint picked off. Dentist tools. Stripper. Steel wool. The brass knob burnished with the oil of her skin.

He leaves his clothes in a pile in the corner. Winces when he steps in. She must have just kept draining, adding more hot. Waiting. Keeping it ready.

He closes his eyes. Fights the initial sting. Feels sweat pop along his forehead. Hears the bubbles' tiny burstings. It's like sliding into a new skin. He breathes. Blurs at the edges. Marnie says, *We so should have finished this bathroom.*

The door creaks. Elmo's face in the gap.

"See what it's like," she says. "Taking a break?"

She steps in, a bowl in her hand. She leans back against the studs, watches him. His knees naked above the water. "If you'd locked yourself in here, too," she says, but leaves it at that.

"Are you going to feed me now, too?" It's the only thing he can think to say.

"If that's what it takes to get you to stop hiding from everything."

Taz looks down at the bubbles.

"I thought they'd make it easier for you. You know?" She sighs. "They never look like they do in the movies."

"What can you do?" he says, lifting his hands in surrender, finding the bubbles cupped there. He spreads them over his chin, up his cheeks. A beard he hasn't made since he was five. Six.

She shakes her head. "Nice," she says. Then, "I'm not doing anymore weekends over here."

"School?"

"No."

He sits there with his bubble beard.

"I think you need some time," she says.

"I know. A lot more."

"That's not what I mean."

"El."

"Time for you to decide where you want to go."

"Go?"

"Forward. Backward." She shrugs. "Past? Present? Hell, *future?*"

She stares at him so long he has to turn to her. Is startled senseless by her tears.

She swipes at them. As if caught. "I can't stand watching you creep out to your shop anymore."

Taz wipes off the beard. First one side. The other. Like shaving.

"For christ's sake." She drops to her knees beside the tub. "Lean forward," she says.

He sits up. "El."

She pushes him forward. Starts rubbing his shoulders. Fingers digging deep. His muscles a knotted mess. "Do you even know what you're doing to yourself? I mean, how long would you have stayed out there? What are you going to build? An ark?"

"I don't know."

"You've got to come back," she says. "Wherever you are, you've got to leave it behind." One hand leaves his shoulders. An emptiness. The other goes still as she swipes again at her face. "And I was even thinking maybe I should get in there with you," she says. "My great big, stupid plan. Like some, I don't know, human sacrifice. Like you and me screwing everything up would solve anything. Bring you back from the dead. Jesus, I should have brought candles. Drawn pentagrams."

"El, it's going to—"

"You just shut up. Please. I don't want to hear one word from you."

She starts again, both hands, but then gives him a shove. Gets up quick. "God. I have to go. I won't get there till dark thirty as it is."

"You can go in the morning," he says.

"What, at four? Great plan."

"I'll drive you."

"So we all three die flying off some cliff?" She picks the bowl off the chair. "I can't even believe I'm in here. I mean, you're in the bathtub. I'm the babysitter. Is it catching? What you've got?"

"We can—"

She shoves the bowl at him. "Here. Just eat your chili."

"Chili?" he says.

"You got it. All No Biggie."

She leaves the door open. The draft sweeping in when she opens the front door.

Marn, all awe, but sounding hurt somehow, sad, says, *You made your Muppet cry.*

He shivers. Listens to Midge, still bouncing, telling some sort of story. To nobody.

DAY 437

Over the next week he works with Midge. Tries to get across the distinctions between *Mama* and *Elmo*, as if she's coming back. He makes no progress whatsoever. She knows *Mo*. She always wants *Mo*. He's not sure if it means *more*, or *Elmo*. Both, maybe. More Elmo. Mo' 'Mo.

Avoiding Alisha, he finishes the cabinets, waits for Rudy to get back from Nevada, does what he can on his own.

He's still out in the shop when Rudy finally calls, still road bleary, asks if he needs a hand.

"Kinda been waiting," Taz says. "It'll be for more than a couple of days."

"Perfect."

"You want to come over? First thing tomorrow? We could use both trucks."

"Why don't we get together, discuss this over a beer? I'm flat desiccated."

Taz spins a square on the surface of the workbench. "Man,

Rude, that's sounds good, but, you know, I'm wiped, I've got to go in, let Alisha go home, feed Midge—"

"Dude," Rudy says. "Just come on in. We'll talk about it."

Taz leans over, pushes open the shop door, looks across the yard to his house. Sees Rudy waving from the kitchen window, phone pressed to his ear, beer raised in the other hand.

"What the—"

"Just you know, being neighborly, getting acquainted." He grins and slips his phone into his pocket, tips his beer toward Taz.

DAY 438

First thing next morning, Rudy backs in toward the shop, nipping the garbage cans. Like any day.

Taz stands aside, waits for him to swing the door open.

Rudy steps down, cradling his coffee mug. "Too nice a day for work," he starts. "We should be out fishing. Teaching the little shaver a solid roll cast."

Used to it, Taz just follows him to the shop, saying, "Mmhmm," and they pull up the overhead door and Rudy whistles. "Things of beauty, Davis," he says. "Things of beauty." They could have been taking trash to the dump. He always says that. He takes a pull on his mug.

"Speaking of things of beauty," Taz says. "Alisha?"

"Friend-zoned. Big time. She's got *things she needs to work through.*"

"God," Taz says. "Who doesn't?"

"Exactly what I told her. I said, 'Man, look at Taz, you know?' But, I'm going African wild dog, run her to ground. Persistence, you know?"

254

Taz says, "Your only hope."

"Cold, man," Rudy says. "Fricking Antarctica. But the Rude does persist." He thumps a cabinet with the side of his fist. "This one?"

Taz looks, says, "The long one first," and they load Rudy's truck. He pulls out to the street and Taz backs in. "Should have used your trailer," Taz says.

"I meant to ask you about that. Last night." Rudy smiles. "Forgot."

"Yeah, well, you were kind of preoccupied. The whole wild dog thing."

Taz dodges inside to say good-bye to Midge and Alisha, and Rudy follows, saying his own good-byes.

Midge waves like a madman still. Shouts, "Bye-bye!"

Back out on the porch, he tells Rudy the address but Rudy says, "Really? I'll forget it before I've pulled out of here. You know that. I'll just follow. Same as ever."

And he does, across the Bitterroot, already winter low, then up the creek, climbing Blue Mountain. Air too rarified for mere mortals. Taz pulls into the circle drive, the fresh asphalt gleaming, and Rudy slides in beside him, backs up to the door. He climbs out, looks around, grinning. "S'pose they've spent a winter here yet?"

He always says that, amazed at the rich, their whims.

"No idea," Taz says. "No interest beyond the check." He always says that, too, but it's never quite true. He makes everything as if it were for his house, his and Marnie's, something he can't help, something they argued about. "We can't afford you building pianos," a line she'd stolen from what little he'd told her of his father, bulling through every job at light speed. "God-damn it, Taz, we're not building pianos!" Though his father would have built a piano the same way. With a chainsaw. An auger. A maul.

"At some point," Marn told him, "you have to consider, you know, profit?" She spoke as if he were twelve, while he stood mixing rottenstone with mineral oil, his buffing slurry, leaning down to catch the reflection, make sure the gleam was even. A rolltop the customer had to have, had to have him make, to match the wainscot he'd put into the den, the raised-panel wal-nut. A piece of Victorian England on a Montana mountainside. "You're not a furniture maker," she said, but he'd only looked down at the desk, worked the top half up, half down. "Looks like furniture to me," he said.

"Aargh." She slapped her forehead. "It *is* furniture. That's not what I mean and you know it. It's weeks of work, you and your hand-sawed dovetails. Your fricking hand-rubbed finish." She tried to ease up, to smile, even reaching out, taking his arm, giving it a little shake. "Save all this goodness for us, Taz. These clowns? They'll never know the difference."

"They're paying thousands," he said.

"Which works out to about a month at seventy-five cents an hour for someone who usually shops at IKEA."

"What?" he said. "You want me to be like—who?" He groped for a name of a hack she'd know. "Taylor?"

"Taylor's not living in a half-demoed fixer-upper," she said right back, and though he saw the blink of her surprise, knowing she'd gone too far, he said, "Maybe you should go live with him then."

Her jaw tightened, eyes narrowed. "Maybe," she said. You couldn't back her down with a bulldozer.

She turned back inside, the bills still in her hand, and he went back to his polishing, but her last jab hung with him, got him wondering if, for the buyers, all his work was only darker stuff in their vacation home, a contrast for the paint. His desk a place to let the junk mail stack up. That IKEA would have done it for them just the same.

That night he'd come in, hoping, but she still sat surrounded by bills, her glasses on, blew some hair back up off her forehead, shook her head. "Your desk has put us back in the hole. Jesus, we can barely pay for all that walnut. Eyed burl, of course."

"I'll ask them for more."

"They don't give *more*, Taz. How do you think they got rich to begin with?"

"Parents?" he said.

"Even so, they work to stay that way."

Clinging to his hope, he stepped behind her. "We're going to be fine," he said. Put a hand on her shoulder. Let it slide down her front, a finger between the buttons.

"You're kidding, right?" she said, leaning away, slapping her hand down on the paperwork. "Which aren't we going to pay this month? The electric or the water? Which do you want less?"

He pulled his hand back. "I'll go knock out some footstools," he said. "Plywood. You and Taylor can sell them at the farmers' market."

"Better make it snappy," she called out after him.

Behind him now, Rudy says. "So, this is close enough? They just wanted all this stuff up here in the back of our trucks?"

Taz looks up at the massive double doors, over to Rudy. Then back at their trucks. "No," he says, "I suppose they want them inside."

"Well, I'm on the clock. Whenever you're ready."

They're moving in the last of the second truck when Rudy says, "Where do you go?"

"Go?"

"When you stall out like that. Like at the front door. Where are you?"

Taz gets the front end of the upper through the kitchen door, backs up while Rudy swings his end around. "Nowhere," he says.

They set the cabinet down in front of the others in the kitchen and Rudy holds up his hands, not quite keeping in a tiny snort. "You don't have to tell the Rude a thing. I respect that."

"Rude," Taz says. "if you have to know, it's Marn. That's where I go."

Rudy's face falls. "That's cool," he says, looking nothing at all like he means it.

They get to work, getting the uppers in first, then start on the lowers. "You talk to her mother at all?" Rudy asks.

"Been holding off."

"For what?"

"Just trying this out. No Grandma, no Elmo. See if we can make it."

"You *want* to make it that way? Alone?"

"It was not exactly the plan," Taz says. "But now ..." He lets it trail off.

"You know how many guys she drove wild, when she was at the Club?"

Taz backs out, stands up, stretches his back. "Rudy, do we have to?"

"Well?"

"One, that I can see."

"Guilty," Rudy says. "As charged. But, well, they all kind of do that to me."

"So?"

"I'm just saying."

"Saying *what*, for christ's sake?"

"That I'd be jazzed."

"Rudy, you ever consider English? Like maybe as a second language?"

"Elmo," he says. "You know, thinking maybe there's a chance there. I'd be jazzed. Seriously."

Taz leans forward, grabs Rudy by the shoulder, leans in close. "Rudy, I know you're not used to ideas, and once one takes hold, it's not an easy thing for you to shake, but this time try, okay?"

"Okay, okay," Rudy says. "But, man, that's just a drag."

"She was the babysitter, Rudy. Midge's babysitter."

"You're killing me with the past-tense stuff."

"Well, she's not here anymore, is she?"

Rudy whistles, slow and sorrowful.

"Jesus," Taz says. "You ready to get the drawers, the shelves?"

"Countertops?"

"The stone guys got those."

They walk through the long hallway, through the foyer, out to the trucks, Taz leading the way.

"Just one thing," Rudy says behind him.

Taz groans.

"No, for real."

"Okay. Spit it out. But if this is about Elmo—" He stops, starts to draw his hammer out of its loop.

"Well, there is a lot I could say on that subject," Rudy says, stepping around to get the truck between them. "But, I was just wondering."

"Wondering what, Rude?"

"Tazmo and Rude. Any chance that much might be a real thing?"

"You're asking me?" he says, "About the future?" Taz drops his hammer back down. "Hell, Rude, I've got no idea about tomorrow, let alone whatever'll come next."

Rudy steps into his truck, leaves the door open. "So, back to the shop? Pick up the next load? That's all?"

"It's about as far as I can get."

Reversing the order, Taz follows Rudy down the mountain, no Mo to the Tazmo, no Midge on the installs, not even the car seat in the truck.

Marnie startles him when she says, *You know, it's not a dirty word.*

He downshifts for the switchback, watches Rudy's bumper.

The future, she says. *It's where you're headed, you can't help that.*

He doesn't answer, just shifts again, letting gravity do the work, pulling him down the mountain.

It's not a bad thing, Taz. Remember? We could hardly wait to get there ourselves.

DAY 443

They work all week, twelve-hour days, more, Alisha helping out a little longer, through dinner, Taz bringing Midge days Alisha's in school. Rudy lifts, holds, runs the level, climbs the ladders, but otherwise plays with Midge, keeps her away from the tool bucket, the nailers. Taz squeezes her food into his lunch cooler. Some toys into Rudy's tool bucket. Changes diapers on brand-new kitchen counters. They'll never know.

Stiff, sore, exhausted, he plods in every night, the house dark, Midge all but unconscious on his shoulder. He sings her a few songs, tells one short installment of Marnie the Mariner, then slides her into the crib, her thumb in her mouth. He tiptoes away, eases the door half shut, flips on a light, sits, gathers himself before reaching down and untying his boots. Toeing them off. Eventually he forces himself all the way up, gets the mail. Bills. Junk.

Trying to stay on top of things, he lines the bills up on the table the way Marnie did. Cuts them open with his utility knife. Knows he has to.

He looks at totals, due dates. The numbers swim, and he leans over, head in his hands. If he closes his eyes, he'll be out where he sits. With all the work, things do look better. Until he lines up the bills. The house payment right on top, crushing as ever. Even with the first-half check folded in his pocket, the owner doing a surprise walk-through this afternoon, ecstatic, pulling out his tooled leather checkbook. He'd glanced over at Midge in her walker, lifted an eyebrow, but didn't ask. Some sordid divorce, no doubt. The working class. The pathetic masses.

He pulls out the check, sets it down on top of the bills. Maybe enough to get him through the rest of the year. He'll have to put the ad on Craigslist for Marnie's Ghia.

He pushes at the mail stack, beyond the bills. A Costco flyer. A credit card app. Something stiff, like cardboard.

A postcard.

He sees the picture. Helena. The bright lights of Last Chance Gulch.

He turns it over. "You going to make it another weekend without me?"

A postcard?

He takes his phone from his tool pocket, changes his mind, puts it down. "Yeah," he says, to the empty room, "we'll make it."

Marn says, *I don't think she's talking just brute survival.*

He picks the phone back up, types, "Got your card. We're hanging in there."

His phone buzzes almost instantly. "Good for you two."

He looks away from Marn's *I told you so*, texts back, "Everything OK over there?"

"Hanging in there."

Marnie says, *Ouch.*

Taz has no idea what to say, holds the phone so long it goes black. He puts it on the postcard, spins it.

I think she's waiting, Marnie says.

Minutes pass before it lights up, buzzes. "Okay then," she says. "Off to bed. A room full of third graders always comes too early."

He picks up the phone, clicks to see if maybe she'd called before resorting to postcards, if somehow he'd missed it. But there's only one from Lauren. He knows he wouldn't have missed it.

Hardly aware of his hands, he pushes call back instead of voicemail, and clicks and clicks to get it to stop, hears one ring before it shuts off. He just doesn't have it in him. Not tonight.

Leaving the phone, he pushes back his chair, wanders into the kitchen, knows he should get something to eat. But he sees his computer, wonders since she's using the post office, if maybe she emailed. He swings the lid up, waits, and waits, and sees nothing but the blank circle of his parents' Skype dot, just two missed calls, both late, his mom waiting until his dad's asleep. He wonders what it's like down there for her, with him, and slowly shuts the computer. He wonders, too, what it's like for Lauren, just sitting, waiting for the life ring of his call.

After looking over El's texts once more, not a lot for analysis or hope, he shuts down the lights, walks through his empty house in the dark, and finds his way into the little bed in Midge's room as if it's the only walk he's ever taken. Listening to her breathe, he drifts off, the night a tangled spin of Marnie and Elmo, even Lauren, his own mother. Midge sleeps through it all and when he wakes in the morning, he's snarled in the sheets and his head aches. He feels less that he's slept than that he's been on a forced march. He drags out, starts the coffee, picks up his phone.

Nothing from Elmo. Not a word.

He looks at the computer, almost afraid to open it, but it's the middle of the night there, maybe his mom's only chance.

The phone rings in his hand, and he smiles, thinks, "At last," like the two of them have this connection, can tell when the other needs them most.

He says, "Hey," almost a sigh, but it's Lauren who says hello, who says she knew she wouldn't be waking him. She says that she saw that he called, that she's been wondering about coming out, just a few days. It's been so long.

He pushes the computer lid open, sits staring at the lighted blip of his parents' Skype, until Lauren goes quiet, says, finally, "Ted?"

"Yeah?"

"So, what do you think? Would now be a good time?"

"Yeah, it would," he says. "It'd be great."

DAY 452

Elmo stays in Helena. Just a single text one morning. "Still hanging on?"

He sits in the dark, texts, "Fingernail stuff." Then, "You're up early."

"School," she answers.

"Ever coming back?"

She says she's got seven weeks left, as if that explains everything. Then she texts, "Got to run," and everything goes quiet. He sits in the dark and waits for Lauren. For Rudy. For Midge to wake up. The day starting one way or the other.

He pulls over the computer, brings up a New Zealand government page. It actually does look possible. As far as the government's concerned anyway. The antipodes. Marnie's word. He's about to click over to Skype when Lauren knocks, peeks in the door, saves him. Taz gets up, says hello, asks about the flights, tells her Midge is still asleep, but adding, "She's going to be so excited." He carries her grocery sacks back to the kitchen, saying, "You know, I actually do eat when you're not here."

"I don't even want to think about that menu," she says, and before Taz can say, "Coffee?" she holds up her Starbucks cup, and behind her Alisha slips through the door, stops, looks as if maybe she's gotten the wrong house.

Taz leaps, makes the introductions, apologizes, then apologizes again, telling her she can take some time off. He writes a check, saying that she's been great, taking on all the extra.

Alisha looks at his check, at Lauren, says, "Is this severance?"

"No, just a break, till Grandma's gone."

"That'll be?"

She stands back by the kitchen, watching.

"I'll let you know," he says.

When he closes the door behind Alisha, Lauren says, "That's not the same girl as last time."

"She had to move. Work."

"Well, you could have called her, saved her the trip."

"Spaced it," he says. "My head these days. But, had to give her the check anyway." He starts for the kitchen, says, "Coffee?"

She holds up her Starbucks cup again. "Ted, are you okay?"

"Just tired," Taz says. "Burning it on all ends."

"Maybe you should have called earlier. Maybe a vacation's in order."

"Work comes when it comes."

"Yeah, but there's more to life, right?"

"It's not something that's really crossed my mind."

She lifts her cup, tips it toward him. "What does then, cross your mind?"

He almost smiles. "Mostly nothing," he says, something

Marnie would swear to. "And when it's not nothing, I'm usually wishing it was."

"She's still here then? All the time?"

He nods. "Of course."

"And you wish she wasn't," she starts, but then, fast, says, "No, not like that. I know. I know. But, you've got—" She turns away, starts to shelve her groceries. "You've got your whole life," she says. She holds a potato that's escaped the bag. "Mine," she says, "mine went with her. But you—"

"Mine, too, Lauren."

"I know, I know," she says. "But you've got Midge, and, and you're not even thirty."

Taz blows out a breath. "You ever get the feeling that taking one single step forward is just, I don't know, wrong? Betraying her or something?"

"I haven't taken a step."

"Me either, but hell, there's Marn, egging me on, pushing me toward anything."

"Marnie?"

"You know how she is."

She almost laughs. "Boy, do I."

Taz smiles. "But, still, you know, even when she's pushing me forward, she's still always there."

There's a tap on the door, the gentle push open. Rudy still in never-wake-Midge mode.

Taz crosses the kitchen, on his way to the back step, his boots.

And, as if she's ready to start her workday, too, Midge begins her crib babble. He's lacing his boots, and before he can make a move, Lauren's gone for her. He hears Rudy's, "Oh. Hey, Mrs. H. Laurie. Looking good."

"It's Lauren, sweetheart," Taz hears, and nearly drops his teeth.

Lauren comes back, smiling, Midge rubbing her eyes, looking around, wondering if any other new people have dropped out of the blue while she was asleep. Still looking for Elmo, probably.

"All her food's in the fridge," Taz says. "Naps around one."

"All right."

"Loves the park. The swings."

"Perfect."

He tugs his laces tight. "You know where it is?"

"Yes. Of course."

"Good."

"Taz, I …"

He stands, starts into the living room, Lauren following, Midge still trying to get her wits about her. "She's got toys all over," Taz says. "Her favorite thing in the world is pulling them out of the toy box. You can just load it, let her unload it. Over and over."

"I know. I've been here before, Ted. But, really, I think you should take that step. See where it goes."

Rudy moves to the door, puts a hand on the knob. "You're welcome to come along," he tells Lauren. "Watch me in action." He flexes a bicep, gives her a wink, and Taz blinks, wonders about all the other, easier ways to commit suicide.

Lauren looks straight at Rudy, considers him, slides her hair back behind her ear, a slick, practiced move. "Maybe when you're finished," she says, "you and I should get a drink, see what develops."

It's like hearing Marnie, but Taz hears the slap of her palm against her forehead, her gasp of disbelief, her amazed *Oh, my, god, Taz.* Then, *Wait, that was a joke, right?* Then, *That better have been a joke.*

Rudy swallows, works on breathing. Taz knows he's thinking, hard, wishing he'd showered this morning. Then wondering, getting suspicious. "The Rude," he says, "is forever at your service," and maybe does a little bow thing before slipping out the door.

Lauren turns back to Taz, dusting off her hands, barely holding in a laugh. "But seriously," she says, "that step. She'd want you to."

"I know," he says, then, quick, getting out of the house, he says, "We'll be late. I'll do my best."

"So will I."

It takes him a few seconds, but he gets out, "I mean, you know, to get Rudy back to you as early as I can."

She does laugh then, so much like Marnie he can't help but smile. She says, "Take him through the car wash beforehand. Please."

Midge leans toward the floor, putting the strain on, one of her oldest tricks. Lauren sets her down and she heads straight for the door.

"She's kind of used to going with us," Taz says. "You might have to hang on to her for a few. Distract her with something. She'll still use the Jump-Up some. Not supposed to, but. Always the toy box."

"She goes to work with you?"

He says, "Haven't had a lot of options."

"What about your babysitter?"

"She moved to Helena," Taz says.

"The new one?"

"She does what she can." Taz pushes through the door. "See you two later."

When Taz gets in behind the wheel, Rudy is still breathless. He turns to Taz. "The Rude cannot control his powers."

"She never stood a chance, did she?"

Rudy shakes his head. "They never do. But, I don't know. Marnie. What would she think?"

"Well, she always liked you. I'm guessing she's going to feel sorry for you. Same as ever."

Rudy looks at him. "She wasn't serious, was she?" he says, sounding relieved and disappointed at the same time.

Taz just turns the key, starts it up.

"The Rude will never understand them. Not if he lives forever."

Taz puts the truck into gear, starts down the drive. "And they will never understand the Rude."

"Yep," Rudy says. He pushes his cap back on his head, slides down in the seat. "Where does she want you to go?"

"Go?"

"Take that step."

"Oh, who knows?"

Rudy gives him a sidelong. "The Rude understands some things."

Taz smiles. "Just, you know, forward or something."

"To infinity and beyond?"

"Yeah, like that."

Rudy takes a sip from his keg of coffee, rests it back on his belly. "Poor Mo," he says.

DAY 454

October deepening to scraping frost off the windshields, crackling it off the tarp when he scrounges through the salvage wood beside the shop, Taz and Lauren fall back into the routine, the switch-off every morning, Lauren shaking out of her coat, her gloves, and every evening like summer again, but the light low and golden, already chilling down toward the stars and moon. Taz spends all day with wainscoting, picture rails, corner cabinets, buffets, doors, windows, whatever. Rudy mostly stays in the truck rather than face Lauren, and only once does he ask about Elmo, mentioning that he hasn't seen her around.

"She's teaching, Rudy. In Helena. Remember?"

"Yeah, but she did that weekend once and—"

"And how are things in the friend-zone?" Taz says, derailing Rudy completely. For the rest of the day Taz listens to tales of injustice and woe.

Then, at last, they're caught up in just the punch-list details, hardly any real reason for Taz to bring Rudy along, but he does anyway. He drops him off at his house every night, turning down

the offers of beer, then gets home, lets Lauren go back to her motel, carries Midge around the kitchen, if she isn't already asleep,
while he finds something to eat. More often than not, Lauren's
left him something. She even, last week, left him a microwave,
after he'd admitted he just ate what was there, peeled off the
plastic wrap, shoveled it in, hot, warm, or cold.

Then, one night, as he peeks into the microwave, the ring of
the doorbell stops him dead. He's grinning before he gets there,
just a feeling it's got to be Elmo, already picturing Midge losing
her mind, lunging from his arms for her, as if she could fly.

Midge calls, "Do, do, do," as they charge over, and when he
swings it open, he's staggered by two little ghosts on his door-
step, a one-eyed pirate standing behind them, reaching out with
his bag. They sing out, "Trick or treat!"

Taz manages, "Just a second," and turns inside, searches
through the house, bootlaces dragging. He's a dead man. Forget
Halloween? Marn will slaughter him. He can't believe Lauren
didn't make a single mention, bring in some sort of cute costume
for Midge. Pumpkins at least.

He finds Rudy's little bags of chips. Things he buys for his
lunch box, then throws at Taz, says he can't eat, that he's getting
fat. "Well, quit buying them," he says. "It's a willpower exercise,"
Rudy tells him.

Taz drops one in each pillowcase. The pirate says, "Yo
ho ho."

Taz turns off the porch light. The living room light. The
kitchen. Sits in the dark with Midge. Reads her the rest of *Sleep
Book*, no need anymore to see the words.

No way, Marnie says. *Not a chance. I will make you walk the plank myself.* Hiding on Halloween. All those kids out there. Simply not allowed. All her costumes. The pregnant mermaid. Pregnant skeleton. All those bones. He can even hear Elmo getting after him. *Midge? No costume? Unbelievable.*

He pushes up, tells Midge they've got a store run to make.

The girl at the checkout bags his candy, raises her pierced eyebrow, says, "It's all half off tomorrow, you know?"

At home he turns on the lights, toddles Midge out to the porch to drop the candy into every bag, but the first mask scares the hell out of her and Taz has to wonder if he's ever had an actual thought in his life. He apologizes to the goblin or serial killer, whatever he is, the mother waiting down on the walk, picks up Midge, pats her back, drops a wicked big handful of tiny candy bars into the kid's bag, shocking him into a breathless "Thanks!"

He sits with Midge, her cries easing into a few hiccupped breaths. "Don't worry," he says. "Pretty soon you'll be out there with them. Won't be able to believe the shit people give to you, for free."

He holds her for the next few groups of kids, but she's rattled, cranky, and he leaves the candy on the porch until he gets her to sleep.

He steps out of the bedroom, thinking he'll just leave the candy out there all night, but Marnie loved handing it out, seeing the costumes, showing off hers, and he can't quite shut them down. He pulls a chair up to the door, so he can see them coming, so they won't ring the bell, and he stays until the last two show up, nine thirty, a pair of teenaged boys in shoulder pads, football jerseys, barely even pretending to try, only one bothering with a helmet, but neither able to let go of what used to be so great. He tilts the bowl upside down over their bags, gets a last gasped "Whoa!" then shuts the door, finds a whole other bag of candy he'd missed. He calls them back, but they don't hear, and, afraid to raise his voice, he leaves the bag on the porch for any pumpkin smashers, and turns off the lights, eases back onto the couch and smiles. He hasn't been up this late in ages.

DAY 455

"Seriously, dude?" Rudy says.

Taz stirs, shifts, opens an eye. He sits up with a groan, looks around the living room, down at the couch he's slumped into. Rudy unwraps a tiny Snickers, chews with his mouth open. "You've got beds, you know."

Taz looks for his boots.

"The head witch not here yet?" Rudy asks.

Taz has to clear his throat. "Guess not," he says. "The little witch isn't even awake yet."

"Long night?"

Taz almost smiles, marveling. "I forgot it was Halloween."

Rudy stops chewing. "For real?" he says.

Taz says something. An *uh-huh*, maybe, he's not sure what.

"The costume party? I didn't tell you about that? Me and Alisha got screwed, second place."

"Only second? What were you?"

"I wanted to be a horse to her Lady Godiva, but she wouldn't go for that."

"Surprise."

"She stuck with the livestock theme, though. I was a cow. She was a cowgirl."

Taz holds up his hand before Rudy can elaborate.

Rudy reaches his mug out to him. "Here. You look like you need this worse than me, which is something, when I got up this morning, I would not have believed possible."

"I had to go to the store last night, for candy."

"Marnie make you?" Rudy says.

"Yep."

"Good girl," Rudy says, and unwraps another Snickers. "Least you got the good stuff."

A car door thunks shut in the street, and they glance at each other. "Ready?" Rudy says, and Taz nods, though he isn't even close. A toothbrush would feel great. But he heads for the door behind Rudy, is there when he swings it open, sees Lauren's face, stricken looking.

He thinks maybe it's only walking into Rudy so early on, but she says, "Ted, we forgot Halloween."

"We did," he says.

"How could I have missed all the decorations? The pumpkins?"

"Entranced," Taz says. "Midge's mad powers."

Rudy holds out a Snickers for her.

"Marnie would kill us," she says.

"Pretty much already did," Taz answers. He steps back so she can come in, says, "Midge had a rough one, too many ghosts and goblins. She's still out cold."

His phone chimes in his pocket, the double, a text, and he says, "Already late, we'll catch you tonight."

"Another long one?"

"Just punch-list stuff. Should be short. And then, who knows?"

"I suppose I ought to start thinking of a return flight," Lauren says. "Get home and knock down the cobwebs."

"We can talk about it tonight."

He follows Rudy to the truck, tosses him the keys, says, "Coffee first." He's pulling out his phone, looking for the text, collapses in the passenger seat as Rudy climbs behind the wheel, saying, "If you saw my night, you might be rethinking this driver decision."

But Taz only sits staring at the phone, until Rudy starts up the truck, pulls out, takes a sip from his giant mug, and says, "What?"

Taz says, "Elmo."

"She coming back?"

Taz reaches up, pats down the tangle of his hair. "It's, I, she doesn't sound like Elmo."

"What do you mean?"

"She wants to know if we're nearly done. If maybe I could come up to Helena."

"Whoa ho!"

"No, says she needs help."

"With what?"

"Doesn't say."

"Well, call her."

"Coffee," Taz says, still staring at his phone.

At the cart, he doesn't answer when Rudy asks what he wants. Rudy orders an XXL. Four shots. He studies Taz, says, "So, I couldn't believe it, but Alisha did it, full-on nude for Lady Godiva."

Taz says, "What?"

"She just doesn't have enough hair for the role, you know?"

"Who?"

Rudy hands him the coffee, says, "Never mind," says, "No power tools for you today."

————

She doesn't call. All day, he checks his phone, Rudy raising an eyebrow. He texts. Leaves one voicemail. Another. Resists, barely, a third.

He and Rudy finish the house. The owner pads the check a little, something he wants to wave in Marnie's face. It's Midge who's earned it, he guesses, but still.

He passes the extra on to Rudy, who passes it back, says only, "Not a chance." He's never asked how Rudy exists, if the tower work is such a gold mine, if there's a trust fund hiding somewhere, a drug cartel, and Rudy has never said.

As they stand in the foyer, loading the last of the tools, Rudy says, "Well, that's that then. Give me a call when you got something else?"

"Right now," Taz says, "there's nothing even on the horizon."

Rudy purses his lips, throws the extension cord higher up on his shoulder. "Nothing?"

"Marko maybe has—"

"I mean Helena. Nothing on the horizon there? She never answered?"

"Nope." Taz starts out the door with the compressor, the broom.

"She in trouble, you think?"

"She would have said, right?"

They get into the truck. Rudy says, "Club?" It's a tradition. End of job.

Taz taps his phone against his thigh, stares out the window.

He puts the truck into gear, rolls down away from all that work. Things he'll never see again.

"You should maybe text her," Rudy says.

"No answer."

"Call?"

"No answer."

"Well," he says, putting a boot up on the glove box. "That doesn't make it any easier." A minute later, Rudy says, "Road trip?"

"And if it's nothing? Me standing on her porch with my teeth in my mouth?"

"She'd do it for Midge and you in a heartbeat. Be here already."

Taz is chewing on that when his phone chimes, the double, and he snatches at it, lifts it to read against the wheel. Rudy reaches over, steers.

"She says never mind. It's nothing. She never should have texted."

"Huh?"

Taz takes over the steering again, drives down the mountain. Wonders.

DAY 456

He stares at the ceiling. The dim glow in the nightlight. The railing bars of the crib rattle. "Daddy!"

"Right here, Midge," he says. "It's okay. Put your heady down."

Silence for a moment. Two.

"Da-DEE!"

He sighs. "Right here, Midge. Put your heady down."

The bars shake again. Like they're coming apart. A wild beast caged.

Then silence. The measuring of effects.

The first start of a whimper.

Taz rubs his temples.

"Mo," she says, incorporating it into a whimper. "Mo, mo, mo."

The mattress bounces as she collapses, sinking into her misery. But it's the tired whimper, not the half-hour brand of anguish, and Taz hopes he can wait it out. The books warn of the endless loop of broken nights created by running to every cry out. But it says nothing of lying in your own sweat, listening, not moving, making your huge mistakes.

He feels Marn pat his arm, nearly afraid to move, but leaning close, whispering into his ear, *You're doing great.*

If he had any guts at all, he'd move down the hall, back into their room.

Midge whimpers herself to sleep, asking for Mo. Again and again until she's down. Mo, mo, mo.

She's asleep, her quiet, steady breathing filling every space in the room, hours before Taz is. And when he wakes up, he wonders if he ever was asleep. The room still dark. Head throbbing. Like the first days.

He eases up, stands over the crib, and goes out, loads what he needs into the truck, fixes coffee, fills the thermos. He readies the diaper bag, a few toys, stops, thinks. Midge or not?

Lauren. Due in any minute. Talking about flights home. She'd stay. He knows that.

He looks up into the gray rift of the morning, thinking maybe it'd be better to bring Midge, that she'd help with Elmo, then almost flinches at the whack Marn gives him over that.

But he sits down, pours a cup out of the thermos, and waits for Lauren.

He's still sitting there when she comes in. She gives him a quick look, a glance to her watch, says she thought he'd finished up yesterday, had a day off, might sleep in.

"Sleep in? Mean, past three? Four?"

"Well, I thought I could help. See her one more day. I've got the late flight."

"Tonight?"

She nods.

He drops his head, says, "I was going to run over to Helena. Check out a job there, maybe."

She looks straight at him. "Helena?" she says. "Going global?"

He smiles. "I don't think so. Not just yet."

"Should I cancel my flight?"

"If, I don't know. I don't really know what's going on over there."

She looks and looks at him. "If there was something going on over there," she says, shifts from one foot to the other. "Well, you know Marnie would only be happy for you."

Taz fidgets at the door. "Like I said, I really don't know anything."

"You think about that, and you'll know it's true." Lauren runs her hand up through her hair, another ghost move that just hollows Taz. "She could be a lot of things, Taz, and easy wasn't always one of them. We both know that. But, this Muppet, Marnie would like her. A lot."

"Lauren."

"She's not here anymore. She'd never want you stalled out for, what, the rest of your life?"

"You're jumping the gun. Like leaping way, way ahead."

"Really?"

"She just asked if I could come over, that she needed something. Then she took it all back."

"But you think you should go anyway."

"She'd do it for me."

Lauren looks away, toward the kitchen, Marn's smiley face maybe. "I believe she would," she says.

"And?" Taz says.

"Well, what else is there? You'd do anything for each other."

Taz blows out a long breath. "Marn used to say that when she was little, in trouble, you'd just sit her down and talk to her. Said she wished you'd just beat her, that there was no squirming out of anything once you started talking to her."

Lauren smiles. "Wishing for beatings? Was I really that bad?"

"Beatings in a good way," Taz says.

"Go to Helena," Lauren says. "See what she needs."

"I—" Taz starts, but Lauren interrupts, says, "And you leave Marnie here with me. It's time I had a talk with her."

"I was thinking of taking Midge."

Lauren shakes her head. "You leave her with me, too. I think this might be something you have to do on your own."

Already packed, Taz walks out to his truck, scrapes away at the frost. The engine stutters, slurs in the cold, but fires, and he waits for a little warmth, then backs out of the drive, turns on the headlights, follows them down the block away from their house.

———

Far from staying behind with her mother, the whole way to Helena, the world an early winter gray, Marnie works him over for leaving Midge behind. He wants to say, "But your mother told me to," but knows how that would go. So, he just drives, listens.

(A) she says, you don't ever leave her behind, and (B), she's who your little redhead is all about. You get that, right?

Taz holds the wheel tighter, goes through the curves in the canyon, the red rock walls. "I should have brought her," he says, and Marnie says, *Better late than never.*

It makes the ride go quick, but even Marn falls quiet when he pulls up in front of Elmo's fourplex.

"Can't just go barging in," he whispers.

No, I don't think that would be wise.

"Why didn't you think of that before?"

He feels Marn's shrug.

Finally he reaches for his phone, texts, "El, you okay?"

He waits minutes. Then minutes more. Then types in, "El? Kind of freaked me out yesterday."

It's another few minutes before she answers. Just, "OK."

"OK you freaked me out?"

"No. I'm OK."

"Busy?"

"What?"

"Can I come in?"

There's a space then, and Taz finds that he's holding his breath, has to let it out, sit panting like he ran over here.

Then, at last, "Are you here?"

"Look out the window."

Oh good christ. What if she's not home?

Do not go there, Marn whispers, sounding breathless herself. The front door of her apartment swings open. Elmo standing there. Just looking out at him. Wearing a T-shirt. Her basketball shorts.

He opens the door. Stands looking back at her.

"No Midge?" she calls out, just loud enough to make it across the street to him.

He shakes his head.

She gives him a wave over, and when he gets close, she says, "I really could have used me some Midge."

He stops, says, "She's having a girls' day with Grandma."

Elmo turns and climbs the steps, says, "Well, come on."

Taz stays where he is, says, "I, I just wanted to see. You got me worried."

She looks down at him and wraps her arms around herself, shivers. "I'm not standing out here," she says.

Taz follows her in and sees she wasn't lying about not moving in. A handful of boxes sort of line one wall, some open, stuff spilling out. There's the same well-worn chair and couch, the chair arm draped with a Halloween costume, angel wings flat, a little ratty, a halo slapped on top. A crimson pitchfork leans across it all.

"So," she says. "What brings you to town?" She stands sideways to him, looking out the window, as if his truck out there might have been dropped by tsunami.

"Like I said," Taz says. "Yesterday, your text, I was—"

"Yeah. Sorry about that. But, I told you to forget it. It was nothing."

"But, still. You never asked me for a thing before, so ..."

She starts to lift her arms, lets them fall down to her sides. She looks at him, just a glance, then away. "You want anything? Coffee or something?"

"Had it on the way."

"Need to pee, then?"

"El, I'm okay," he says, glad he stopped before getting here.

"Well, at least have a seat."

He picks up the halo, the white dress, moves the pitchfork aside.

"What's a girl to wear, you know?" she says.

"El. What's going on?"

She takes her braid, runs her hands along it, starts undoing it. "Big party up here the other night."

"And?" he starts, but Elmo interrupts, says, "Do you still tell Midge about her mom?"

Taz rocks back a touch. "Um, yeah, I do."

She looks at him for real, eye to eye. "How do you do it?"

Taz tries to figure out an answer, but Elmo runs over him. "I mean, like, how, you know? What way do you make up the stories? If you make them up."

"She's this big adventurer," Taz says quietly. "Like a pirate, kind of. Sailing around. Not able to get back yet. Like this fairy tale or something."

"Okay," she says, standing there, finger-combing her hair, separating it, starting to weave it back into a braid. Over, under, across.

Taz waits, begins to pet, without knowing it, one of the wings, smoothing down the feathers.

She drops down on the couch across from him. "Once upon a time," she says, but stops, looks at him. "Do you do that? That whole 'once upon' thing?"

"Nope," he whispers.

"Okay, forget that then." She does the rubber band loops, then lets go of her hair, puts her hands in her lap. "So, there was just this girl, you know? And she was kind of fun, her friends said, and kind of okay-looking—her friends said that, too, she didn't—and she was in this new place, like the youngest person there, and there was this guy, this new teacher, who wasn't that old either."

Taz holds up his hand. "What if I don't think I like this story?"

She stops, fixes him with a stare. "Does Midge say that to you? *Ever?* 'I don't like this story?'"

He shakes his head.

"Then you just—" she lifts her fingers to her mouth, works the key, tosses it over her shoulder. "I'm the one telling this story. And don't forget, I didn't ask you to come here."

"Well, technically, you did."

"Okay, there was that. But still." She twists the lock shut again, and holds his eye, making sure.

She's pale, Taz sees, maybe even more than usual. And the braid, even redone, looks slept in. If she slept.

"So, anyway," she says, "this girl, she just minds her own business, does what she has to, because far away, in another land, there's this beautiful little princess, who has stolen the girl's heart."

"Like bad stolen?" Taz can't help a smile.

Elmo drops her hands in her lap, sighs. "No, ass, good stolen."

"Okay then."

"But the little fairy princess, she lives with this terrible, mean, ogre."

"Hey!"

"Okay, okay. She lives with her father, who, who ..." Elmo's voice trails off. She clears her throat, looks into her lap, winds her fingers around one another. "... Who a horrible thing has happened to."

She takes a shivery breath. "But, he may have a piece of this girl's heart, too," she says, so quiet Taz has to lean closer just to hear.

"But, the other guy, he doesn't know anything about this far land, and he sends a glass slipper to the girl, and she doesn't know what to do, so she sends it back, but he sends it back, and so does she, until finally, she doesn't know how to keep sending it back, and she goes to this party with him, gets all dressed up, and this guy is a good guy, and he asks her about her life, and he listens, and—the girl tells him stories, all kinds of things from her life, but never once does she mention the far land. Not once."

Elmo stops, and Taz looks up in time to see her wiping her cheeks.

"And this girl, she wonders why she does not say anything about that land, and, when this guy, who is a good guy, not some creep, at the end of the party, on the way home, at the girl's door, asks if he can kiss the girl, I mean, he freaking *asks*, she cannot even look at him, cannot even answer him, only just suddenly realizes that she misses that far land more than she misses anything in the world, so, she panics, runs away, suddenly does not want to waste one more second away, drives halfway over the mountains before losing her nerve, wondering what if that land is not as friendly as she'd hoped, that maybe her heart had been stolen, but not taken in, so she turns around, drives back, one wing sticking out the door, which the policeman is kind enough to point out, sends a lame text instead—"

Taz reaches across the little gap between the chair and the couch, over one of the unpacked boxes, and takes one of her hands, which has been busy strangling the other, and says, "El, breathe."

"And then, what if the father shows up at the girl's door, and the girl has been hiding from him, because she doesn't know what to do, what to do about him, or about the guy, or about herself, or about one single thing, and—"

"Breathe," Taz says.

She looks up, then down to her hand in his. She pulls it away. "I just don't know if I've been a dumb ass, sending back that stupid slipper. If that far land isn't anything real at all."

"It's real," Taz says.

Elmo blinks, looks at him, away. "What if that man, what if that horrible thing that happened to him, what if he never comes back from it?"

"I don't know," Taz says. He reaches back, doesn't take her hand, just pulls her little finger a touch away from the others, lets its tip rest on the side of his finger. "Maybe somebody in glass slippers will show up and, I don't know, pour him a big-ass bubble bath."

Elmo laughs, just once, a kind of blurt. She wraps her finger around his. "I mean, I just want to know if I'd be stupid, you know, to hope."

Taz takes a breath. "You've been making me wonder the same thing, but, man, wanting in on this? I figured, who'd want to? So, no, not stupid, but I'm guessing there's a name for it that's not far off."

Elmo smiles, says, "Don't think I haven't thought that myself. More than once."

"Great," Taz says, and they sit there looking at each other, away, not quite holding hands, until Taz sits up a little, says, "Well, Grandma's flying out tonight, so I better—"

"Wait," Elmo says, and Taz stops. He fiddles with the staff of the pitchfork.

"As long as we're airing out all our fairy tales," Elmo says, quiet again, "when Marnie talks to you—"

Taz jerks like he's been shocked. "I told you that?"

"A guess."

Taz stares.

"When she talks to you," she says, still quietly, "what does she say about me?"

Careful, Marnie whispers.

Taz says, "She says a lot of things."

"About me, Taz."

"She says, 'Don't be a fool.'"

Elmo sucks in a breath.

Taz can feel Marnie holding her breath, too. "She says, 'Don't let her get away.'"

Elmo leans forward to look him in the eye.

"Everyone tells me that, El. Rudy. Even the wicked stepmother. Marn most of all."

"And she's the one you listen to most of all?"

Taz nods, smiles a little, one side of his mouth.

Elmo lets out a breath, one it seems she's been holding for ages. "I am so sorry you lost her, Taz."

"I know. Everyone is."

"And you think ..."

"I think no one would be anything but happy to see me pull some sort of Lazarus."

"Lazarus?"

"I've been given up for dead for a long time, El. Maybe by myself most of all."

————————

Marnie doesn't say a word on the drive back, and he's glad for that. It's just the way they get sometimes, quiet, cool with it, each looking out the windows, thinking whatever they're thinking.

He's back in time for Lauren to catch her flight, but she's already canceled. "I was worried," she says. "Your job in Helena."

Taz is standing at the door, Midge climbing his legs, yelling, "Daddy home!"

"Worried?" he says.

She smiles, draws herself up. "If it worked out all right."

It's like talking to Rudy. Then he gets it, smiles himself. "She's teaching till Christmas," he says, and doesn't miss the touch of color that comes back to her cheeks.

Midge grabs Taz's fingers, tugging on them, climbing up onto his feet. She tugs again, like putting her heels against a horse, shouts, "Go!" Taz starts walking her around on his feet, her new favorite game.

"I didn't just sit around all day myself," Lauren says.

Midge steers by pulling on one finger or the other. She directs him into the kitchen, around, back out. "Spending a day with Midge isn't much like sitting around."

"Ted," she says, serious enough to stop him.

He turns.

"I talked to some realtors today," she says, out with it, fast.

Taz blinks. Midge keeps after his fingers.

"There is nothing for me anymore that is not right here." She waves toward Midge, still on Taz's feet, pulling him toward the toy box.

Her living here?

"I won't even start looking if it's not something you think you can handle."

He staggers over to the toy box, lets Midge loose to do her worst. "Sounds like you've started already."

"Ted," she says. "I'm trying here."

"I did some looking, too," he says, before giving it a second's thought. "Back in the darkest days. Talked to my parents."

She goes blank, as if he's left the planet, zoomed off into a whole other world.

"They live in New Zealand. I don't know if you knew that."

"Marnie said."

"I, my dad, he nosed around, about getting me work down there."

She puts a hand down, steadies herself on Marnie's gigantic table. Where she wanted to entertain the multitudes. At least build forts underneath with Midge.

"They've never seen Midge," he says. He glances up to her. "They never even met Marnie."

Lauren takes a second, collects herself. "They could come here if she meant anything to them. Could have at any time."

"It was just talk. Like what you're doing with the realtors."

She's shaking. "But I am talking about moving here. *To* Midge." She stares at him. "You would, would you really take her that far?" she says, like she might come across the table at him. Fight him to the death for her.

Taz shakes his head. "Like I said, it was a long time ago."

She doesn't say anything, but drops her gaze, the stare down.

"Truth?" he says. "I don't really think I could move. Away from here?" He waves his hand around. "After all we did? All the work? The whole fell swoop?"

She looks down, brushes some invisible crumb from the table. "I was afraid you'd leave just because of all that."

"I know," he says. "And maybe I should. Still can't face the bathroom. Even after tearing it out. I can't even go into the mountains for a Christmas tree. The way she'd eye about a thousand, finding all these invisible flaws, then pick the perfect one, no different, far as I could tell, from any of the rest."

"She was good on invisible flaws," she says.

"Wasn't too bad on visible ones either."

"Good god, no. I had all mine paraded before me, believe me."

He keeps nodding. The way she could pick a thing apart. A person. The way she could put him back together.

"So," her mother says, "my talking to realtors?"

"It'd be a big step," he says, "just to be the grandma. You know, the old lady down the block she'll visit less and less?"

Lauren coughs as if punched. "Well," she says, "Marnie gave you the gift, didn't she. *The old lady down the block?*" She smiles. "And you know who you'll be, don't you? The dad. The old man who embarrasses her. Who she'll fight to get away from. Who she'll *lie* to, to run off with boys. Right to your face. All your trust. Whose heart she will break as surely as if—"

Taz chops the air between them with the edge of his hand. "Enough!" he says, but he gives out a long "Phew," says, "Mercy," says, "Maybe we've both got the gift."

Lauren raises an eyebrow. "We'll both be obsolete before we know it. It's in the job description."

"She's not even two," Taz says. "Not even one and a half. Let's give her a while."

"Well on her way," Lauren says. "Believe me. I've raised one before. Didn't even see the sidelines until I realized that's where I'd been left."

"That's our job, though, right? To make sure they leave us behind?"

"It is," she says. "But who on earth would ever take such a job?"

He says, "Who'd be begging for a second round?"

She spreads her hands flat on the table, bows her head. "Touché," she says.

They stand that way for a minute, just looking at the table-top, their hands, the room quiet around them, just Midge's babble as she searches through the bottom of the toy box, looking for any last thing she hasn't hurled out into the world.

DAY 461

After most of a week of no work, Marko calls, out of the blue, talks his ear off, another job, a meeting in the morning, another rocket launch, the sky the limit. Taz hangs in there, letting him wear himself down, and when he's finally finished, Taz clicks off and falls into the chair at the kitchen table. Can't believe the raw stupid luck of it.

He calls Lauren, tells her about the new work, and she just says, "Well, thank god I didn't get that ticket." She's all but laughing.

But she snoops enough to learn that Elmo might be back for the weekend, and maybe that's why she tweaks her back, or says she does, why, Friday afternoon, as soon as Taz gets back from meeting with Marko, she's off to her motel, says she might just get a hot pad, watch movies all weekend, maybe venture down to the hot tub.

And, an hour or so later, there's a knock at the door, so tiny Taz might have missed it if he hadn't spent a week hoping. He eases the door back, and they stand smiling at each other, until Midge comes to see who now, and cries, "Mo!"

Elmo drops down and they cling to each other. It goes on and on, the two of them recharging.

Midge eventually begins to squirm, to pull away. Elmo lets her go, and Midge takes her hand, takes her back to her room, showing her everything that's changed, which is pretty much nothing except a new stuffed toy from Grandma. A Cookie Monster to go along with her disheveled Elmo. There's no difference between the two, as far as Taz can tell, other than color, but the Monster has sat pretty much untouched since Grandma brought it out of her bag. Midge only calls it "Blue Mo," kind of like one word.

From the living room, Taz hears Midge cackle, cry, "Mo, Blue-mo!" and barely Elmo's, "Seriously?" and he smiles, knowing that's what she'd say.

When they come back out, Midge drags the stuffed Elmo by a leg, still laughing, tugging at him, saying, "Mo," then tugging on the real Elmo's hand, saying, "Mo," cracking herself up no end. Elmo gives Taz a what-can-you-do?

They take her out, a milk shake, then back home they set up an elaborate block castle together—Taz has made her more blocks than any ten children should possess—and when Midge finally settles into bed, Elmo hits the couch like she's ended the longest day of her life. "You can't believe how much I've missed her," she says.

"I can," Taz answers.

Elmo smiles, says, "I guess you could." She closes her eyes, sighs. "Where's Grandma?"

"Motel. She, I think . . ." Taz wonders, but goes on. "I think she's giving us space."

"No lie?"

Taz says, "I think so," and Elmo pushes herself up, says, "Well then," and takes two quick steps forward, and kisses him, a quick peck, and just as quickly steps back. "There," she says. "Couldn't let Grandma's deal go to waste."

She pulls the door open, slides most of the way out. "I'll see you tomorrow," she says.

———

Sometime middle of the night, that kiss lingering into his dreams, the nightlight flares and Taz, not quite awake yet, feels his blankets being pulled back, and then the light crush of his mattress, and his heart does a leap that comes out as a gasp, and he turns, lifting his arm for Marnie, only to feel Midge crawl up and in with him.

He says, "How?" and then, "Midge?" and then, "Sweetie, what?" and she only crunches in tight against him, and says, "Toady," which means that she's cold.

He props himself up on an elbow in the dimness and looks down at her snarl of hair, her eyes already closed, and then over to the crib, imagining the high wire/prison break/mad ninja moves she must have used. He grins, picturing her concentration, her effort, and eases back down, puts an arm around her, and though she's already almost completely out, he starts another installment of Marnie the Mariner for her, Marn running up the rigging, leaping along the masts, swinging back down to the deck, all of it just exactly like the Mighty Magnificent Midge rappelling down the face of her crib.

She's still curled tight to his side at dawn, and Taz gathers his breath, holds it, begins to sneak toward the edge of the bed, moving his legs inches at a time, rolling over and out, but keeping his arms pressed against the mattress, squelching any bounce. He throws the little blanket from the crib over his own blankets, and tiptoes around the bed, gathering clothes, and slips into the kitchen, starts the coffee, wondering if Midge is finally going to use her own big-girl bed. He remembers bringing in his stupid blind fox joint, wanting Marn to marvel over it as much as he had himself, and Marn maybe already seeing how the real marvel—their daughter coming into that bed and making it her own—was still years in coming.

DAY 504

Finally, Christmas looming, the schools wrap up classes, the streets suddenly deserted. Old snow blows along the empty pavement, and Taz warms up the truck before strapping Midge into her car seat, Lauren shivering beside him in the driveway.

"Really, Ted, I can watch her. There's no need to drive her all over the country."

Taz cinches the belt, turns out of the cab. "She likes going places. She'll go nuts when she sees El."

Midge, on cue, starts chanting, "Mo, mo, mo!"

Taz says, "Look at her."

Lauren looks down the street instead. "But it's so far, and it's winter."

"Roads are fine. I checked."

"But ..."

"Lauren, we'll be fine."

She looks down at the frosted ground. "I just—once she's—I just don't know how many more days I'll have her to myself."

Taz puts a hand up on her shoulder. "You're not being replaced. She's just done with her student teaching. She's moving back home. She's going to be looking for work."

Taz glances over at Midge, double-checks that the diaper bag is there, her new book, the extra blankets. "We'll be fine, back by this afternoon." He slips in behind the wheel, the heater charging the whole cab. "I'll shoot you a text," he says, "when we hit town." Then he closes the door, tells Midge to wave, and puts it into gear.

The roads are clear, other than the pass, though the sky is ominously low. Midge conks as usual, leaving the cab empty but for the push of air out the vents, the rush of road around them.

He pulls up in front of Elmo's apartment, walks around the truck, drops the tailgate, and Elmo charges down the walk, already carrying the first box, skidding to a stop when she sees Midge. "Taz?" But Midge is pounding on the arms of the car seat, shouting, "Mo!" and Elmo hands the box over to Taz and hauls Midge out, both of them laughing as they go up the stairs.

They've emptied the whole apartment before Taz asks, "Your car?"

Elmo winces. "Um. In back. Dead. You okay with driving?"

"Great with it," Taz says, and Elmo grins, bundles Midge into the cab, Taz climbing in after them, turning the key.

"Rudy's better with cars than wood," he says. "Maybe we could—"

"Tazmo and Rude goes all auto mechanic?"

Taz says, "Why not?" and Midge grabs Elmo's hand, swinging it up and singing that they're all going for a drive, a drive, a drive.

Elmo says, "And what brings Midge up here? Grandma too busy?"

"Just thought it'd be fun. Even before I knew you'd be joining us."

"Driving to Helena and back? True fantasy vacation stuff."

"So," Taz asks, "once the fantasy is over, then what?"

"Start putting out apps. Big time."

But Midge won't take any divided attention. She points to the diaper bag, says, "Mo, book," and as Taz gets back on the highway, Elmo starts to read *One Fish, Two Fish*.

———

It snows on the way back, nothing predicted, and Midge doesn't give Elmo a second of peace, telling long, indecipherable stories, wanting her to read Bish again, and again, asking for snacks, the front of the truck a sudden fog of Cheerios. Taz works the wipers, squeezes the wheel, drops the speed down once, then again, so it's dark when they get into town, Midge cranky, head drooping, too thrilled to be riding with Elmo to nap, the drive failing to do its knock-out trick.

Taz glances over to Elmo, catches her eye, and she says, "My place, I suppose," and Taz doesn't say a word, just eases through the dark and the snow, Midge finally dozing off three blocks before Taz pulls up in front of Elmo's, the porch light on, a few Christmas lights draped in behind the window glass.

"Homey touch," Taz says.

"Rudy's, probably."

Taz smiles.

"Don't worry, we'll get yours up to speed," Elmo whispers. "Unless, you know, you've already gone all Griswold over there."

"No, saving that for you, for sure," he says, and reaches up and switches the dome light off before Elmo opens her door. "I'll back it into the shop," he says. "It'll keep your stuff dry. We can unload tomorrow."

Looking just as worn-out as Midge had, Elmo says, "Thanks, Taz, for everything. Especially for bringing her."

Taz thinks it has been his biggest mistake of the day, hardly a word exchanged between them, but he nods, says, "We'll see you tomorrow," and she reaches over Midge to hold his hand for an instant, give it a squeeze.

"I hope she sleeps for you," she says, then slips out, carrying her coat, one box she'd been resting her feet on for the whole ride. Taz watches her up the walk, until she's got the door open, turns and waves. Then he gentles out away from the curb, onto the nearly trackless street, keeping Midge asleep until he backs up his drive, parks, and undoes the car seat's straps.

She murmurs something when he lifts her out, so warm under her blankets she's almost hot to the touch. Her face hits the cold air, the touch of snow, and she scrunches in against his sweatshirt. "Home?" she says.

"Home," he says.

He carries her up onto the porch, reaches, turns the knob, pushes the door in on the darkness.

"Mo?" she says.

"No," he says. "No Mo."

She whimpers, pushes away from him. He sets her down, on her feet. She goes straight for the toy box. Drags toys out, barely over the lip, scattering them behind her, across her lap. But she's not really awake, not really into it, and she comes back to him, holds up her arms. He lifts her, carries her into their room to get her jammies.

She says, "Want Mo."

He gets her down, knows, with the sleeping on the way over, he's maybe in for a night, then finds his phone and punches in a text to Lauren. "Home again, all safe."

It seems he's hardly hit Send before the phone chimes back. "Thank you," then, "Welcome back."

He goes out, opens up the shop doors, moves the saw out of the way, the jointer, and backs the truck in.

He leans against the truck seat, drops his head against the glass separating him from all Elmo's stuff, everything in its place, a truckload of decisions to be made. He sits long enough for the cold to seep in, his breath starting crystals of frost climbing the windows.

Taz? Marn whispers.

He smiles, knew she'd show up.

It's time to go, she says. *You'll freeze out here alone.*

He nods, his head still against the glass, his eyes closed against the glare of the shop lights. Midge will feel like a furnace when he goes in, makes sure the blankets are right. Maybe he'll move her to the big-girl bed. Make the move back down the hall way. Finish the bathroom.

DAY 505

Midge stays in her crib, asleep, all night, and when Elmo comes over the next morning, she doesn't knock, just slips inside the door, sees Taz on the couch with his coffee, says, "Morning, Ralph."

Taz smiles. "Night, Sam."

"How'd you sleep?"

"Okay."

"Me too. Any more coffee in there?" She gives a wave toward the kitchen.

"Should still be hot," he says.

She comes back with her cup, sits down beside him. "How's our little terrorist," she says.

"Still out cold."

"The big one?"

"Not here yet. Should be though, any sec."

"Work? Pretty busy?"

"Not too bad."

She nods, as if the two of them have never spoken a word to each other before.

Taz keeps looking into his cup. "So," he says, but then they both hear it at the same time. A little rattle of crib bars. No babbling. And only a moment later there's the plasticky shush of feet pajamas, a slow shuffle across the floor. El turns first to Taz, then peers over the top of the couch, toward the bedroom door as Midge comes out, rubbing her face, dragging her stuffed Elmo. She comes around, flops against Elmo's leg, worms her way up onto the couch, into her lap.

Elmo rubs her back, blinks at Taz. "How long has this been going on?"

"Second time right there. The first time just a few nights ago."

"Wow," El says, "check out my big girl." She looks to Taz. "What are you going to do?"

"Do?"

"Sleep. Where? She's pushing you out of the nest."

Taz shrugs. "There's always the couch."

"Oh please," she says.

"Save the big room for guests, you know. Drunk drop-ins."

"Cute," she says. "And I think Alisha has got other plans for me, anyway."

"Such as?"

"Rudy shield."

Taz gives a little laugh. "Really? Damn, I thought he might be on to something there."

"He might be, but, you know, we're old-fashioned girls. We don't rush into things."

Taz stands, says, "Come on, Midge, how about some breakfast?"

She slides off of Elmo, but grabs her thumb, tugs her toward the kitchen.

Lauren's got grocery bags stacked all over the counter, something he hadn't noticed the night before, something totally unlike her. He pictures her standing here, hearing some truck rumbling up the street, panicking, fleeing the way he used to, afraid to see what might come through the door.

He peeks into a bag, starts shelving turkey broth, stuffing mix. He sets a bag of oranges on the table, another of potatoes. Elmo works Midge into the booster seat clamped to the edge of the table and scatters Cheerios for her to play with. Taz slides a banana across to her. Midge cries, "Nana!" and Taz says, "Half at a time, or she tries to put the whole thing in her mouth."

"I know."

"Right," he says, and hits the gas under the water. "She's on an oatmeal kick," he says.

"She has been since July," Elmo says, and a potato bongs against the side of the stove.

Taz bends down, picks it up. "A throwing kick, too."

Elmo rolls another potato across to Midge. "Looks like she could use some practice," she says. "Missed you by a mile."

Midge rolls the potato back, laughing, a mouth full of banana. Elmo rolls it back and Midge snatches it up and unleashes a pop up that almost lands on her own head.

"You're not," El says, "not teaching her to throw, are you? Because she's a girl?"

"She'll start for the Mariners."

"*I* could start for the Mariners."

"El," Taz says, "you know, you could stay here."

She looks at him. "Here?" she says. "But what about Grandma? My reputation?"

"Your *what*?"

"I don't know," she says. "You mean like, what? Roommates?"

"Makes sense to me," he says. "If that's what you want."

"Yeah," she says.

"But I'd pay you. For babysitting."

"Which is where it gets slippery. Like, you know, kept woman kind of thing."

"Please. I work, I get paid. You work, you get paid."

Midge throws the potato. A line drive, barely missing Elmo. "There you go, girl," Elmo says, rolling her another one.

Taz leans in the kitchen doorway, tilting from one shoulder to the other. "You're not going to talk about this?"

"Well, I'd like to think about it first, if that's all right with you."

"So just leave all your stuff in my truck? In my shop? While you think about it?"

The doorbell rings, Lauren being all obvious about being careful, and as soon as he starts for the door, a potato bounces off the casing, just beside his head. He turns, and Elmo points to Midge, and Midge points right back at Elmo, giggling.

———

Lauren says her hellos, apologizes about leaving the groceries out, says something about being addicted to *Downton Abbey*. "I just realized the time," she says, laughing at herself. "I still missed the first few minutes."

She takes a sip of her Starbucks, looks around, and finally can't not turn to Elmo, says, "So, you're all moved back now?"

"Last night," she says. "But my stuff is still in Taz's truck. Spent all night talking to my roomie." She lets that sink in before adding, "I just got here myself."

"And you'll be here for Christmas?"

"If I'm invited," she says, giving Taz a glance.

"Of course you're invited," Lauren says, "and your roommate."

Taz finishes working on the oatmeal, puts a bowl on the table for Midge to paint with, warns Elmo that it's still a little hot.

She looks at him, like she'd never fed Midge before.

"So, Ted," Lauren says. "The bathroom?"

"It's, I'll get to it, really, but anybody who comes here won't be surprised it's unfinished. I mean, look at this place."

Lauren turns to Elmo. "He insists on not finishing the bathroom. Insists nobody minds stepping into that dark room, all the wiring hanging out. No sink."

Elmo smiles at Lauren, nodding. "He says he's going to hire me to help."

Taz says, "What?"

"Tazmo and Rude," she says. "Ready when you are, boss."

"That's great," Lauren says. "Finish in time for Christmas?"

"The bathroom?" Taz says. "When's Christmas?"

"The twenty-fifth," Elmo says. "Almost always."

Taz tries to smile.

"Wednesday," Lauren says.

"Not a chance."

"Even with the two of you?"

"Even with twenty of us."

"Call Rudy," Elmo says. "Get the crew together. We can sure give it a try."

"All right, then," Lauren says. "I'll be on Midge duty. Once she's ready, she can go shopping with me."

"But, you just went shopping," Taz says.

"It's the holidays, Ted." She gives a wave toward the groceries. "Tip of the iceberg."

DAY 508

Christmas Eve Taz and Elmo work side by side, screwing down Durock, every six inches in the field, screw guns whining, door closed, the walls already up, taped, a couple coats of mud. The bathtub sits in the living room, behind the couch, each clawed foot holding down a stack of cardboard, protecting the floor. El had draped it with garland, a last string of lights, Midge helping. Lauren standing shaking her head, unable to hide a smile.

Reaching for another screw, Elmo gives a nod toward the door holding out the living room, the world out there, Lauren and Midge, but not the smell of roasting turkey. "Smells good," she says.

"It's some OCD thing she's got."

"Cooking?" she says, about to push the trigger, drive in the screw, but she stops, staring at him. "Listen, if you've got a problem with cooking, you better say so right now."

Taz says, "Christmas is tomorrow, right? And she's cooking a turkey today?"

"She must be planning on a crowd."

"You. Me. Midge."

"Her. Rudy. Alisha." She drives the screw. "You know about them now, right? Finally?"

"Trying my best not to," Taz says. "That whole African wild dog thing."

"The *what?*"

Taz says, "Never mind. It's a Rudy thing."

"I don't want to know," she says. Then, "Anyway, there's maybe Marko, too. His wife. What's her name?"

"Jeannie. But still, two turkeys?"

"You heard her. One to have all ready to cut. Make gravy or something. Leftovers for everyone to take home."

Taz, laughing with Marnie about it, her food thing, early on, before he was sure laughing about her mother was safe. He says, "She might cook a third, before she's through."

"It's nice," Elmo says.

"It's nuts," he answers.

She does her half-shrug thing. "I think it's great. Like this big, huge family thing."

He starts to tape the joints, the corners, and Elmo says, "You ever think of that? That she just wanted to be part of something like that? Maybe always has? You know, instead of just her and Marnie, always just the two of them?"

Taz runs another line of the mesh tape. It's a jolt, hearing her say Marnie.

"And you?" Elmo says. "You ever think that way?"

"What way?"

"That you'd like more. You know, more than just you and Midge."

"You mean you?" he says.

She smiles, dips her head toward her shoulder. "Well, yeah, that might be cool. But, you know, maybe more? I mean, it'd just have been so different without my brother."

Taz stops his trowel, the thinset oozing. He realizes his mouth has dropped open, and he closes it. They'd always talked two, maybe even three. Never an only. He and Marnie, the paired onlies. He nods, unable to quite look at her.

Elmo bursts out laughing.

He looks up, fights up a grin, and she points her screw gun at him. "I'm not talking signing up for Lamaze or anything," she says. "But, sheesh, take a breath or two, nothing to panic about. I was just wondering, you know, if something like that was ever even on your radar. For, like, way out there, future-wise."

"Always was," he manages. "Yours?"

"Oh, hell yeah," she says. "Someday."

Taz scrapes up the thinset mess, starts spreading again.

"Well, anyway," Elmo says, stretching it out almost like a gasp. "You know, after the last couple nights, Rudy staying over, having to listen to that rodeo, I've been rethinking a few things."

Taz runs the tape along the vertical seam. Starts the trowel down, glances over. The muscles in her shoulders bunch as she bears down, driving a screw. She fixes another onto the point. "Like?" he says.

"My little place is getting a little crowded."

"Oh," Taz says. "Well, the guest room is still open." Then, before Elmo can say another word, he says, "But, do you, um, think you can finish this taping?"

She looks at what he's been doing. "Is it somehow harder than it looks?"

He shakes his head.

"Well, then I think a monkey could do it."

"Perfect," he says. He's already setting down his tray, his trowel, the roll of tape. "Once it's done, we've got to lay off, let it dry. So, the rest of the day off. I've got to make a run now."

"The rest of the day off? Like, there-goes-my-paycheck off?"

"The Christmas bonus will cover it."

"Ha," she says.

He opens the door. She says, "Where are you going?"

He dips back into the room. "It's Christmas," he says. "There might be, you know, surprises?"

He starts to close the door, but she says, "Taz!" sharp enough to stop him. He peeks back in.

"I haven't scared you off, have I?"

"No, no, I just, there's something I have to do."

"Right now? In the middle of this?"

"I should have done it a long time ago."

"Seriously?"

"Yeah, no, I mean, no, you haven't scared me. At all. I just have to do this thing now."

He smiles at her, eases the door closed between them, already pulling his phone out of his pocket.

She gives it a minute, then another, then just can't stand it anymore, steps out of the bathroom to investigate and is all but knocked flat as Taz blows out of the big bedroom with an old double mattress. She leaps back into the bath, saying, "What on earth?"

"Sorry," he says, maneuvering the mattress across the living room, almost taking himself out on the tub before finding the door.

Elmo follows after him, standing in the door. "You're moving out?" she says. "That, I'd say, is pretty similar to panic."

Rudy's backing up the drive, like it's something they've choreographed. He gives her a wave from behind the wheel. Taz, hidden behind the mattress, arcs it up over the side of the pickup.

She stands in the open door, turns back around to see if she's missed something. Midge sits on the floor, crayons, a coloring book with a riot of scribbles. Lucky she wasn't trampled. She gives a shiver, says, "Toady," and El pushes the door nearly shut. Lauren pokes her head out from the kitchen, a giant spatula in her hand. "Where's he—" she starts, but Elmo just shrugs, and Taz shouts, "Back soon," and slams the truck door and Rudy takes off.

But he's not. Hours and hours, the whole day, nearly dinner. And when he crashes back through the door, his entrance is nearly the same as the exit, barging in blind behind a new mattress, the plastic wrap crinkling. "Clear?" he says.

Elmo runs out of the kitchen, swoops Midge up. "Clear," she says. "Watch the tub."

Taz staggers across the room, turns through the hallway, to the bedroom. She hears the fall and bounce. The tear of plastic. He comes back out, closes the door behind him, creasing and folding the plastic. "You never saw a thing," he says.

She follows him into the kitchen, watches him disappear into the broom closet, the Hogwarts entrance to the basement, back a moment later, something hidden behind his back. He edges around her, keeps whatever it is hidden, goes back into the bed-

room. Lauren follows them both out of the kitchen, looks at
Elmo, gives her what could only be a wtf?, and Elmo says, "Who
knows?"

"Men," Lauren says, and turns back to the safety of her
kitchen.

When Taz reappears, Elmo says, "So?"

"So what?"

She waits, then waves toward the big bedroom. "Are you
moving back in? Giving Midge her own room? Her own bed?"

He smiles, half his mouth. Zips his lips. Throws away
the key.

She peers up at him. "Have you been to a bar?"

He smiles wider. "Rudy made me."

"Oh boy. The Club?"

"Of course."

"And this is the plan you two came up with? Buying a mattress? Like that'll seal the deal? And then you tear off to the Club
to celebrate your genius?"

Taz blinks. "He said he'd only help if I bought him a beer."

She looks at him. "Well, thanks for the invite."

"You were still working," he says.

"You got that right," she says, pointing to the kitchen. "All
day long. My top-secret stuffing recipe."

Taz blinks. "You and Lauren?"

"She knows what she's doing in there."

"That's what Rudy says."

"Rudy'd say that in front of a pig trough."

Lauren comes out, says, "Elmo, are you going to use all those
onions you chopped?"

"Just got carried away," she says. "Have at 'em."

Lauren stands a second, watching them, smiling. "Your babysitter knows her way around a kitchen," she says.

Taz says, "That's what I just heard about you."

As soon as she retreats, Elmo all but skewers Taz on the finger she jabs at him. "Don't even think this is the way things work," she says.

"What?"

"You and Rude out tearing it up, *the girls* in the kitchen."

Taz blinks. "Are you even close to being serious?"

She squints, studying him. "I don't know," she says. "But I am not going back anywhere near pre–glass slipper days."

"Oh no," Taz says, "all princess, all the time." He gives a wave around the room, Marn's smiley face leering from the kitchen. "Your kingdom."

DAY 509

Midge is zonked. They've cleaned her up, gotten the dishes, if not washed, at least stacked. Lauren's run off to her motel, Rudy and Alisha off, too, Marko and Jeannie.

Taz and El sit for a while, just watching the Christmas tree lights, Midge sagging between them in her new Santa jammies, until Taz lifts her up, carries her into the bedroom, tells her she's going to sleep in her big-girl bed.

Midge sings, hardly more than a whisper, "Big gull, big gull," until she switches to, "Mo, Mo," and Elmo comes in and sits down with them on the little bed. They sit a while longer, watching her curl in, fight it, go out. They sneak out into the hallway. Elmo turns toward the living room and Taz says, "She thinks you're her mother."

Elmo stops. "No," she says. "Never."

Taz raises an eyebrow. "You're the woman she knows. Practically since birth."

"There's Grandma."

"There's you," he says. "Just you."

She looks around, like for exits. "So?"

Taz puts a hand up on the wall. "What'll she think? When she's older? Mom in one room. Dad on the couch."

"You're making assumptions, bub, but she won't think I'm her mom. You tell her all those stories about her."

"She's not even two. She doesn't know those stories from any other fairy tale."

Elmo blinks.

"I don't mean fairy tale," he says. But, yes, he does. "They're just made-up stuff. Her out there traveling. Away. Exploring. Doing bold stuff. On her way back."

"That's really what you tell her?"

"She's a baby. I wasn't even really talking to her."

"Well, who were you …" She stops, lets it drift away.

"It was nice," Taz says. "Picturing her that way."

"Coming back," Elmo says.

Taz runs a finger along the door casing. "Yeah."

"And now?"

"She's talking. It's going to start sinking in."

"What? Your mom stories?"

"Everything."

Elmo eyes him. "That'll be cool, her thinking her mom is some kind of hero or something."

"Her thinking her mom just stays out there? Instead of coming home to her? No, El," he says. "She's never going to know her. I can't pretend that away. You can't."

"And, you want her to think I'm her mom?"

"I'm just saying it's what she already thinks."

"But that's what you want her to think?"

He whispers, "No," then, "I just think it's inevitable."

"And you're going to tell her about Marnie."

"Of course. But right now?"

"It'll just be one more story," Elmo says. "The best one. The way it's always been. 'I never knew my mom, but there was always Elmo.'"

"Is that what she's going to say?"

Elmo winces. "Walked into that."

"El."

"Well, what, you just think we should move in together, for her sake?"

Taz says, "Not just for her sake."

He walks down the hall, opens the other bedroom door, waves her after him.

She sees the bed, the new mattress covered up by the blankets, the comforter. Rudy's gigantic old bow on top. "Merry Christmas," he says.

"You got me a *mattress*? For Christmas?" Elmo laughs. "Wow. I guess the whole princess phase is over. What next year? Tire chains? Vacuum cleaner?"

"I was thinking maybe a new kitchen."

She eyes him. "And what, Taz? This new bed's for me? And you're going to sleep on the couch? Set up some cot or something? Some faithful dog nest at the foot of the bed?"

"No," he says. He looks straight at her. "I'm thinking ahead here. About the future."

"You and me?" Elmo says.

Taz touches her nose with the tip of his finger.

"I won't do it for her sake," Elmo says.

"That's not what I meant, I—"

"I won't even do it for your sake," she says. "Only ours. The future's."

He smiles, lets out a breath. "*That's* what I meant."

"And I'm not ever pretending I'm her mother. Like, biologically speaking."

"No. Just the woman who's always been around. Always loved her."

"And you."

He swallows. "That would be good, too."

"But you keep telling her about her mom."

"Right," he says.

"And let's screw that princess stuff, okay?" she says. "Who really wants all that? The balls, the magic wands, those gigantic dresses. Pain in the ass."

"We can just be peasants?"

"*We*," she says, smiling.

DAY 1

EPILOGUE

"Tazmo and Rude has never done finer work," Rudy says, and El stands up, stretches, the last of the hex tile in, just the grout waiting, moving in the gigantic cookie-making stove, the sink, all the cabinets out in Taz's shop, gleaming, more stashed in Rudy's garage.

"We deserve a break," Taz says.

"Beer thirty?" Rudy says.

Elmo smiles. "That'd be good, but it's pretty early."

"God," he says. "How old are you? Ninety?"

"Don't you have shopping to do?" Elmo says, and Rudy gives her a blank, then a slow dawning.

"Right you are," he says. "See you guys later."

Taz watches him tear out the door, glances to Elmo, says, "What's that all about?"

"Probably the same thing that kept you awake all night."

He still can't get used to it. How she knows everything.

"He's getting the party stuff. I told him we had other birth-day things to do."

Gated off from the tile work, Midge calls, "I am two!" from the living room.

"Other birthday things?" Taz says.

"I think the water will be perfect," she says.

Taz says he guesses so.

"So?" she says.

He nods, and she flips him a thumbs-up, says, "I'll pack lunch."

They don't say a word to Midge about where they're going. With the wind roaring through the windows, Midge's hair a whirlwind, they hardly say a word to each other, a word at all, until they're off the highway, the pavement. Taz rolls slow, not bouncing Midge the way she likes, but at the last turn she remembers. Her raven call is gone, but she smiles so wide it looks like it could hurt. Begins to bounce in her seat, the seat belt straining as she cranes.

They get out of the truck, and they're not looking at each other. Quieter even than the ride out. They walk around the far end of the chokecherries, leaving no trail.

It's like it's always been. No new fires, no burns, no change at all. But everything is different. They stand back from the water, the slow circling of the big eddy. Elmo holds her cooler.

Midge takes off her own clothes. Doesn't need help any more. Dances out of her pants. Peels back the Velcro ties of her dry diaper. Elmo starts racing her, clothes flying. The two of them, giggling, right at the edge of the water.

Taz says, "Wait for me." Clears his throat. Says it again.

Midge turns to El, says, "Wait, wait, wait."

Elmo sings, "Wait, wait, wait. He's sooo slow." And they laugh and start into the water together.

Midge shivers, draws her elbows into her ribs, her fists up to her chin. "Toady," she says, though he thinks she knows how to really say it now.

El takes her hand and walks beside her, and Taz has not made a move to even take off his shirt. He just stands and watches. Wants it to last forever. Behind him, Marn whispers, *You do good work, Taz.*

Midge punches her feet into the water, one after the other, splashing. She tugs on El's arm, says, "Swim!"

Taz stands in his sandals, his shorts.

Elmo dips under, stands back up, water streaming. Midge dunks, jumps back up, shrieking and laughing, two years old. He starts taking off his clothes.

When he's done, he looks up to see Elmo just standing there, holding Midge on a hip, water thigh-deep, one eyebrow raised, checking him out. Behind them the eddy curls in, and the willows edge the far bank, the cottonwood, the mountains and ponderosa rising up, the canyon upstream.

"Ready?" he says, and Elmo says, "And waiting," and so does Midge, and Taz dashes in and dives, the world gone to bubbles, to rush and silence and broken light, until he sees their arms, hands open and reaching down, ready to pull him back into the air.

ACKNOWLEDGMENTS

With many thanks to Joe Millar, for years of friendship and for the poem that gave this story its title. Thanks as well to my agent, Gail Hochman, who found the right home for Taz and Marn and Elmo and Midge, and to my sister, Ellen, proofreader par excellence. And, finally, to Dan Smetanka, the kind of roll-up-your-sleeves-and-get-to-work editor long rumored to have gone extinct. This story would not be the same without them.

© Emmanuel Romer

PETE FROMM is a five-time winner of the Pacific Northwest Booksellers Association Book Award for his novels *If Not for This*, *As Cool as I Am*, and *How All This Started*; the story collection *Dry Rain*; and the memoir *Indian Creek Chronicles*. He is on the faculty of Pacific University's low-residency MFA program, and lives in Montana with his family. Find out more at petefromm.com.